The Needle Shower

Don Heywood

Contents

for Nanette
best of days

1.

September, 1974

Dutchess County, New York

What would you do for love? A simple question, really, with no simple answer. Each and every person has a different response, as unique to them as are their thoughts, their DNA. Family, friends and life experiences would all play a part, certainly. But also trust, loyalty, passion and intimacy. And religion. There are as many influences on, and answers to, this question as there are stars in the universe. And every one would be right, in its own personal way.

Would you fight for love, or let it slowly sink into the deepest recesses of your being like a stone cast into this river? Would you lie for love? Would you steal for love? Would you be dishonest for love? Would you kill for love?

Is love permanent, or does it come and go like the tides in this river? Does it stay or can it be carried away like a piece of driftwood, ending up in an eddy, forever swirling in the opposite direction of life's tides, tantalizingly close yet unreachable?

What would you do for love?

I've been sitting on the beach in this small cove staring at the agitated lead-colored river for hours. Its foamy whitecaps, driven by the earlier storm, have swirled, crested and fallen as far as my eyes can see. They've rumbled and roared as they've collapsed onto this glossy pebble beach, their spuming fingers reaching out as if to drag me in. The cool mid-September wind bites at the waves and tugs the gulls sideways with invisible strings like some crazed puppeteer.

The sun charges into the western skyline, slinging the last horizontal red and tangerine rays like arrows. My shadow grows longer by the minute as the shy full moon peeks above the eastern horizon as if checking to see if the sun has completed its job.

Shivering in my rain-soaked clothes, I bury both hands a little deeper into the pockets of my sweatpants seeking warmth like a burrowing animal, but it is not there.

Earlier in the afternoon, I had watched two boys up the shoreline holding on for dear life to their multicolored kites as they flapped and darted up and down in the wind, the tails desperately tried to keep the kites facing into the breeze, as effective as a broken rudder on a floundering ship. The wind on the paper drew out a slapping sound, like a hand landing flush on a cheek, and threatened to rip them apart at any moment. Now all that remains is a deserted river's edge slowly being lit by silver moonlight as the sunset reluctantly retreats.

The elephant gray hues from the rain storm appear to be waning, giving way to a clear evening sky and a calming river. I can smell the moist air. I can taste it on my tongue as it stings my tired eyes.

A metallic blue dragonfly appears at eye level as if inspecting me. It hovers for a few seconds and then is gone in a flash as the cooling air makes my eyes tear. Wiping them with my sleeve, I close them and briefly rest. Exhaustion settles in. Even so, it is comforting to be back here where I have spent so many wonderful summer days. This beach is where, as a small child, I met the water for the first time, heard its song, experienced its magic, felt its life. It is where I learned how to love it, fear it.

Reaching into my pocket, I remove an orange plastic vial. Twisting off the lid, I pop out two purple pills, each the size of a bullet, and swallow them one after the other. It's just another in a seemingly endless parade of anodynes I have been given over the last few years. Recapping the vial, I stuff it back into my pocket with a sigh.

Gazing back at the blackening river, I spot a maroon tug highlighted by both the rising moon and the last straggling rays of sunlight. It is thrusting a corroded barge through the water, seemingly making little progress, appearing almost still in the water, despite the waves clawing at the front. From where I sit now, it seems as if I have always been like that barge, constantly pushing ahead but seemingly getting nowhere. Living can be like that.

That all will change tomorrow.

Looking up, I see the blinking lights of a jet passing silently overhead leaving a fluffy white contrail as soft as love in the moonlit sky. Life goes on for others.

Gazing back at the now gentle, frothy waves kissing the beach, I realize that there has only always been this. Water. My one constant source of enjoyment and love has been water. To be near it, to stare at it, dip my toes into it, jump into it. It was my home.

And my real passion was swimming. As a kid, I would look for any excuse to steal away to a cool forest lake or to this tempting river to jump in and swim. It seems at times that I spent most of my early years wet. I absolutely loved it, especially in the early morning, as the sun rises, before the world comes alive. There is something you can't describe about being in water with an untroubled surface, smooth as glass, surrounded by total quiet, as a new sun rises, full of promise, warming your face. You have to experience it, spend time with it, get to know it; only then can you come to love it.

That love was taken from me, stolen in my youth in an instant. It has been years since I have really enjoyed the water, and with good reason, but tonight it is once again flirting with me, enticing me. It beckons me like a lost love, I can feel its sultry pull. Sometimes, against all common sense, it is difficult to say no to love. Once it has penetrated and grabbed your heart, it never really ever releases you.

A lone seagull floats by screeching like a rusted hinge, before gliding further down the river as I rise to stand. To the north, a lonely lighthouse blinks its cautionary beacon. Looking at the water again, it's almost low tide.

A meteor streaks across the ebony sky, dissolving into darkness. It's time.

2.

February, 1964

Dutchess County, New York

We live inside a giant snow globe that someone has just shaken. Small, scattered flakes of crystal snow fill the cerulean sky as the sun peeks in and out of the wispy clouds as if it can't make up its mind to stay or go. Lenter's Hill is a packed sheet of ice, perfect for tobogganing. The snow pack, however, isn't all that deep and hay stalks poke up through the surface like an old man's whiskers. Barren trees line both sides of the hill from top to bottom like skeleton sentries.

The walk up the hill was strenuous, especially with toboggan sleds in tow. The three of us sit at the top, catching our breath as our exhales swirl around us like chimney smoke. The only sounds are our collective breathing and the whirling wind. It is late in the afternoon and we're alone here at the top. The view is, as always, magnificent. From up this high you can see Mirror Lake below us, an abandoned, oval shaped limestone quarry that has filled with crystalline clear water over time, now frozen and smooth as glass. White pines surround it, except for a cleared shore area at the bottom of this hill, reflecting off of the smooth icy surface as if viewed through cataracts. On the opposite side of the lake you can see a worn path that leads up a hill and then down to the county road. To the east are fields with stone walls as far as the eye can see.

Nag's Boulder starkly protrudes skyward in the middle of the lake, discarded there by the ancient glaciers like an afterthought. In the heat of summer, we take turns swimming from an old wooden dock. We swim out and circle the rock before returning, our seconds ticking by underneath competitive eyes on my beat-up old Timex. I hold the record time and have for as long as I can remember.

Directly below us to the west is our single stop light village. From up here, you can clearly see snow-covered roofs of the crowded houses that sit along the leafless, elm-lined streets. The black spire on Saint Vitonus Catholic Church on Market Street is spotted with white as it rises majestically above all else, pointing to the heavens like a symbol of hope. On the south of town sits the war memorial, and beyond it, balanced on a high hill, is a forsaken red brick school house that was abandoned when a new school was built in town across from Saint Vitonus. Behind the unused building, sits the sports field bordered by Farley's Stream, a frozen meandering gray and white line.

A lazy county road snakes out of town towards us, past the Oakley's farm, twisting and turning around the drumlins. Just before it passes by the hiking path that leads up here, an unpaved road juts off to the south. It's a long-abandoned road, but it used to guide traffic in and out of Lenter's Limestone Mine, which sits on the backside of the hill we'd summitted with our toboggans. The road is barricaded about a half mile in by a sagging rusty chain that blocks further access.

Further out to the west, beyond the town and below the Catskill Mountains, the frozen Hudson River can be seen snaking lazily down through the valley. The Coast Guard cut a jagged channel in the ice and it now stands out like a massive scar. The sun dips dangerously close to the horizon coloring the landscape light orange, making the world look as if everything is made of marmalade. The temperature rapidly drops.

"Hey Tommy, are you okay?" I ask.

"Yeah. It's just that this old toboggan has a loose board on it and it slows me down more and more on every run," he says in a high-pitched voice like a piccolo. Being twelve, he is the youngest amongst us by two years. He sports large pink protruding ears like a Volkswagen with its doors open. His ever-present grin exposes bad teeth with gaps that look like a broken gray picket fence badly in need of painting. The old winter coat he wears is ripped and patched with duct tape; his orange cap sullied with dirt.

"Tell you what, I'll fix it for you later when we get home, okay? Now, whose turn is it to go first?" I ask.

"If you're asking then it's your turn!" Billy says and laughs. His reed like body towers above us all, his dirty blond hair slapping in the breeze at the acne on his cheeks, his ever-present confidence glowing in his hazel eyes. I don't think I have ever seen him back away from anything, be afraid of anything. He attacks life like a daredevil.

"Yeah!" Tommy chimes in. His tight overcoat is several sizes too small and seemingly ready to burst under pressure from his rather large stomach that looks like a soccer ball. You would never know it by looking at him, but he is a smart kid bordering on genius.

Looking at my friends and the views, while breathing in the intoxicating winter air, I feel life will never be any better than this.

They all are smiling and yelling dares at me.

"Pansy!" shouts Billy as he pulls his hair away from his cheek with his gloved hand.

"Chicken!" bellows Tommy as he attempts to making clucking sounds, his high-pitched voice sounding more like a castanet.

What can I do? Pulling my snow cap firmly down, I feel the hairs of my crew cut frozen at attention like porcupine's quills. The cold makes my teeth ache and my braces feel like frozen metal shavings in my mouth.

Grabbing my toboggan, I start racing downhill as fast as I can, the ice-covered snow snapping and cracking under each footstep like popcorn on a stove. Just before I feel as if the snow will grab ahold of my feet, I jump onto the sled and take up the rope in my hands. Already zooming, I can just barely hear the fading whoops and yells of my friends behind me. The wind whistles in my ears like it's announcing quitting time at a factory as a startled squirrel darts out of my path in a frantic zig-zag through miniature swirling snow twisters. The snowflakes blind me, sticking to my eyes as I wipe a gloved hand across them. Holding onto the rope for dear life as the sled increases in speed, the bottom slaps a beat on the rough snow like a jazz drummer keeping time as the hay stalks stroke the sled like drum brushes.

Advancing towards the half way point on the hill, my sled is careening towards a rapidly approaching jump. Here the terrain angles suddenly downward so that a sled at any speed becomes airborne. I hold my breath and the rope as I leave the ground and, for a few fleeting seconds, I am flying. After what seems like an eternity, the sled finally crashes hard onto the snowpack, jarring my teeth as the descent continues. I can't hear them, but I'm sure that my friends are still yelling down to me.

The goal of every run down Lenter's Hill is to have enough speed to cross the twenty or so yards of relative flat at the bottom, to then glide out onto Mirror Lake. No one has ever done it before, so when I hit the flat and start towards the lake, I suddenly become excited. This could be the day. The icy conditions are perfect. Pulling hard on the rope, I lower myself to cut the drag. My speed is slowly decreasing, but so too is the distance to the lake's edge. I'm no more than ten feet away when suddenly I see a very slight knoll in front of me. My sled reaches it, angles down ever so slightly, and I pick up a tick of speed that pushes me out past the would-be water line and out onto the frozen surface of the water. The ice is smooth as a fingernail and my sled seems to float across it like a curling stone. I quickly glide by Nag's Boulder, coming uncomfortably close to the jagged rock. I don't increase in speed, but I also don't seem to be slowing either. Instead, I just glide along until the opposite shore is all of a sudden racing towards me. Sliding off the solid ice into the bank, my jaw jerks forward, punching against the lip of the sled before I am thrown forward over the front into a rather hard snow pack, face first.

Lying still for a few seconds, I gather my senses before rolling over. From the flat of my back, I reach up and wipe the slightly bloody snow from my face. Sitting up, I can see the distant silhouettes of my friends waving and jumping up and down back at the top. Seconds later, as I see two distant dots start to slide down the hill, I start to laugh. And laugh. And laugh.

Walking back to town in a spitting snow, our pulled sleds follow us like obedient dogs. With each step the story of my ride becomes more and more exaggerated.

"Man, you must have been ten feet in the air when you went over the jump!" shouts Billy.

"When you hit the shore, it looked from up top like you would fly over the pine trees!" says Tommy.

"Yeah, it was a cool ride," I say enjoying the ever-growing legend as we walk through town. We round the A&P at the corner and turn onto Oak Street. Dragging our sleds down the middle of the street, we stop in front of Tommy's weathered yellow house. It always looks sad and lonely, even in the summer, but with the steel sky and dying light of the winter, it looks especially forlorn. The faded green trim around the windows looks like a poor mascara job, the peeling yellow house paint like aged makeup. This street is filled with neglected houses and littered lawns, the driveways filled with rusting and dented cars. This is what the town's people refer to as the poor side of town, and evidence to support that statement is visible everywhere. Next to Tommy's house, I see an old familiar Bonneville sitting in the driveway.

Looking down, Tommy scratches the snow with his boot toe and asks, "Hey Danny, do you think it would be okay if I stayed at your house tonight?"

Billy and I exchange knowing looks, both this car and its driver having been the subject of many discussions between us.

"Sure, Tommy. Sure thing. After dinner we can fix that loose board on your sled," I say and pat him on the back. "Let's go."

With that, we all turn and start the walk back to downtown as the silver snowflakes turn to a gray spitting rain.

3.

March, 1964

Dutchess County, New York

The winter sky is dangerously dark and ominous, the wind blows increasingly hard. Billy and I are walking to school together as we always have since the second grade. Turning the corner onto Market Street across from Lawson's Lumber Yard, we see Tommy walking towards us as a stiff gust of wind hits us. As a truck pulls out loaded with plywood, its springs screech as the driver turns right onto Market Street heading for the county road out of town.

"Hey Tommy! Hurry up before the sky opens up," I yell as he gives a broad smile and starts to run toward us. We first met Tommy years ago at the summer little league field where he used to show up by himself and retrieve wayward balls. He must have been around eight years old or so and always had on old, tattered clothes that never fit him. Always smiling, you could still see the loneliness, the desperate need for friends. Billy and I felt sorry for him, befriended him and, to our surprise, found he was not only a great kid but extremely smart. He has been our constant companion ever since and we love him like a kid brother. Either of us would do anything for him.

Suddenly, the sky rips and hail begin to fall, steadily increasing in size until they are like mothballs dropping out of the sky. Laughing, we start to run to the school's front door and safety.

Upon entering the main hallway, it seems as busy as Grand Central Station with students heading in every direction to get to their respective classrooms on time. Feet scuffling, lockers banging, talking and laughing all merge into a kind of mellifluous melody. Shaking the wetness off of my jacket, I say, "Later, guys. See you at lunch."

"See you," says Billy.

"Yeah, later," says Tommy.

Four hours later, Billy and I are standing in the lunch line impatiently waiting for pizza, the aromatic scent everywhere. "I'm going for the jumbo lunch today. How about you?" I ask.

"Hey, look over there," Billy says ignoring my question at the sounds of shoes scuffing and bodies being moved. Peering down the hall, we see the enormous back of Sandy Stewart, a loser who flunked several grades and takes his failures out on others. Several years older than his classmates, and much bigger and stronger, he walks around with whisker stubble on skin like burlap. Sandy has a younger, much smaller kid backed up against a locker and every time the kid tries to move forward, he pushes him back with both hands generating a fleshy, metallic thud. A crowd has gathered around but no one intervenes.

"How about it, jackass?" shouts Sandy, knowing he has an audience. "You bump into me without saying sorry, tough guy? Come on, do something."

"Crap! That's Tommy he has against the locker!" exclaims Billy as he starts walking quickly and with purpose with me in tow. As we approach, he yells, "What do you think you're doing, jackass?"

Distracted, Sandy turns to look and is in total disbelief that some-one has challenged his authority. "What in the hell did you just say?" he asks. Forgetting Tommy, he starts walking towards us. They stop face to face, with me on the side. Billy towers over the shorter Sandy like a redwood. Though Sandy is much heavier and stronger, there is absolutely no fear apparent in Billy's eyes. In fact, his narrowed eyes look ominous.

"I said, I believe, what do you think you're doing, jackass? Isn't that what I said, Danny?" he asks as he turns towards me.

"Yeah, I do believe that is exactly what you said."

"Okay wise guy, I'm going to close that big mouth of..." Sandy's words stop as quickly as they started as Billy, a confident grin on his face, lands a punch squarely on the side of his jaw. Sandy drops like the bag of crap that he is and the whole hallway, that was quiet as a funeral parlor while watching, suddenly explodes in conversation and laughter. This is not unlike Billy. I have never seen him afraid of anything. He is the type who would gladly charge into a burning building to save someone he didn't know. Sandy sits up and tries to get to his feet but Billy kicks him as soon as his legs are under him and he falls for the second time.

"If I ever see you picking on Tommy, or any other kid for that matter," he tells him menacingly as he can muster, "You won't be able to walk again when I am finished with you. You got that?"

Dazed and still lying on the floor, he does not respond. Billy leans over and yells, "You got that?" As he nods his head, we both turn and walk over to Tommy.

As we walk across the hall, I spot a girl in the crowd who I know is new to our school. I have seen her in the hallways before and I know she is two grades ahead of me and that her name is Jo. It seems that everyone else turns a blur, her face being the only one I can see. She has high cheekbones, a strong jaw with glaucous, olive shaped eyes like steel. She has a blue bandana on her head, tied off in the back with her auburn hair poking out in a pony tail. Small gold earrings dangle from her lobes, sparkling in the light. I smile at her and she smiles back without losing eye contact. I feel a rush of color come to my cheeks.

"You alright, Tommy?" asks Billy.

"I think so. Thanks, guys."

"No problem. If he ever bothers you again, you come get me okay?" Billy says, showing no visible sign of what just happened, calm as a windless sea.

4.

April 1964

Dutchess County, New York

Walking down Market Street early Sunday morning, I am enjoying the peace and quiet on my way to the A&P to pick up milk and bread for our breakfast. Glancing into the dingy diner window, on the counter several half-eaten pies sit under glass covers like ancient Egyptian archaeological treasures. Looking through the opening to the kitchen, I see a bored chef with a heavy five o'clock shadow lazily turning the pages of a newspaper as over his shoulder smoke curls towards the ceiling from the unattended grill. A waitress with made up eyes like a raccoon, white bleached hair piled high in a stiff looking chignon that could pass as a bale of hay, wanders amongst the patrons as old Bus holds court with a group of older men at their usual spot. Their table top is littered with empty dishes piled high with silverware and balled up napkins. Bus has his ever-present cigarette in one hand, a cup of coffee in the other, while his agitated mouth opens and closes like a trout out of water, engaging in some heated conversation I can't hear. The aroma of coffee has snuck outside and mixes pleasantly with the pollen of budding spring leaves.

Crossing the street in front of the five-and-ten cent store, I see someone peering into the Western Auto store window at a bright red Truetone *Speed Master* guitar. I recognize the auburn ponytail immediately as I step up onto the sidewalk. It is the new girl, Jo. Mustering what little nerve I have, I say, "You play?" *What a stupid thing to say,* I think.

As she turns, I see blue-gray eyes the color of slate widen slightly as a sliver of a smile comes to her face. "No, I'm just window shopping."

A slight breeze ruffles her hair, blowing a few wispy strands like thread across her face.

Stammering slightly, I say, "I've seen you around school but I don't think we have ever been properly introduced. My name is Danny. Danny Fosse."

"Yes, I know. Jo Nelson," she says as she extends her hand. Pleased to meet you Danny Fosse."

Taking it, I give a firm squeeze, holding onto it probably a little longer than I should. "I take it you just moved here?" I say, trying hard not to be overwhelmed by how much I'd like to keep holding her hand. Her beauty is making me nervous and I start to sweat. *I'm way out of my league here,* I think.

"Yes. My dad works for I.B.M. and he was transferred from Burlington, last fall. I stayed in Vermont with my aunt until Christmas break and then came down here to join my dad."

"And your mom?"

"Mom passed away a few years ago."

"Oh, Jo, I am so sorry."

"It's okay. Dad and I have gotten through it together. He gave me these earrings to always remember her by," she says as she turns her head exposing a tiny gold rock axe, smaller than a pea, dangling at the end of a very short gold hook. "Mom loved the outdoors, hiking, climbing, and exploring."

"They're beautiful," I say, followed by awkward silence. I'm really sweating now.

Trying to begin the conversation again, I say, "Tough being the new kid in school?"

"Oh, it's not so bad. With Dad's job we have moved several times so I am sort of used to it now."

Standing in another uncomfortable silence, I hear the deep roar of Bus's voice from behind me as he and his friends exit the diner still in a loud discussion. Moving in the opposite direction, their voices get fainter and fainter and then disappear as they turn the corner. The sound of one of their pickups backfiring rings out before it comes around the corner, a grayish black smoke choking the air as it rolls towards us.

Smiling, I shrug my shoulders.

Awkwardly, she laughs a bit. "There sure are some local characters here."

"You get used to them eventually. It's a small town. Once you have been around here awhile, you'll get to know most everyone. Sometimes it feels like old Bus thinks he was elected mayor the way he carries on about everything," I say. She's smiling at me again even though I'm not sure what else to say. In the distance the bells of Saint Vitonus ring for the start of the ten o'clock mass. My armpits are soaked. *What in the hell am I doing here?* I think.

"So, have you seen everything there is to see around town?" I ask.

"Pretty much, I think. It doesn't take long! I guess being from Burlington, getting used to this small town could take some time."

"What about outside of town?" I ask.

"A little. I just got my driver's permit and on weekends Dad lets me drive for practice. We have gone on several back roads around the town but I can't say I really know the area. Why?"

Here goes nothing, swing for the fences, I think. "Well, if you aren't doing anything this afternoon, there is something you should see," I say nervously. My mouth is suddenly dry, my palms now wet with sweat. I can't believe I am actually having a conversation with this beautiful, older girl. I feel anxious that this might be a dream and my mother will shake me awake any second.

"What is it?"

"Tell you what, if you can meet me here around one, I'll take you there. It's is a bit of a hike, so wear good shoes."

Giving me a look that is somewhere between curiosity and caution, she smiles and shrugs. "I guess you will have to come back at one to see if I show," she teases.

"Your smile says I will see you here," I say calmly while my heart races in my chest. *That one is going, going, gone, out of the park*, I imagine.

"What beautiful scenery out here," Jo says as we walk leisurely past the Mobil station on the county road heading out of town. Lenter's Hill looms in the distance. "It reminds me a little of the area in Vermont we used to live in."

"Well, I'm sure the hills and the mountains here can't compare in size, but we have a lot of beautiful things here in the valley," I say while looking at her. A slight crimson color comes to her cheeks and I feel a little less nervous.

As we walk past the drive for Oakley's Farm, I say, "My dad has his shop in a barn behind the farmhouse over there."

"Really? What type of business is he in?" she asks.

"Blacktopping. I help him on weekends with repairs and equipment maintenance."

"That must be interesting," she says.

"It really is. I like working side by side with my dad. You said your family moved often? Where were you before Burlington?"

"Raleigh, North Carolina. My mom and dad lived in other cities, but Raleigh is my earliest memory. It was nice there, and I was not happy when we moved to Vermont. Once we got there, I fell in love with it and couldn't imagine a better place in which to live. That is, until now," she says followed by a short laugh. She is easy to talk to and, even though I have just met her, I now feel at ease and comfortable around her, and am becoming less and less nervous.

"What did you do for fun in Vermont?"

"Well, my family has always been adventurous, loving the outdoors. We used to hike, swim in mountain lakes, rock climb and explore caves. I have come to love doing all of these things," she says as she walks at a brisk, yet unhurried pace, her athleticism apparent.

"Swimming and hiking are two of my favorite things also," I say with a grin. Pointing straight ahead, I say, "That path on the right leads up to Mirror Lake, which is at the base of Lenter's Hill. In the winter, the hill is a great place to sleigh ride. In the summer, my friends and I go swimming. I'll take you up there once it warms up if you want," I say before quickly continuing, not giving her a chance to say no. "We are going to take the road up there to the right that leads back to the entrance of an old mine."

"Cool," she says, a bit to my surprise. "What type of mine was it?" she asks, snapping me out of my own head.

"Limestone," I say. "It was closed and the entrance walled off back in the forties during the war."

"When my family would go on our climbing trips, we would often find small caves and explore them. Once they took me to Howe Caverns and I just fell in love with it. Do you know it?"

"Sure. We took a class trip there just last year. It was breath taking and, to be honest, a little frightening being so far underground."

"It's too bad the mine here is sealed up. I'd love to see inside."

Hesitating, I say, "Well, it was sealed but someone pried the hasp off the door and you can get it. Me and my friends Billy and Tommy went in last fall but we couldn't go far because we didn't have flashlights. We're actually planning on going in again next weekend if you're really interested. You have to promise not to tell anyone though. No one is supposed to be in there."

"Really? I could go with you guys?"

"Definitely. I mean, why not? I'll talk to my friends and give you a time to meet us next Saturday if you give me your phone number."

"Okay!" she says, grinning as we continue walking. *Another one out of the park!* I think.

"I want to show you something before we go up the mining road," I say and point to a small dirt path on the right that cuts through towering brown reed grass. "Follow me."

Walking down the trail, the reeds soar over us on both sides like buildings on a Manhattan street. Above us, the looming tops look like feather dusters and I feel so very small amongst them that I half expect to see a white rabbit in a waistcoat run by looking at his pocket watch. The footpath flattens out and emerges from the reed forest onto the edge of a fast-flowing stream, the water tumbling over rocks causing rapids and gurgling sounds. Forsythia bushes grow randomly on both sides, glowing the color of fresh lemons.

As Jo comes along my side, I say, "This is Farley's Stream. It starts close to the Connecticut border, flows below Lenter's Hill, through here, and winds through the southern part of the town eventually emptying into the Hudson."

"I love the sound of water washing over and around rocks, it is so soothing."

Smiling, I say, "This way," and we set off parallel to the stream. The tall reeds thin and give way to small birch trees lining the creek's edge, their bark curling like the edges of a yellowed photograph. The ground is mostly stone and pebbles, the topsoil having been washed away over the years. With each step it feels like walking on marbles. As we come over a small rise, I point to the stream and say, "There it is."

Watching her, I see her face twist in confusion and wonderment at the same time. In front of us is a whirlpool, maybe twelve feet in diameter, swirling counterclockwise. Towering over it is a huge weeping willow, its branches hanging down like beaded curtains, the tips all frosted white. The turbid swirl is full of small sticks and leaves and is spinning so fast that the vortex has been pulled down about a foot below the stream's surface level. Like the tips of the willow branches, both banks and all the low vegetation are bleached white like some crazed confectioner had used his sifter to spread flour.

"Why is that here?" she asks.

Laughing, I say, "Let's see if you can figure it out after what I am going to show you next! Follow me," as I turn to head back up the path.

Heading up the mining road, birch and maple trees hug both sides, sporting tiny spring buds. The wind moves the limbs about in a soft lazy sway. After about half a mile, we come to the rusty chain that's been strung across the road. A tarnished lock secures it to maple trees on both sides. Tire tracks can be seen preserved in the softer dirt on both shoulders where cars have parked.

Stepping over the chain, we walk through locust trees that have claimed stake to the abandoned road, like homesteaders, leaving only a worn foot path that weaves amongst them. Small limbs litter the trail, twigs and last year's leaves crunch and snap under our footsteps. The footpath turns sharply to the left before the slope increases dramatically. Going up, my legs tire quickly but Jo hardly seems bothered by the hill at all.

Climbing to a higher elevation, the locust trees give way to evergreens and smaller saplings, their scent is surfing on the breeze. As the wind picks up, limbs creak and moan like stairs in an old house. Coming over a small ridge, I say, "We're going down there," my finger pointing into the woods to the right.

"I don't see any route."

"That's because there isn't one! I love to hike off trail, that's how I found this place the first time. I told you this was the best kept secret in the county!" Looking at her, I sense something. "Is anything wrong?" I ask.

Hesitating, she gives a laugh and says, "No, everything is fine. I was just thinking how much these woods remind me of the hikes I used to take with Mom and Dad."

"Listen, we can do this another day if you like."

"No, you lead and I will follow," she says much to my relief. "By the way, how much further up this path is the mine?"

"Not far. I would guess about another ten-minute walk," I respond as I head off track, gingerly pushing through purple stemmed pricker bushes with thorns as sharp as prison wire. As we proceed through the evergreen forest, the ground gradually turns from dirt to rock. Lime and avocado colored ferns are sprinkled about, along with weeds and a few wildflowers, some covered with gossamer. Beefy roots muscle up and over the rocks, twisting and turning like brawny wire cables. The hillside above us abruptly gets very steep. White pines tower above us, filtering the sun's rays as if through a colander. The forest is so dense that visibility is reduced as if in a heavy fog. The whole area is littered with fallen dead trees criss crossed like pick up sticks.

Without thinking, I grab Jo's hand, helping her up and over a large boulder. Standing on top of it, I give her an awkward smile and release her hand. Thankfully, her face lights up with a radiant smile. *I don't want this day to ever end,* I think.

High up on an overhead limb I spot a bald eagle, which I point out to her. Below frenzied chipmunks scurry up, over and around the rocks making a warning sound like a stick hitting a hollow piece of wood.

White head, piercing eyes stun us both with its beauty. "It's magnificent," she whispers, trying not to frighten it to flight.

"I have often seen eagles here. Billy, Tommy and I have also spotted them up at Mirror Lake, so they probably nest in these woods and hunt there."

With a gentle whooshing sound, it suddenly takes flight, its massive wings propelling it gracefully as it glides up through the trees and is lost to sight.

After scrambling around in the rocks and brush for a bit, we come to a sheer shale wall about twenty or so feet high. It extends left and right as far as we can see. Directly in front of us, pines soar high above the cliff top and have grown so thickly together they seem to have been crocheted.

"I wish I had my climbing gear with me. This wall looks like fun!" she says.

Smiling, I say, "Follow me. There is a small open space behind these trees. I'm afraid we have to crawl a bit here." Grabbing Jo's hand, which I now feel more comfortable doing, I duck down under the lowest branch and fall onto my stomach. Releasing her, I wriggle and crawl until I emerge at the cliff wall behind the dense trees. Standing, I turn and grab her hand as she appears, helping her to her feet. She gives me a grin as she slaps the pine needles and dirt from her jeans.

In front of us the entire rock face is covered in vines that intertwine and criss cross all the way to the top like a giant spider's web.

"My, God! They look like hawsers!" she says.

"What are they?"

"They're huge ropes," she explains. "One time, my dad took me down to the docks in Boston to look at the cargo ships. They all had these huge ropes called hawsers that were looped together and hung off the sides. These vines look just like them."

A little bit dumbstruck, I can't think of a single thing to say as the sounds of the forest settle over us.

"Anyway, I can see why this place is the best kept secret in town. This is unbelievable. I can't wait to see what is at the top!"

"Ready?" I ask.

"For what? Are we going to climb these vines?" I nod and she casts her eyes up the rockface once more. "Born ready!" she says laughingly as she reaches up, grabs a firm hold on a vine and starts to climb. Watching her ascend with remarkable speed, her ponytail swinging side to side like a pendulum, she scales up the cliff effortlessly like a human spider.

Lunging up, I take a vine in my hand and start to follow. We reach the top after a strenuous effort and scrap our way onto our feet. We stand together on the cliff top and I am noticeably out of breath. The woods up here slope gently away from the cliff edge upwards as far as we can see, making the trees seem impossibly tall.

"What is that distant noise?" she asks.

"I am going to show you. Follow me, but be careful," I say as we start to walk along the cliff rim. The shale we hiked up on now has given way to limestone covered in soft olive colored moss like carpet which silences out footsteps. As we walk on, the distant muted noise becomes louder and louder until it sounds as if a stampeding herd of buffalo is just over the ridge.

Cresting over a small moss-covered rise, Jo walks to my side and stares wide-eyed at a stunning waterfall tumbling and roaring right in front of us. We are standing on a corner of a cliff where the water has cut into the limestone through the years. The water cascades over the edge some forty feet above us in a powerful stream about the width of the old mining road, then crashes straight down onto a pool of rocks below us, a fine gray mist drifting up and enveloping the whole falls like a morning fog.

"It's so beautiful! Absolutely beautiful!" she gasps.

"Notice anything unusual?" I ask.

Looking up and down, she scans the falling water. Her head jerks up after staring at the bottom of the falls. "Where is all the water?"

"Bingo!" I say with a laugh. Near the base of the falls you can clearly see a dry gulch running down the mountain side where water used to flow. Now, it is arid.

"I noticed it my first time here too. Then I came back again and hiked along the cliff base to the bottom of the falls. The force of the falling water evidently eroded the ground until it found a vein in the limestone. Now the water flows straight below ground. Then I came back another time and hiked the top of the falls. There's no feeder stream there.

"Really? Jo asks. "Where does the water come from then?"

"The water emerges from another vein about ten feet from the top of the falls and flows over. That's why hardly anyone knows about these falls; there is no water to follow in or out of here," I say.

"I guess that also explains the whirlpool we saw in Farley's Stream and why the banks were bleached so white?"

"Bingo again! Years ago, I hiked down the dry gulch below and came out almost directly above the whirlpool. The bleaching on the banks is from the limestone. Turn around and take a look."

Twisting, Jo looks and sighs. Below us is our town with the majestic Saint Vitonus spire dominating the village, the old abandoned red brick school house seemingly standing solitary sentry on its hill south of town, Farley's Stream curling along the wood line behind it. Far off in the distance, the Hudson River twists down through the valley with the Catskills in the background. The whole scene is ablaze in a late afternoon sun that casts a variegated magenta light that blinks in and out of the clouds, giving the illusion that we are watching a motion picture.

"It's beautiful, like a dream," she says with a sigh. "Can we sit awhile?"

"Sure, we have plenty of sunlight left for the hike back," I say. Sitting, I think to myself *I never get tired of this view, especially so today.* After looking at the view in silence for several minutes, I ask, "Do you have any dreams?"

Smiling, she unconsciously picks up a twig and starts dragging it back and forth across the moss. "Gee, I don't know. I guess I would really love to study abroad. I am fascinated by Europe and its history. Mom was from France and we still have relatives there. She spoke several languages and taught me both French and Italian. Though I am not fluent in either, I can read and speak both. I guess it would be a dream of mine to live there, even for a short while."

"What would you like to study?"

"Well, my mom was a teacher and I always dreamed of doing that. What I would really like would be to work with children with learning disabilities. I think I would find that rewarding. What about you? What is your dream?"

"You'll laugh."

"Try me."

"I love swimming. I have dreamed about being in the summer Olympics. Realistically, I know that won't happen because I have never had any training. I guess a more sensible dream would be to swim competitively in college someday."

"I think that is a terrific dream, and one you can make come true, if you really want to. What about a career? Do you know what you would like to do someday for a living?"

Laughing, I say, "I think I would love to teach swimming at the college level."

"I have a feeling that you will live your dream someday."

I glance at Jo. I like that she is so easy to be with, so natural in everything she says and does. Her eyes are wide as if she is trying to drink in all the scenery at once. I can't help but smile, feeling something within me that I have never experienced before, and, whatever it is, it feels wonderful. I feel as if I might be in a dream now and, if it is so, I hope I never wake.

"You know, Danny, I think I am going to like it here," she says. Again, I smile. Somewhere above us, deep in the woods, a woodpecker starts pecking on a tree sounding like a miniature jackhammer, but it is nothing compared to the pounding of my heart.

5.

April, 1964

Dutchess County, New York

Under duress from pea-sized raindrops, the four of us cautiously hike up the old mining road on the backside of Lenter's Hill on a stormy spring afternoon. Lightning snaps out of the dark, putty gray sky like sparks, thunder rumbling like a battery on a dreadnought. Carrying a cornflower blue duffel bag containing a change of clothing for everyone, my arm starts to ache from the weight. From our brief last visit, we learned how the white limestone dust clings to everything like fly paper so we have brought a change of clothes to hide the evidence from our parents. Jo has volunteered to launder everything the next time her dad is at work.

The newly emerging lime leaves on the few deciduous trees here seem muted today like we are looking at them through wax paper. I continually take furtive glances around. We're trespassing, yes, but we're also going to a location all of our parents have forbidden us to go to: Lenter's Mine. Everyone has raincoats and boots on except Tommy, who is sloshing along in old sneakers and has a garbage bag pulled over his upper body with holes torn for his arms and his head. The rain that started as slow as a snail is now falling with the speed of a cheetah out of a miserable sky. Newly formed streams slither here and there on the hillside like baby serpents. The windy air smells of mud and decay like an overturned garden, yet still fecund.

"Here it is!" shouts Billy as he waves for us all to catch up.

Walking to his side, I see the large scar in the hillside with several "No Trespassing" and "Dangerous Mine" signs half-heartedly extending their warnings. The entrance to the mine abandoned long ago. A faded *"Lenter's Limestone"* black sign with yellow letters leans against the entrance wall like it only reluctantly acknowledges ownership. The disk-shaped opening is boarded up with riven plywood and six by six boards. A Judas door built into the center is partially open with the hasp dangling out like a broken limb and the padlock hanging on impotently.

"Tommy, do you know what this mine was for?" I ask.

Unsurprisingly, he does. "Cement mostly. Unlike the dolostone that was mined from Ulster County and used to fashion the locks of the Erie Canal, this limestone mine was used mainly for cement. It was closed down in the forties for two reasons. First, bigger mines with better access to transportation opened in Ulster County. And secondly, miners here at Lenter's started to hit veins of shale which made the mine unstable." Billy and I shake our heads knowingly, no longer surprised at his encyclopedic brain. "This particular mine actually started as a natural cave. I read somewhere that the mining company enlarged the entrance, but otherwise used the cave mostly as it was, digging their own tunnels as needed."

"How you know this stuff I will never know!" says Billy. Jo looks at me, gives her head a slight shake and smiles. Though she has known Tommy nowhere near as long as the rest of us, she already is impressed by his wealth of knowledge.

"Ready?" I ask as I pull the door fully open, rusted hinges moaning in protest. Moving, we all pull out our flashlights and turn them on.

"Let's do it!" Billy yells as he enters first, striding through the door into the unknown with his usual fearlessness. I go in next, followed by Jo and Tommy, whose garbage bag outer garment swishes with each step. Inside, I shine my light on the cave wall and see a rock ledge about five feet above the floor. Walking over, I deposit the heavy duffel bag onto it.

We each shine our flashlights around the tunnel, the beams frolicking on the walls as we walk further and further into the mine. Running along the ceiling are electrical metal conduits and flexible armored cables. There are wire baskets for lights spaced every ten feet or so.

Most of them are either empty or contain broken bulbs. Spider webs hang like angel hair, seemingly from every surface. The walls and ceiling are roughly cut like they were chewed by beavers. Condensation drips from the walls and ceiling as if the tunnel is perspiring. Glancing back over my shoulder, I can no longer see the entrance but I can still hear the roar of the storm now raging outside, the sound of pounding rain echoes in the tunnel like a train rumbling on tracks.

"Guys," Tommy says. "I don't want to be a spoil sport, but caves are notorious for flash flooding. It's been raining all night and it is really coming down now. Maybe we should save this for a nicer day?"

Feeling apprehensive, I look around and say, "What do you say that we continue and at the first indication of flooding we will get out?"

"Okay," he replies but does not sound at all convinced. Looking at Billy and Jo I see neither concern nor fear.

Walking to the end of the entrance tunnel, we come to a wooden ladder. We all shine our lights down the shaft. It is about a twenty-foot climb to the muddy floor but the ladder seems sturdy enough. Shining my light to our left, I see a rusting metal framework slightly canting to one side like the Leaning Tower of Pisa. A fraying metal cable attaches to the mining cage below, goes up to a pulley hanging from a gantry, runs to a pulley outside of the framework, then back down to a rusting motorized winch that sits atop a concrete plinth. It goes through the winch and back up and around a final pulley where it supports a huge metal counterweight, similar to a construction wrecking ball, which hovers ominously in space.

There is a brass plaque on the railing reading "*Lenter's Limestone*" that has turned verdigris green over the years. Glancing to the right, I see the electrical metal conduits and cables running down the ledge wall towards the floor ending in a huge electrical box. Conduits and wires twist and turn out of the bottom, disappearing into all the tunnels.

Shining my light downward onto the mine cage, four steel posts rise in each corner from the platform floor up to the protective metal mesh cover, two of which have a coil of rope on a hook. The platform itself appears weathered and cracked, powdered white with limestone dust.

"Look over here," says Jo as she shines her light down on the ledge to the far right of the ladder.

"What are those?" asks Billy.

"They are rock anchors normally used for climbing. Strange that someone would put two here. I guess they were practicing climbing? Or maybe they are from before the ladder was put here," she says.

"Or maybe after. Maybe someone didn't trust this rickety old ladder," Billy says. "Last one to the bottom is a rotten egg!" he shouts as he boldly darts down the slippery ladder.

"Billy!" I shout. "Wait!" He doesn't acknowledge me and continues to the shaft floor.

"We have to keep him in check or we all could get into serious trouble," Tommy offers.

"Come on guys! You have to come see this!" Billy shouts.

"First sign of water and we are all out of here," I say. "Agreed?" Both Jo and Tommy nod an affirmative. I, however, am getting apprehensive about continuing on.

At the ladder's bottom, we step onto a soft, muddy floor where six sizable separate tunnels go off in different directions looking like the warren of a giant rabbit. Scattered along the edges only are hoary ice stalagmites the size of traffic cones, part of the original cave, that look like tombstones. The second tunnel from our left has a railroad track disappearing into the darkness. Several piles of chains, tools, old fraying lengths of rope, blasting mats and other discarded artifacts are scattered around each entrance, as well as up on wall ledges. By the entrance to the tunnel with tracks, a corroded loading cart sits on its side exposing its rusted metal wheels. The air is much colder here than outside. It's damp and musty too. Like the entrance tunnel, all of the walls and ceiling weep with condensation.

"Why are there so many tunnels?" asks Billy.

Tommy, of course, knows why. "For every tunnel that was used for limestone recovery, there is also one for ventilation. I would imagine that at one time huge fans would have been located in those for airing," he says.

"Why are the stalagmites only along the wall edges?" asks Jo.

"I imagine that they originally covered the floor, matching the stalactites on the ceiling," he says as he casts his light upwards, highlighting what looks like a snow-covered, upside-down mountain range. "To be able to recover the limestone, most on the floor would have been leveled."

"I bet you know how they got these carts to move too, don't you?" Billy says with a look towards Tommy.

"Are you asking me to see if I know or are you asking me because you're actually curious about them?"

"Ha! So, you *do* know how they move!"

"Well, yeah," Tommy says before continuing. "Generally, the tunnels were made sloping downwards so gravity would help move the carts. To get them back, they had cables attached to a winch which would wind the cable up and pull the carts to the start of the mine shaft. The winches had to have been powered by some source of electricity, so I'd bet that there was a generator of some sort around here at one time," says Tommy.

"What about stopping the carts as they rolled down the slope?" I say, not really all that interested. Showing off his brain is one of the few chances Tommy gets to shine. Who am I not to lob him a softball question?

"They had something called a dead man's stick, which basically means that someone had to grab this bar and push forward to release the brakes. If something happened to that person and the stick was released the brakes would engage and the cart would stop," Tommy explains.

"Tommy Willott, master of the mine. Is there anything you don't know?" laughs Billy.

"Hey guys, look at this," says Jo. She is shining her light on the soft ground in front of the tunnel to the far right of where we stand. "Footprints," she says.

Walking to her side, I shine my light onto the same spot. There are several impressions of shoes in the mud and I follow them with my light until they disappear into the tunnel.

"I guess we aren't the only ones who have come to explore," I say.

"Do you think there is somebody else here?" Jo nervously asks.

"Not possible," says Tommy confidently.

"How can you know that?" she asks.

"When Danny pulled open the entrance door, it was warped so that it made a mark in the dirt. I noticed the ground around the door was smooth before he opened it so no one else could have pulled or pushed the door recently. Rain most likely erased any previous marks." Keeping his light on the tunnel, Tommy says, "Guys, see that there?"

"What are you looking at?" asks Billy.

"The stone. That's a shale vein which means that tunnel could be extremely unstable."

After much discussion and further inspections, we decide to follow the tunnel to the far left since this is the only one that doesn't show shale veins. Walking in, the roof of the tunnel tightening above our heads and at our shoulders. The only sound is our echoing footsteps sloshing through the puddles. Reaching out, I touch a wet wall. It is sticky from the limestone. Concerned about the narrowing tunnel and how far into the cave we now are, I am just about to suggest we turn around when Billy yells from in front, "Hey guys! Come look at this!"

Catching up to him, I see that the tunnel has opened into a massive sepulchral cavern that houses a huge lake. A huge blasting mat is stretched across the floor on the rock ledge. Walking on top of it, we come to the end, shining our lights down to the water which is about fifteen feet below us. Our flashlights move back and forth looking like World War II searchlights combing the sky in search of bombers. The water against the limestone is of robin's eggs blue and the giant stalactites hanging from the ceiling look like colossal, jagged dog teeth.

"Did miners build this lake?" I ask.

"I don't think so," says Tommy. "Look up. You see those stalactites on the ceiling? They take thousands of years to form, so this cavern and lake must have been here naturally. The miners must have punched through to this room on accident," says Tommy.

"Hey guys, look back here!" Jo shouts. We all turn to see a small rivulet of water coming down the tunnel we just emerged from. It makes a burbling sound as it drops lazily over the edge, making a pat-a-pat-pat sound on the water's surface below.

My stomach sinks, thinking of Tommy's words about a flash flood.

"We should get out of here now!" cries Tommy.

"Come on! Don't be such a wuss!" shouts Billy as he shines his light around the cavern. "This is too cool." The word fear is not in his dictionary.

"Damn it, Billy! We need to get out of here. Come on," shouts Tommy. Jo and I look at each other and I now see worry in her eyes.

Ignoring us, Billy says, "This looks almost as big as Mirror Lake! That is, without Nag's Boulder." Shining his light to the tunnel on our right, he traces up the front end of a loading cart that is half way out of the tunnel. The rail tracks that are in front of it go to the rock edge and extend a few feet past, hanging in air unsupported. Addressing Tommy, he says, "I suppose you can explain that also?"

"Easy. That tunnel used to be longer than the one we came out of. Over time, the ground underneath the tracks eroded away until it collapsed and fell into the water, snapping the rails off where you now see them end."

"Is there anything you don't know?" teases Billy.

Ignoring him, Tommy says, "Look here, as he shines his light on the walls. "More shale veins. Now, let's get out of here and fast," he says as he starts back up the tunnel.

Suddenly the ground vibrates. Before anyone can move, the ledge we are standing on gives way. We all slide down with it into the gloomy water with a grumbling splash. It's ice cold and when I surface, I spit out a mouthful of it. I still have my flashlight in my hand but it is starting to fade. I can't touch bottom and start treading water. Holding the light above my head, I shine it around. I spot Billy and Jo but no Tommy.

"Where is Tommy?" I shout.

"Up here guys!"

"Tommy! Thank God," I say as I turn my weakening light on him. Turning the light around the room I see no other exits. "Tommy, go get help! Quickly!" I yell as I continue to tread water.

"You guys will never be able to last in that cold water. Hypothermia would set in long before I get anyone back here. Hang on," he says as he disappears from sight.

"Tommy!" I shout. "Where are you going?" Already I feel the cold penetrating my skin, quickly chilling my body as I start to shiver. But I also feel something else, something getting stronger and stronger. Fear.

Shining my light up the rock in front of us, I can see why the ledge we were standing on collapsed. The rock from the water up to the top has eroded away so that it is recessed. Even with the collapse, the ledge that remains still extends well over the water like a diving platform, the blasting mat now hanging over the edge like a panting dog's tongue.

"Jo," I say. "Do you still have your flashlight?" I ask.

"No, I dropped it during the fall."

"You, Billy?"

"Same thing."

"Crap," I say.

"Hey, guys, I can touch bottom over here," shouts Billy who is about four feet to my right. Both Jo and I swim over until we also can stand, but the water is still up to our waists. Shining my fading light on Billy and Jo's faces, I can see alarm and panic building. This is the first time in my life when I have seen Billy afraid. And that makes me even more afraid than I was. Quickly I decide I must do something to keep them focused on survival.

"All right," I say. "Move close together so that we are touching. This light is going to go out any second. We need to be in physical contact with each other when it quits." Jo moves over so that our bodies are touching. I can feel her body shivering. I reach down and grab her hand as Billy moves over close to Jo.

What was a small trickle of water now is coming over the edge like from a garden hose, the rushing water making a sonorous sound in the cavern. The tumbling water sluices over the limestone ledge and falls with the randomness of rain.

"Damn," says Billy as my light slowly fades and then goes out. Dropping it into the water, we are left in absolute darkness as I give Jo's hand a reassuring squeeze. The blackness and the cold are frightening, and it is all I can do to stay calm. The thought occurs to me that we could die here and I can feel my whole body shaking from cold and fear.

At first, the only sound is the newly created waterfall hitting the lake surface with a vigorous slap-slap-slap. Then, in the distance, another sound emerges.

"What the hell is that?" I ask.

"It sounds like metal or something," offers Jo.

A few seconds later, I hear a loud metal clank and see a faint light in the tunnel up to our left. The light is bouncing like it is on a trampoline as it continues to get brighter and brighter. Suddenly, Tommy appears from the tunnel shining his light down on us. "You guys still okay?"

"Yeah, Tommy, but we are freezing. We have to get out of here now!" shouts Billy. I can literally hear his teeth chattering.

"Calm down, Billy. We need to keep our wits about us if we're going to get out of here," I say. "What are you doing, Tommy?" to which I receive no answer.

I can see and hear him doing something to the back side of the loading cart, but the cold is numbing my brain. Tommy's movements and sounds are the only thing tethering me here, as my vision starts to cloud. Standing, he runs back into the tunnel as his light gets fainter and fainter and then disappears leaving us once again in total darkness.

Above me, I soon see a faint light in the tunnel we came out of. It slowly becomes brighter and brighter and is accompanied by a clanging sound. Suddenly, I see Tommy standing above us on the edge of the ledge that just collapsed.

"Hey, guys! I am going to lower down a chain that has three rope loops tied into it. Each of you put a loop under both arms and then hang on the chain as tightly as you can," he says as he starts lowering it over the edge. Suddenly my quiet desperation leaves and I feel that there might be a chance that we will get out of here. I silently thank God.

Grabbing the chain, I pass it onto Billy who in turn hands it to Jo while Tommy shines his light on us. We each pull the rope loops over our heads and under our arms and then grab the chain in front of us.

"We are all set, Tommy. What's the plan?" I ask.

"I'll pull you up, but remember to let go of the chain when you reach the blasting mat. If you don't, your hands will be caught between it and the chain. The rope loops should hold you until you are pulled over the ledge," he replies as he races down the tunnel as his light disappears, once again leaving us in blackness.

"What? How the hell is that kid going to pull the three of us up?" yells a distraught Billy. His obvious fear is becoming more and more disconcerting to me. If he is afraid, then I know we are in a dire situation.

Looking up at the other tunnel to our left, I see the light bouncing again as Tommy reemerges. Placing his lit flashlight on a rock shelf so that it shines into the cavern, he climbs up into the cart while yelling, "Hang on, guys!" With that I see him push the dead man's brake lever forward as the cart jerks almost imperceptibly, then starts inching towards the cut end of the sloping rail.

Realizing what he is doing I yell, "No, Tommy! No!" as the cart reaches the track end and then plummets over the side.

Suddenly, the three of us are being pulled straight up towards the ledge. Just before I reach the blasting matt, I let go of the chain and feel the rope loop take my weight. My chin catches the end of the matt as I am pulled up and over it and then I find myself being dragged along the muddy tunnel floor. My mouth fills quickly with water and I start choking and gagging as I try in vain to pull my arm free of the rope.

Hearing an enormous splash from below, I realize Tommy and the cart have hit the water. I'm dragged another few feet before I finally come to a stop. At first, I can't move. Slowly pushing myself up on my knees, I spit up water as I remove the rope. It is totally dark and I can't see anything. "You guys there?" I ask.

"Crap," says Billy. "My knees are killing me. It feels like the skin has been pulled off. God it hurts," he moans.

"Jo?"

"I'm here," she says weakly.

"You okay?"

"Yeah, I think so. Feels like I have some cuts and bruises, that's all."

"How about you?" Jo asks.

"Like Billy, my knees feel pretty banged up and I have a cut on my chin. Other than that, I'm okay, I guess. You guys stay here. I'll go get Tommy's light." Standing, I grab the chain and cautiously edge my way forward in total darkness. Eventually, I see a very faint light to my left as I bump into something. Feeling around, I realize it is the overturned cart we saw when we climbed down the ladder. I feel the chain is wrapped around both of the bottom wheels and then heads back down the adjacent shaft. Shuddering, I think of what would have happened if I had been pulled into it.

Edging around it, I slowly turn myself one hundred eighty degrees and move back down the adjacent tunnel towards the lake where I can see faint light. Soon, Tommy's light on the ledge comes into view. Dropping the chain, I stumble towards it, grab it and then run back the way I came.

Reaching Billy and Jo, I yell, "Come on!" as we carefully edge back to the lake ledge. Shining the light out onto the lake below us, it lights up the stalactites on the ceiling making them look like the teeth of a giant bear trap. Shining it down on the water, all I see are the waves created by the cart slapping at the mine walls sounding like an offbeat drummer.

"Tommy! Tommy!" I yell.

"Down here!" I hear.

Shining the light to the right, I see Tommy's pale face sticking out of the surrounding dark water looking like an abandoned volleyball. The water surface is starting to calm as the waves dissipate. The water is now flowing over the tops of our feet in a torrent, creating a noisy waterfall in front of us.

"Danny, behind you on a ledge to your right is another chain I found along with some rope. Tie a rope loop into it and drop it down to me. You guys should be able to pull me up."

"What?" I shout in desperation. "I can't hear you Tommy! The water is making too much noise!"

Tommy begins to frantically point behind me while yelling something I still can't make out. Turning, I shine the light along the wall until I see a ledge with a rusty orange chain coiled on itself like a garden hose. Next to it is a small section of rope. Grabbing it, I slosh over to the ledge and hand Jo the flashlight. Tying the rope onto the chain, I lower it down and yell, "Here it comes, Tommy."

Tommy reaches up a hand and grabs the chain and guides it down until he can grab the rope loop. Since we can't hear him, he makes a thumbs up gesture indicating that he is ready.

Jo places the flashlight on a ledge as the three of us get in line each holding the slippery chain. We start to pull, but as soon as we feel Tommy's weight the chain slips through our hands. After several tries, I lean over the ledge. "Tommy! Tommy, I'm sorry. It's too slippery. We can't hold onto it."

Tommy slowly drops the chain and swims away from the falling water as I move to that side of the tunnel.

"Danny, can you hear me now?" he asks.

"Yes, Tommy, I can," I say.

"Go back to the area where the loading cart is flipped over. I saw on top of it a couple of small pieces of rebar. Grab three and then put them through the chain links and then hold the bar…" Tommy continues but I can see where he's going already. I grab the light and take off in a sloshy sprint through the water to grab the rebar.

Splashing back through the swiftly flooding tunnel, I find the over-turned cart, quickly grabbing the rebar pieces. Looking up at the ladder we climbed down, I see several runnels coming over the top ledge. We're running out of time. *What next?* I think.

Heading back, I hand Billy and Jo a rebar piece which we each slip through the chain links. Laying the flashlight back on a shelf, it shines towards the ledge. Once we've all grabbed ahold, I yell, "Okay, Tommy, hang on!" Here we go!" Pulling hard and leaning backwards, the chain lurches toward us and we start shuffling our feet away from the ledge. I can feel Tommy's weight as we keep pulling and taking small steps backwards. After backing about twelve feet, a set of hands come up over the ledge. Another few yanks and I see Tommy's head with a painful looking grimace on his face.

"Keep pulling, guys!" I yell. We walk a few more steps backwards until I see Tommy's body spill over the edge. "Stop!" I scream.

We all drop the chain and move to him as he is pulling the rope loop over his arm.

"You all right, Tommy?" asks Billy as we all grab and hug him.

"Yeah guys, I'm fine. Thanks! Just some minor cuts and scrapes. You guys look worse than me. Danny, you have quite a gash on your chin," he replies.

I had forgotten about it in the rush to get Tommy out of the water. Reaching my hand up to my face, I pull it away and see it covered in blood. Jo takes her bandana off, folds it several times, then gently places it under by chin and says, "Hold pressure on this and it should help stop the bleeding.

"Thanks Jo."

"God, that was close!" says Billy while I am thinking *we are all lucky to have gotten out of the lake alive but we still are not out of danger.*

"Let's get the hell out of here!" Tommy says as he points to the rising water which is now well over our ankles.

Grabbing the flashlight off of the ledge, I turn and we all start wading back down the tunnel against the current with increasing difficulty. The water, rapidly rising, is now just below our knees. The sound of gushing water echoes off of the tunnel walls sounding like a jet engine as we finally reach the entrance chamber.

"Damn!" says Billy. "Look!"

Shining the light across the room, I see that the ladder that was there moments before is now gone.

"Crap! The water must have pushed the ladder over. What do we do now?" says Billy as he looks at Tommy.

An awkward silence follows and Tommy seems to be concentrating on something. The sounds are the booming water and our heavy breaths. From where we now stand, I can see six thirsty tunnels drinking at a furious rate. On its churning surface the current is carrying debris-rope, wood, and even discarded clothing that roars past us. It is getting increasingly difficult to even stand against it as I reach out and grab Jo's arm to help support her as Billy stumbles and falls face first.

"Crap!" he yells distraughtly. I think I detect panic. Letting go of Jo's arm I reach down and help him to his feet.

"You alright?" I ask.

"Yeah. Yeah, I'm fine. Thanks. Let's just get the hell out of here!" Reaching out, I grab Jo's arm again.

Meanwhile, Tommy is in stern concentration as his eyes go up and down the metal elevator framework. The water is now just over our knees, and I feel myself continuing to shake involuntarily from the cold. Looking at Jo, she appears pale with bluish lips and she is likewise shaking. Billy has his arms wrapped around himself, shivering, his skin clammy, his eyes darting around like a trapped animal. No one will say it, but we are all scared to death.

"Come on, get on the platform," says Tommy.

"Are you crazy, Tommy? That thing looks like it is ready to fall apart and probably hasn't been used for years," says Billy with terror evident in his tone. His rising anxiety is evident.

"Stop wasting time! Get on it!" he yells. "Danny, give me the light."

Handing him the light, we wade over one by one to get on the platform. Looking at the rope hanging from a hook on the platform, Tommy says, "Danny, take that down and give me one end and tie the other to the railing. Grabbing the rope, I give it to Tommy then watch him tie it around his waist. Handing him the rest of the coil, I tie off the other end to the platform railing.

"What are you doing, Tommy?" I ask.

"There is no time for an explanation. Just stay on the platform, all of you!"

Standing there holding onto the railing, we all watch Tommy splash back down the roiled water into the tunnel we just emerged from, his flashlight illuminating the rugged walls before disappearing, leaving us once again in total darkness. Feeling along the rail, I locate the rope and reach over, placing both hands firmly onto it.

After a few minutes, the rope goes taut. "Tommy! Where are you?" I scream. Instead of an answer, I only hear the increasing growl of rushing water.

"Billy, Jo, I am going after him," I say as I carefully duck under the railing while holding onto the rope, stepping into water now half way up to my thigh.

"No, Danny!" screams Jo. "It's too dangerous," apprehension evident in her voice.

"You two just stay on the platform as Tommy said," I say as I slowly waddle down the black tunnel while firmly holding onto the rope. The current gnaws at my legs. Shortly, I trip over something and fall face-first into the swiftly moving water, losing my grip. Suddenly I am being swept down the current, my knees and arms banging off of the stalagmites along the wall. In total darkness, I have no orientation of up and down, direction has no meaning. Desperately, I roll over and feel my hands flailing out of the water, searching for the rope. Nothing. Now tumbling over and over, I see a faint light that becomes brighter and brighter. Water is forced up my nose and into my mouth, I am coughing and gasping, growing weaker, confused. I am in total distress.

Suddenly, I feel a tremendous force on my arm and my whole body is jerked across the current. Feeling something under both arms, I am lifted up out of the water and see Tommy's face inches from mine, lit by the bright flashlight sitting on a rock ledge.

"Danny, you okay?" he hollers.

Steadying myself as I continue to hack and cough, I nod an affirmative.

"What the heck are you doing?" he says as he guides me to a rock outcrop that shields us a bit from the current.

Finally regaining my senses, I cough again and say, "I felt the rope go tight and then nothing happened so I thought you might be in trouble. What are you doing, Tommy?"

Grabbing the light, he shines it behind me. "Look."

Turning, I see a rusty old sledgehammer, the metal head the color of a pumpkin, and a long piece of rebar sitting on a rock ledge about four feet from where we are standing.

"We need those, but the rope was about two feet short and I couldn't reach them. I thought about it, but I didn't want to untie myself. I moved back here by this outcrop and was just turning to start back when I saw you."

Analyzing the situation, I say, "Stay here and I'll go back and make extra slack so you can reach them. When ready, I'll give two tugs on the rope."

"Got it. Be careful, Danny."

Grabbing the rope, I trudge back into the strong current and start back with one hand sliding and then gripping the rope, over and over. I'm totally petrified. Shortly, Tommy's light fades and I am once again in total darkness. Seconds pass like minutes as the frequency of rushing water intensifies sounding like a burst steam pipe. I am sightless and have never been this frightened in my life. I feel as if my pounding heart will burst through my chest.

Hearing the resonance of the whooshing water suddenly change, I guess that I am back in the chamber where all six tunnels start. "Billy! Jo!" I scream.

"Danny? We're still here, Danny! Thank God you're back!" yells Jo.

Continuing on, I trip again over a submerged stalagmite and fall, but I manage to keep my grip on the rope. Standing, I continue to inch forward until my hand slides up the rope and hits the metal railing of the platform.

"I'm here. I have no time to explain, but someone untie the rope!"

"Got it," shouts Billy. A few seconds later, he says, "It's free, Danny. What now?"

"Feel along the railing until you find my hand".

A few seconds later, I feel cold flesh on my right hand. "Give me the rope. I'm going to give it two hard tugs to let Tommy know it is okay. You and Jo grab my hand and, please, don't let go. I have to stretch out holding the rope to give him a few extra feet. Ready?"

"Born ready!" Billy says, suddenly sounding like he has his emotions back under control, confident even. "We've got you. We'll not let go." Smiling, I think *that is the Billy I know. Welcome back.*

Feeling both of their hands on my right hand, I stand sideways and give the rope two quick yanks. Spreading my feet and arms as far apart as I can, while still maintaining my balance in the current, I grip the rope like death in my left hand and wait.

Minutes later, I see a dull light bouncing off of the tunnel walls and boiling water. Soon, the light brightens and Tommy materializes holding a sledgehammer, its head rusted orange, and a long piece of rebar high over his head with his left hand while holding the rope in his other, the flashlight stuck in his front pocket shining upwards, the water level just inches below it.

Watching as Tommy wades up to the platform, Billy screeches, "Way to go, Tommy!"

"Thank God!" Jo howls.

Coming up to me, he has a sheepish grin on his face and I simply smile back and nod. His whole body is shaking from the cold, as is everyone else. Gesturing back without speaking due to the thundering water, he immediately heads to where the top part of a submerged motor is partially visible above the water. Motioning for me to get onto the platform, I duck under the railing and stand. Handing the flashlight to Jo, and the sledgehammer to Billy, he holds the rebar in hand, takes a deep breath and suddenly disappears under the rushing water.

"Tommy! Tommy!" yells Billy.

"Oh, no! Not again!" says Jo as I stare in horror at the spot where he was only a few seconds ago.

After an agonizing amount of time, he breaks back through the water's surface, inhaling a deep breath. Not understanding, I shout, "What are you doing Tommy?"

Standing, he doesn't seem to hear me either because of the rumble of the water echoing throughout the mine or because of his extreme concentration. He is holding the end of the now vertical piece of rebar as he wipes the water from his eyes. He points to me and grabs ahold of the rebar a few inches from the top. The water is now halfway up my chest.

Nodding, I reach under the rail and grab it where he indicated. He ducks under the railing and stands. I watch as he takes the sledgehammer from Billy and positions himself against the railing close to where I grip the steel. He motions to Jo and Billy to grab ahold of the railing, which I also do with my free hand.

With that he positions the sledgehammer, raises it back over his head and then comes down hard on the rebar which makes a sound like a radar ping. The resulting vibration causes my hand to go temporarily numb. The platform does not move and the water is now just below my shoulders.

"Shit," I see him mouth. He raises a finger indicating he will do it one more time.

As if in slow motion, I watch as he raises the sledgehammer yet again and then comes down, whacking the rebar end. I feel it move and my hand goes down with it. At the same time the whole platform vibrates and starts to rise. Dropping the rebar, I look up as the massive metal counterweight is soaring down towards us. We all scream as it goes wheeling past us, missing us by inches, followed by an explosive splash as it hits the water. The whole metal framework suddenly groans like an old man trying to get out of bed and cants slightly.

The platform stops with a jerk and we all fall to the floor. Tommy frantically points to the ledge and motions for everyone to jump. I help Jo up as Billy pulls himself up by the railing. We all turn and run, duck under the railing, and reach safety on firm ground. Turning around, Jo shines the light on Tommy who is now running across the slippery platform towards us. Suddenly, one of his feet breaks through one of the rotten floorboards. At the same time there is another metal creak, so loud it can be heard over the booming water, and the framework tilts a little further.

I desperately motion with my arm for him to hurry, then extend my hand out.

Pulling his leg out of the hole, he darts towards my extended hand. Just then, the metal framework gives way and the tower starts to crumble before me like a building being demolished. He takes one last step and jumps towards me, his whole body now suspended in air.

As gravity starts to do its work, I lean out a little further and grab Tommy's hand, which pulls me face down to the ground with a thud and sends a searing pain into my chest as water goes up my nose. I have Tommy's hand and he is dangling just over the ledge, water flowing around us. Squeezing with all of my might, I feel his hand slipping free. Just then Billy and Jo flop down on their chests and reach over and grab his shoulders.

"Okay, on three pull!" screams Billy so he can be heard. "One, two, three!"

With that, we pull with all of our strength until Tommy's upper body is on the ledge. Billy reaches over and grabs him by the back of his pants through his plastic covering and we pull him the rest of the way to safety. We all quickly stand to get our bodies off of the flooding ground as we listen to the cacophony of water. Luckily, the water flow here at the cave entrance is only a few inches deep whereas below us the tunnels are all raging, muddy torrents.

Suddenly, Tommy starts to laugh and laugh. It is contagious and the first thing I know we are all laughing uncontrollably.

"Tommy," I say, "You are one smart son of a bitch! How in the world did you do that?"

"I noticed when we first climbed down the ladder that the lift operates on an electric motor. It was common in these types of mines to have a backup method of operation in case of an explosion, power outage or other issues that affected its operation. They had to have another way of getting out besides just a ladder. In this case it is the counterweight that was hanging alongside of it. When the winch brake is released, the weight drops and as a result pulls the platform up. I positioned the bottom of the rebar into the latch that held the brake in place. When I whacked it with the sledgehammer, it released the counterweight and pulled the platform up."

"Damn, you are smarter than the average bear!" says Billy.

"You saved all of our lives. I was scared to death and was sure we were not going to make it out alive. Thank you," says Jo as she embraces him, tears wetting her cheeks. Billy and I join in.

"I hope someday, somehow, I can repay you for this Tommy," I say.

Abruptly, there is another noise in the tunnels besides the surging water. At first it is only a very distant, indistinguishable susurrus and then it becomes a thrumming. Steadily it becomes slightly louder, clearer and closer. Even above the roaring water I can distinctly hear the screeching and squealing coming from the bottom of the mine.

"Quick!" Tommy yells. "Get outside as fast as you can! Now!"

There is a moment of confusion and hesitation, but then we see what looks like a black cloud coming out of one of the tunnels below us. The clapping sound now is deafening. Turning, we all skate down the slimy tunnel shaft, slipping and sliding past the duffel bag, out through the entrance into the fading twilight. Peeling off on the other side of the mouth of the mine, we all plaster our bodies to the wall as a black cloud blows out of the tunnel and explodes up into the leafy trees.

"Bats?" I say.

"Thousands of them. Maybe tens of thousands," Tommy says. "When we first entered the lake cavern, I saw a few bats roosting from the ceiling. The rest of them must have been deep inside the tunnels."

I realize that it is close to night out now. With all that happened inside, time has slipped away. I am emotionally spent, freezing and hungry. My chin is sore and raw, but the bleeding has thankfully stopped. I am also grateful to be alive. My whole body is involuntarily shaking and my teeth are chattering along with everyone else.

The violent, petulant rainstorm that was raging when we entered has been replaced by a clearing night with velvet colored sky along with a sliver of a crescent moon. We stand in silence looking at it and the millions of sparkling stars that are emerging when Tommy suddenly says "What a terrific night!"

"What a terrific night to be alive," says Jo.

"I'll second that, Jo," says Billy.

Putting my arms around Tommy and Jo, while looking at Billy, I say, "What do you all say we step back inside, grab the duffel bag and change into dry clothes before we freeze to death? You guys ready to go home?"

"Born ready!" they say in unison as we all laugh and head back inside.

6.

May 1964

Dutchess County, New York

Saturday morning breaks like a clap of thunder. I'm fast asleep when a loud explosion awakens me and I shoot out of bed. After standing quickly, I have to grab onto the pine bed post to keep from falling from dizziness.

Pulling the faded blue and white gingham curtains aside, I look down from my second story bedroom window through the rain streaked glass to see our neighbor Joey standing beside his old black thirty-nine Chevy. His hands are on hips while he shakes his head. Black smoke is curling up from the carburetor like a genie, an indication that he has once again poured a capful of gas into it in an attempt to start the car. The ever-present Camel is hanging from his weathered mouth, his joyless eyes squinting from the smoldering ash as he surveys the damage. A large black crow swoops low inspecting the scene like an insurance adjuster then, evidently satisfied, flies up and disappears into the branches of a maple tree.

Letting the drapes fall back into place, I turn and head to the bathroom while rubbing a hand across my face. Turning on the cold water, I reach down and cup my hands. Splashing water on my face, I attempt to remove the cobwebs from sleeping. Grabbing a hand towel, I dry myself. Looking at the mirror, I see the shiny silver from my top and bottom braces reflecting like a warning from a lighthouse. Grabbing the butch stick wax, I glide it over my brown crew cut like I am varnishing a table. Pushing a brush towards the back of my head, the short length hairs come rigidly to attention like a private saluting a general, ready for another day.

Heading down the creaking wooden stairs, I glance at the portrayal of the Last Supper that was put up by my grandfather when he owned the house. Smelling the intoxicating aroma of the brewing coffee my mother is preparing, I walk down the remaining stairs.

I started drinking coffee when I turned thirteen, with my dad's permission, and now a year later I can't imagine starting the day without some. I love going shopping with Mom at the A&P. As soon as you walk in, the smell of freshly ground coffee attacks your senses like a swarm of bees. She purchases the Eight O'clock Coffee brand beans and then lets me grind them at the register. Even though I never tasted it, because we can't afford it, the Red Circle Coffee is something I dream about. I mean, if it is better than the Eight O'clock it has to be unbelievably good, right?

"Good morning, Mom," I say, grabbing a chipped cup and pouring the dreamy mysterious liquid from the dented silver percolator. Breathing in the aroma, I head for my metal chair. In the background the Beatles pound out 'Can't Buy Me Love' from the green Emerson radio on the countertop.

"Good morning," Mom says without looking up from her newspaper. "Your football pants and shirt are on the living room table. And if Buck is on the couch again, get a folded newspaper and chase him outside!"

"Thanks. I'll let him out," I say as I look up at the pendulum clock on the crooked brick chimney that indicates it's eight forty-five.

"Good lord, not again!" says Mom.

"What?" I ask.

"Another young boy has gone missing in Poughkeepsie. That's the second one this year," she says, her lips drawing together tightly in a grimace. "Make sure you go to the shop after the game. Your father has some work that he wants you to help him with."

"I will."

"We both really appreciate your helping out with the business."

"No problem, Mom," I reply.

"I'll give Dad clean clothes for you and you can shower and change at the shop after the game."

"Thanks, Mom."

Looking up at the small chalkboard on the wall, I see that Dad has written the day's high and low tide times as is his custom. Since retiring from the Coast Guard, this is his one tenuous connection to the water and a daily ritual. Everyone in our house knows when the daily tides occur, always.

Next to the chalkboard is Dad's depth chart showing a section of the Hudson River from Poughkeepsie up to Catskill. Studying this chart through the years, I learned that after the 'World's End' by West Point, one of the deepest sections is just off a small cove where I learned to swim. At low tide there, you can walk out about fifteen feet or so in water that's a few feet deep until eventually you reach the top edge of an underwater cliff that extends downwards over one-hundred and ten feet.

"Oh, and Danny, try not to get hurt this time. Now eat your breakfast, but don't forget to say grace."

Saturday morning football is a standing date for all the boys in our small town. No pads, full contact tackle football. It has been played for as long as I can remember. I'm not sure who started it, or when, but it is the highlight of all our weekends from April until June when little league starts. Then we recommence in September and play until either the cold or snow, or both, drives us all inside for the long winter wait for spring.

Today's game is different. Once a year the 'The Herd' comes to play us. This team is comprised of a group of boys who are in our same class at school, but who live in a neighboring town. It is an intense, hotly contested game and our town has lost the last seven in a row, all by a wide margin, dating back to before I even knew the game existed. We've looked forward to this game every year since I can remember, and our excitement for this particular matchup is at a fever pitch for a few reasons. First and most obviously, we want to end the town losing streak. In addition, the school thug Sandy Stewart is a member of 'The Herd,' as is Paul Agnos, their star running back. Agnos has single handedly torn us up the last two meetings and this year we're finally going to stop him. *Or so I hope,* I think.

The day started rainy and cloudy, but it's now giving way to a warming sunshine. I meet up with Billy, Jo and Tommy at the town war memorial. Both Billy and Tommy at first were reluctant to accept the newcomer Jo into our group as an equal. After their shared experience in Lenter's Mine, however, a new bond was formed, forged like steel. They both now respect Jo and have taken on the role of protective brothers. Today she will be our cheerleader, as well as keeping a fresh supply of towels and water at the ready.

We short cut through the woods up the steep, rock covered path on the south side of town that emerges at the old brick schoolhouse. Walking around the deserted building, the field presents itself down a steep hill behind a row of protective, towering elm trees with Farley's Stream on the far side. The first flowering buds have popped, the smells of spring are everywhere. Black and yellow butterflies bounce amongst the dandelion tops on the hillside, mingling with honey bees.

Even though the field is technically owned by the town, the residents are the ones who keep it up, mowing, weeding, shooting woodchucks and filling in their holes, whatever needs tending to. It's still spring and the field hasn't been mowed yet this year. The grass is thick and bent over like an old man from the winter snow and ice. Today's game promises to be a muddy affair.

Known as the 'Dock Rats,' everyone on our team is jacked for this game. Our teammates are already on the field tossing balls around. 'The Herd' has not yet arrived.

"Hey, guys," we all yell as we toss a football amongst us like a hot potato.

"Hey, Danny, are you going to finally stop Agnos today?" Chucky kiddingly asks. Chucky is a pitcher on our little league team who has hit more batters than he has thrown strikes over the past two seasons. When on the mound, his eyes bulge and his head unconsciously rotates from side to side, making him look like a crazed Rat Fink bobble head doll. These two things make him the best pitcher in the league since no one can stay in the batter's box. Fear, I have learned, is a powerful motivator.

"You can bank on it, brother!" I reply, feigning a confidence I don't actually have while rubbing the forearm that Agnos fractured last year when I attempted a late game tackle. He scored, I fractured. After that, it took a lot of convincing of my mom to let me play again. An assist goes to Dad on that.

I play running back on offense and middle linebacker on defense which pits me against Agnos in man to man coverage and I have a sinking feeling that today, like last year's game, could be a long day. Billy is our quarterback, and he is quite good. Taller than almost everyone else, he can easily see over the defense and spot his receivers. On defense, he plays next to me in his outside linebacker position. Tommy, the smallest boy on the field, we try to keep hidden and out of harm's way. He plays at the back of the defense at safety and is a wide receiver on offense, though most of the time Billy goes another way with the ball. We all do our best to look out for him out there, but he's fearless and finds ways into the action more than anyone would like.

The sound of closing car doors draws our attention and we see 'The Herd' walking down the hill as their parents start removing chairs from their trunks. Towering above the rest of 'The Herd' are Sandy and Agnos. Agnos, like Sandy, has flunked a grade or two and as a result he is also bigger and stronger than everyone else. Sandy is just shy of six feet tall and solidly built. He has the slight shadow of a gut that I'm sure will expand exponentially in the coming years. Of course, his hair is sand colored.

Agnos stands about six feet even and is all muscle. His nose, several times broken, is slightly crooked. His russet eyebrows are thick as steel wool and give him a menacing look as do the muscled arms. We probably shouldn't let either of them play, but what can you do?

"Hey, Danny. You ready for your annual ass kicking?" Agnos jokes.

"It's a new year," I say.

"Hey, Jo. If you get tired of these losers, you can come with me after the game."

"You got to be kidding, right? You're lucky I'm not playing. You could never catch me," Jo says.

"Well, if you do get into the game, make sure you take off those gold earrings you are always wearing. I would hate for them to get bloodied," he laughs while giving her a wink.

After a few more friendly insults shouted back and forth we get right to it. Billy and I go to the center of the field and meet the two muscular rivals for the coin toss. Since they are the visitors, they get to make the call.

"Heads," shouts Sandy as the quarter rises and then falls with a splat on the ground. I notice that he keeps his eyes on me and not on the coin. He evidently has not forgotten the beating Billy gave him at school and I guess I am guilty by association.

"Heads it is," I declare. Do you want the ball or to defend?

Laughing, Agnos replies, "What do you think Danny? We receive." Knowing the south end of the field is where the water always drains to, I choose to defend the north end. That means in the second half when the field will be at its sloppiest, their offense will be going towards the muddiest goal. If we can keep it close in the first half that may be our best chance.

"Danny, are you still bleeding?" asks Tommy as Jo hands out towels and passes around a canteen of water.

"I thought you weren't going to get up after that hit," says Billy. It is half time and, despite being down 16-6, we are feeling pretty good about it. Since there are no goalposts, everyone goes for a two-point conversion after scoring a touchdown. They have converted both of theirs and we were stopped on ours.

The mucky field has definitely helped us, slowing down their two bigger runners. We've been able to gang tackle, something that on a dry field we wouldn't have had the speed to do. Towards the end of the first half, Agnos broke loose and was lumbering down the far side-line, mud flying up from his feet like a thoroughbred as he chugged towards the goal line. Tommy was the only thing between him and a touchdown. *This could get ugly*, I thought before picking out a spot in front of Agnos and running as fast as my legs would carry me through the slimy, chaotic grass. As the distance between Agnos and Tommy closed, so did the distance between them and me. Just before the three of us were about to reach the same spot I yelled for Tommy to duck. With mud at his feet, and Tommy's lowered body just a few steps in front of him, Agnos has no way to stop himself or change directions. When his feet find Tommy, he helplessly trips. At the same moment, I flew through the air to put him down, but not before his infamous straight arm caught me on the jaw as we both landed in the cold, wet mud-spattered grass together. I rolled over and felt warm blood gushing out of my mouth and down my chin. The half ended with me lying on the two-yard line.

Agnos had quickly gotten up and extended his hand to me to help me rise. "Bet you can't wait for the second half, eh Danny?" I just smiled silently as he pulled me up and then I helped Tommy to his feet.

"Way to go, Tommy," I whispered to him. "You stopped him cold."

"I did, didn't I?" he exclaimed as he walked towards our teammates beaming.

The second half follows the pattern set in the first half, but the field continues to disintegrate beneath our sodden Converses. Keeping your footing is a chore, and stopping once you've gotten some momentum behind you is almost impossible to do without falling. With less than five minutes to go, with us still trailing 16-6, Sandy grabs a toss from the quarterback and bursts through our line so fast that he's directly in front of me before I even realize it. I brace for the collision when a blur comes from my right side followed by a cracking sound and a splash of mud. For a moment what has just happened doesn't register, but I can see the ball lying on the ground. Next to it is Billy and the injured Sandy, who is already yelling and crying out in pain.

"Danny! Danny! Grab the ball! Grab the ball!" implores Billy.

Snapping out of my daze, I scoop the ball up and start running as fast as my legs and the muck will allow. My teammates are throwing blocks for me up and down the field, and I'm closing in on the goal line with one obstacle in my way, Agnos. I warily veer to my right and just as suddenly change direction gingerly to my left. He bites on the fake and as I streak by him applying his patented stiff arm to his chin, I can hear his body hit the ground like a sack of flour. Crossing the goal line, I turn to see all my teammates charging towards me while both Sandy and Agnos are still crumpled up on the muddy ground. I grin like a Cheshire cat.

We make the two-point conversion but still lose the game 16-14. However, it somehow seems like a win and we celebrate wildly after time runs out. Just to be competitive, in light of our history of lopsided scores, is a victory to us. Sandy has a dislocated shoulder and Agnos has lost a front tooth. This more than anything feels like a victory, pay back for the continuing losing streak. *There is always next year*, I think.

Climbing the hill towards the old schoolhouse with my friends, I think *we are a team*. It took teamwork for us to make it safely out of Lenter's Mine as it did to keep today's game close. This is a good feeling, to be a part of something, and I smile.

Walking towards Market Street and the Sugar Bowl store for celebratory birch beers, Chucky asks, "You guys hear that the church is looking for more altar boys? I became one over the winter and it's great!

"Oh yeah?" Billy says skeptically. "Why's that?"

"Well, you get out of classes during the week to serve morning mass, but the best part is that on Thursdays Father Donovan takes us to swim at the convent and they have an indoor pool! It was the former mansion of some rich guy and after he died, he left it to the church."

"What, you get to swim in the winter?!" I exclaim.

"Uh huh," Chucky replies.

"Sounds great to me!" exclaims Billy.

"What do we have to do?" I ask, too busy thinking of the warm water of the pool to notice Tommy standing silently by, his hands in pockets, staring at the muddy ground.

After our celebration at the Sugar Bowl, I head east on Market Street. Passing by the Mobil Station, I head out of town on the county road amongst the drumlins for about a half mile until I reach the dirt drive for Oakley's Farm. By the rusting, slightly canted mailbox is a white sign with pictures of violets and the words "*Oakley's: Wholesale Only*" printed in a bright red script. Below it is a smaller black sign with "*Fosse Blacktopping, Stan Fosse Owner*," hand written in white letters.

Walking down the long dirt driveway, the sun reflects off of the glass on several of the greenhouses causing me to squint. Both sides of the drive are planted with cattle corn, the stalks beginning to bust through the tilled dirt surface. Several crows are scattered like litter amongst the stalks, lounging in the sun. In the distance I see the old two-story farmhouse surrounded by an island of towering white pines. The air has a sweet smell of freshly tilled earth and pollen.

Seeing the farm's owner, Mr. Oakley, out in the field on a tractor, I give him a wave. He takes off his straw hat and flaps at me, replacing it as he returns to concentrating on his work. His sheepdog Bullet is further out in the field chasing the crows to flight.

Passing by the house, I follow the road out back where a huge red barn sits, immaculately painted, and meticulously cared for. It looks like a picture. White trim is around each door and window and on top is perched a white weathervane in the shape of a divining rod. A roller and blacktop spreader sit to the right of the barn. To the right a dirt road leads to parking area where five massive greenhouses housing violets fan out like the fingers on a hand. Oakley's Farm is said to be one of the largest wholesale suppliers of violets in the entire country.

Dad has been leasing space here for his shop since he started his business. I have been coming here for as long as I can remember and I love the place. On each visit I am filled with anticipation. There always seems to be something new to learn, something new to see.

Opening the side door, the smell of diesel oil, tar and grease greet me. Stepping inside, it takes my eyes a few seconds to adjust. The inside is one huge space with all the rough sawn framework exposed. Huge twenty-four-inch square beams extend wall to wall supported by identical vertical ones. Small fixed windows located ground level shuffle in limited light. A row of pigtail lights is strung across the center beam providing additional illumination.

Most of the barn is full of farm equipment, fertilizers and tools for the growing of violets. Ropes and chains hang from hooks attached to the vertical beams. In one corner are stacks of shipping boxes of various dimensions for the delivery of violets.

Seeing the door to the office ajar, I walk in and spot Dad hunched over his desk, a pile of papers in front of him. An International Harvester calendar displaying the newest backhoe is on the wall in front of the desk. On the opposite walls are pictures from his time in the Coast Guard. Though my mother is the one who taught me to swim, it was Dad who first fascinated me with his stories of the sea with the Coast Guard. I would listen in rapt wonderment as he described sailing in a storm, waves as tall as buildings that would swallow ships whole, spit them out as twisted and mangled wrecks. Or of a glass smooth sea that went on forever into the distant horizon. It was from him that I first learned that water is not inert, that it has a pulse and a life of its own and needs to be respected.

Hearing me enter, he swivels around in his chair. His thin build belies the layers of hardened muscle, but his thinning hair shows the years are advancing. His tan face surrounds brown eyes that can look both friendly and cautious at the same time. There have been many times when I have misbehaved and withered under their staring scrutiny.

"Hey, son. How did the game go?" he asks.

"We lost, 16-14."

"Wow, that must have been some game. I'm sorry I missed it." Truth be told, Dad has never seen any of my games due to the long hours he always works. But he always asks about them, always interested and sorry he could not be there.

"Yeah, it was a good one. Tomorrow most of them will know they were in a game."

"Put a hurt on them, did you?"

"You bet we did."

Smiling, he says, "Give me a few minutes to finish up here and we can get started. If you want, you can get the tools ready. But first, get cleaned up. Your clothes are in the shower."

"Thanks, Dad."

Handing him a socket, he expertly twists lug after lug on the front truck tire on the International Harvester Loadstar 1600, leaving them on a few turns. He bought the green Nineteen fifty-seven truck used and it is a constant battle to keep it on the road. The heavy loads of blacktop have taken their toll.

"Stand back, son. The locks are under pressure and could severely injure you if you got hit by one." With that, he takes a rubber mallet and whacks each lock which blow out stopping after hitting the lugs. He then twists the lugs the rest of the way off and removes the u-shaped locks.

"Okay Danny, you grab the right side and I'll get the left so we can slide it off the axle. Watch your feet when it comes off."

Tugging on the enormous tire, we slide it off. It bounces on the dirt floor and flops over causing dust to blow out.

"Alright, let's get the new one over here," he says. We both grab the tire by the edge, stand it on end, and roll it over to the axle. Lifting it with great effort, we slide it in place. Handing Dad the locks and then the lug nuts, he ratchets them tight and then secures each firmly with the breaker bar.

Finishing, he hands me the ratchet and breaker bar to return to the work bench. The workbench is immaculate, everything organized and labeled. Everything Dad owns is well cared for and organized. He once told me that you should take as good a care of your tools as you do your shaving razor.

"Thanks, son. That was a big help. Think you could change a tire by yourself now?"

"If I had help lifting it I could," I answer while smiling.

"Well, hopefully you'll go to college so you don't have to do this type of work," he says as he wipes his dirty hands with a rag.

"Don't you like your work?" I ask.

Smiling, he says, "Sure I do, son. I actually love it. I'm just saying, this doesn't have to be your future also. This was my dream, but it doesn't have to be yours. College can open so many doors for you, you can't even imagine now."

"But you went to college. Mom said before I was born you used to work in New York City and had a very good job. Why did you end up doing this?"

Laughing, he throws the rag in a trash can saying, "That, son, is a long story. But the short version is that there came a day when I realized the rat race was not for me. I was spending a good portion of each day commuting and working in a windowless cube. I asked myself, *what kind of life is that and what for?* Suddenly I realized that there was more to life than money. I wanted to be able to spend time with your mother and not on a train. And after you were born, I wanted to be around as much as possible. I wanted to be able to have dinner every night with my family."

"But couldn't you have found an easier job locally?"

"Well, I suppose I could have. I think, though, that everyone, at one time or another, dreams of owning their own business. Most people never get the chance. Or, more likely, don't have the courage. Anyway, I took a chance on starting this business and I have never regretted it. Believe me, there is nothing in the world like being your own boss. I do know that is something money can't buy."

Outside, the sound of an approaching tractor gets louder and louder and then turns to a softer engine idle.

"That must be Mr. Oakley. Do me a favor Danny, go pull open the door so he can get his tractor in here."

"Sure thing," I say as I walk to the door, grab the handle, and slide it left on its track to open it. Looking up at the tractor Mr. Oakley gives me a nod of thanks with a huge grin on his face. In his lap sits Bullet, wearing a straw hat.

7.

June 1964

Dutchess County, New York

The three of us wait anxiously in the sacristy, with its walls of distressed oak wainscoting, wearing our black cassocks and white surplices. The pilasters in each corner give the room a smallish, boxed in feeling and it smells faintly of incense and burnt candles. Having muddled through several weeks of after school and weekend classes, this is our first day as official altar boys. To ease our nerves, Father Sipp has us doing this weekday morning service which is sparsely attended. Additionally, he is allowing the three of us to serve the first time together when normally there would be two altar boys.

We got to Saint Vitonus early to perform before-mass duties which were assigned to us by Father Sipp after completion of our training. He has instructed us to set up by ourselves today, without guidance, and we are ready. Billy was delegated to wash the cruets and fill one with water and one with wine. I don't think the tasting we all participated in was part of our appointed assignments, but it certainly helped us relax. Tommy's responsibility was to place the filled cruets, the prepared chalice, and washing bowl and towels onto the credence table. I had the detail to light all of the appropriate candles on the altar and elsewhere in the church. Tommy has been chosen to lead the procession as cross bearer. Billy and I are to be candle-bearers.

Outside we hear down shifting and the rumbling engine of a car that we don't recognize. We all rush to the slightly opened stained glass sacristy window and peer through the narrow opening above the sill as a brand-new white Mustang convertible charges into the rectory driveway. Father Sipp is at the wheel, and he pulls the pony to a stop and shuts off the ignition.

"Wow!" exclaims Billy. "Look at that car! That is the coolest thing I have ever seen!"

"A Mustang convertible!" I shout.

Speechless, we all just stare and listen as the cooling muffler clicks like high heels on tile. Tommy silently backs away from the window, his eyes aimlessly looking around.

Seconds later the sacristy door opens and Father Sipp appears with a beaming smile.

"Morning, lads! Are you ready for the big day?"

"What a car, Father!" I bellow. "What happened to the old Bonny?"

"Now, now lad, let's keep it down. This is a church, after all. She is a beauty I must admit," he says as he casts his eyes back to the sparkling Ford through the window opening. "I feel ten years younger when I'm at the wheel! The priesthood doesn't supply us with too much in the way of extravagances, but I have the good fortune of having a very wealthy sister who sees to it that at the very least I have a new vehicle every few years to enjoy," he explains. "As for the Bonneville, Danny, I donated that to the convent for the use of the Sisters."

"Can we go for a ride after mass?" Billy asks.

Smiling, Father Sipp replies, "Let's see how well you all do today, lad. We can discuss a ride afterwards." With his slight frame, small, slightly curved nose and piercing green eyes, he looks more like a hawk than a man. His entire presence is bird-like and something about him makes me the slightest bit uncomfortable. He does, however, have the Mustang.

"Have all the preparations been made?" he asks as he pulls off his herringbone and hounds tooth tweed flat cap that has a colored patchwork like a quilt. Hanging it in the closet, he removes his alb and pulls it on.

"Yes, Father, everything is ready," I reply.

"We will see," he pronounces while securing his amice while whispering, "Lord, give me strength to conquer the temptations of the devil."

The mass is relatively dull with the exception of me accidently blowing my candle out while tripping on my too-long cassock and Billy juggling his candle while hot wax dripped onto his hands. To his credit, he doesn't make a sound as the molten wax cooled on his skin, though he later admits that the potential ride in the new car was forefront in his mind and he didn't want to do anything to throw our chances into jeopardy.

After we all reenter the sacristy, Father Sipp silently surveys us as we nervously wait. Watching him as he eyes, I feel like we're in a police lineup and I shift my weight anxiously. There is something off about him that I can't quite put my finger on. The smell of incense and burnt candles seems stronger now than it was before, the room a little darker.

Finally, a smile cracks across his face. "Well done, lads, well done," he says. "Though, next time let's try not to breathe directly on the candle, eh Danny?"

"Yes, Father," I whisper.

"And Billy, how are your hands? I am sure that hurt but because you didn't make a sound and showed such respect for the mass over your pain, you all get a ride after you change!" he announces.

"All right! Way to go Billy!" I roar as I pat him on the back.

"And one more thing, lads, let's leave all the wine for me next time, okay?" We all silently nod with mischievous grins upon our faces.

As he removes his amice he speaks again. "Before we go lads, I have a little something from the church in appreciation for your dedication in becoming altar boys." He reaches into the closet and removes a plain brown paper bag. Inside are three small, fabric-covered boxes. As he hands each of us one, he places his left arm on our shoulder and gives a firm squeeze. Catching Billy's eye, he makes a furrowed frown as I nod.

"Give it a look. We haven't all day."

Simultaneously, we all open our boxes revealing sparkling silver Saint Christopher medals on matching chains.

"Do any of you know who Saint Christopher is?" he asks. Seeing our blank look, he continues. "Christopher is the patron saint of travelers. He will protect you all as you travel through your lives as long as you wear this medal."

"Now, there is one last order of business, lads. As I am sure you are all aware, you are now invited to the weekly swim. Every Thursday, Father Donovan picks a small group of lads up here at the rectory and transports them to the convent's indoor pool for ninety minutes of swimming. Since we now have twelve altar boys, you lads will get to go every third week. On your day make sure you are here promptly at six forty-five p.m. Again, thank you for your work today. Run along outside, I'll meet you out by the car in a few minutes," he says as he exits the room with his cap in hand.

"Wow. Indoor swimming! I can't wait," Billy exclaims. My attention, however, is on the medal in the palm of my hand.

"I have never seen anything so beautiful," I utter while fingering my medal. It makes me feel honored, proud and special, like I am a member of an exclusive group within the church. Also, I know it will make my parents pleased.

"Hey, guys," whispers Tommy. "I have an idea. Why don't we put these on now and pinky swear to never, ever take them off? Friends forever."

"Great idea," I say as I pull the chain over my head and extend my pinky. After an awkward silence, Billy follows suit and likewise extends his. Smiling, Tommy inserts his pinky amongst ours as he shouts, "One, two, three friends forever!" The three of us bend our fingers down and then point to the sky until we are released from each other.

Ten minutes later, we're standing in front of the silent car with our mouths hanging open like a row of empty airplane hangars. It is the first time any of us have been this close to a brand-new car and the Mustang is flawless. It is a spotless. The polished white paint is unblemished and the silver letters spelling out 'FORD' gleam on the front of the long hood. In the middle of the chrome grill is the sprinting logo, racing from right to left. The two slightly recessed oval headlamps sit slightly above the chrome bumper and seem to suspiciously watch us.

Walking around to the driver's side with its single long door, we peer in at the twin red bucket seats, a white knobbed four speed gear shift between, matching bench seat in the back. The fold down top is secured just behind on the short rear deck. The chrome wire wheel covers look to be fresh from an ancient Grecian chariot.

"Tommy," Father Sipp calls from the doorway of the rectory. "Can I see you for a moment before we go?" As he emerges, the screen door makes a hollow thud as it swings shut. Behind Father Sipp is the rectory housekeeper, Mrs. Armstrong, with an armful of laundry to hang. Spotting us, she gives a quick wave before returning to her work.

As Tommy sheepishly walks to the rectory steps, Billy says, "I'm guessing he wants to talk about his mother."

"Probably. She seems to be getting worse. I saw her coming out of the A&P last week and it looked like the shopping cart was the only thing holding her up. It must be tough on Tommy seeing her self-destruct."

"Yeah. I can't imagine what that poor kid is going through."

Placing his hand on his shoulder, we hear Father Sipp inquire, "Your mother, Tommy, how is she doing?"

"Fine, I guess," he answers while looking at the ground.

"Tommy, please look me in the eye. That's better. She missed the group meeting last night so I am concerned," he explains.

"I know."

"Listen Tommy, this is not your fault and nothing for you to be ashamed of. Your mother simply has a problem and I am trying to help her. Do you understand?" he says.

"Yes, Father," he utters.

"Good, lad. After we drop off the others, I will bring you home and pay her a visit. Now, let's go for that ride," he declares as he guides him towards us with his hand still on his shoulder.

"Okay, lads, everyone grab a seat and let's go!" he says as he pulls his cap on.

Billy and my eyes meet with the recognition that we each want to ride shotgun and we both take off like it is the starting bell at the Kentucky Derby. He runs towards the front and I to the rear. Fortunately, the Mustang has a short rear end, so I make the two turns and am at the passenger door a split second before him. Plus, I have the advantage that the door opens towards him. What I didn't expect was for him to jump over the door, landing on the seat and then spinning down into a sitting position while laughing. Father Sipp gives him the evil eye but can't help grinning. Billy opens the door to allow Tommy and me to clamber into the back seat.

"Seatbelts, please," says Father Sipp which is immediately followed by three successive clips as all lap belts are secured. Inserting the key, he turns the ignition and the pony's engine roars to life. Adjusting the rearview mirror, he turns while placing his right arm on the rear of Billy's seat as he cranes his neck while backing into the street.

"Ready, boys?"

"Yes, Father!" we roar back.

Stopping the car, he shifts into first gear. As he releases the clutch, he punches the gas pedal almost to the floor as the straight six engine responds like a horse being whipped, tires squealing and the smell of burning rubber filling our nostrils.

For a few stunned seconds the only sounds are the wailing engine and Father Sipp's laughter. "Lads, this car will be the death of me!" he shouts as our bodies are temporarily sucked back into the seats. Then we fill the air with our whoops and hollers as we stretch waving arms and hands to the sky. He turns the car left onto South Street, which merges with a county road on the edge of town just past the Mobil station. The car thunders out into the open countryside. We snake through the drumlins, past the Oakley Farm, with Lenter's Hill looming in front of us as the warm summer sun is caressing our smiling faces as Father Sipp tugs his cap tightly down.

"Father, can I turn on the radio?" asks Billy.

"Help yourself, lad."

Billy leans to his left, and begins turning the tuning knob. A blur of music, static and voices follows until he stops on WABC 77. Peter, Paul and Mary are soulfully singing 'Blow'in in the Wind' and we all start to sing along badly out of key and not caring in the least. A white streak, we race down the open county road as we sing with voices thundering, hair blowing in the wind, smiles as innocent as a lamb.

8.

July 1964

Dutchess County

Father Donovan pulls his car slowly off of Fishing Grounds Road and starts up a crushed bluestone driveway lined with towering oak trees. Verdant emerald-colored lawns cascade into the expanse on both sides. In the distance I can see the convent, the mansion left to the church by a wealthy railroad baron. The single-story structure glistens a bright white like a movie star's teeth. Identical floor-to-ceiling windows wrap around the entire structure. The top of each window has a semicircle of stained glass that look like giant Japanese fans. The recessed front entrance is protected by two grooved marble columns that extend from the floor to the roof, each with a diameter of a mature oak tree. A single-entry-light hangs from the ceiling over black and white diamond patterned granite tiles that shine like a happy memory.

Exiting the car, we all shadow Father Donovan through the front door like ducklings, our gym bags in hand. Upon entering the main hall, we all stare in wonderment. The room seems larger than the gym at school. The same black and white diamond-shaped tiles from the entranceway gleam like gems throughout the mammoth room. A hefty lone crystal chandelier hangs from the center of a coved rotunda in the middle of the room, its many lights glistening like stars. Comfortable looking furniture is scattered around the room amongst end tables with shaded lamps, a lonesome piano sits by itself in the corner, a sterling silver eight-branched candlestick on its top.

Father Donovan, pointing to our far left, says, "The pool is that way, boys. Watch out for the step down from this level to the pool. Go and have fun, and no running!"

Walking the way indicated, I glance back over my shoulder and see

Father Donovan heading in the opposite direction where a group of nuns are sitting and enjoying what appears to be tea or coffee.

Stepping down onto white marble tiles, we enter the pool area. We're all so excited for our first visit that we wore our swimming trunks under our faded and ripped Lee jeans. Our clothes are quickly discarded and set down against the wall on top of our gym bags.

Standing at the brink of the pool, my toes hang over the marble edge as I inhale the strong aroma of chlorine. Along the eastern wall to my right are three expansive floor-to-ceiling windows identical to the ones I saw in the front of the building. Outside, I spot avocado-colored trees standing guard on the expansive lawn with low-trimmed hedges protecting them. A groundskeeper can be seen in the distance hunched over his tractor wearing a white pith helmet like some ancient British explorer.

White marble columns, spaced evenly along each side of the pool, are identical to the ones at the front entrance, and they sparkle in the low evening sunlight like jewels. Three ceiling lights, equally spaced in line with each window's center, reflect off the surface of the sapphire water. The coved ceiling gives the impression of a cave. Shadows and light fight for station. Outside the air is heavy with July languor, but in here the marble floors and columns together with the cool water seem to soak it in like a sponge, leaving the air very comfortable. The whole room is painted a light, subtle blue which is relaxing.

Dipping my toe into the water, I smile. It's cool, but much more comfortable than the chilly waters of my usual swimming spots at Mirror Lake or the Hudson. The crackles of laughter from my friends echo through the labyrinth halls of the mansion like shouts in a deep canyon.

Thinking back, I remember the first time I ever swam in the Hudson River with my mother. She parked the car in a lot next to an octagon picnic pavilion before we walked down the dirt access road that paralleled the river. Tall and twisted white pines stood on both sides, making a soft carpet of dropped orange-brown needles. Coming upon the small cove that we would often picnic at later, we carefully stepped off of the road with our eyes peeled for treacherous black water chestnuts.

The cove was enclosed on three sides with shale cliffs, each about fifteen feet high and about twenty feet in width. We walked down to the beach on a gentle incline that was cut in the middle of the north cliff for easy access. Cedar trees grew out of the shale ledges with tenuous footing, seemingly defying gravity.

The smooth, glossy gray and brown pebbles on the beach were no larger than a fingernail and as thin as paper, having been scoured by tides and waves for centuries. Picking one up in my fingers, it snapped in half like a twig in winter. Setting a blanket down, Mom pulled out my faded and tattered orange life jacket that was so large that it made swimming almost impossible. I remember Mom sitting before me on her beach towel patiently demonstrating her version of the Australian crawl: one, two, three and breathe; one, two, three and breathe; one, two, three and breathe, she had told me over and over and over again until I had it memorized.

Our first visit coincided with low tide. At low tide, you can wade out in water that is only a few feet deep for about fifteen feet or so until you came to the top edge of an underwater cliff which dropped straight down for over a hundred and ten feet, making this spot one of the deepest on the entire river and a channel edge for the tankers and tugs.

On that day, and on each subsequent trip to the beach, she would swim out into the river. With her head face down, her graceful arm effortlessly would come up from her leg, angled at the elbow, reaching over and far out in front making a powerful pull as her body surged forward as if propelled, her dimpled white swim cap reflecting in the bright sunshine. This was followed with the other arm and then repeated by the first, followed by a half head turn, just enough to breathe in air, her face then again turning into the water as the whole process would repeat itself. She would swim out about twenty yards or so, turn, and while treading water, yell for me to come to her. I would walk slowly into the cold water, hesitate, and then slowly wade out as the water approached the level of my neck, carefully feeling for the cliff's edge with my toes. Finding it, I would leap forward like a dog jumping in for a stick. The muddy river water would get into my eyes, blurring my vision as my small arms rubbed and chafed against the life preserver while my legs kicked furiously as I tried to mimic my mother's form. It would take time, but I always would make it to her where she would snatch me up protectively into her arms while I struggled to catch my breath, a huge satisfied smile on my face.

By the time I was eleven we would swim out together, side by side: one, two, three and breathe; one, two, three and breathe; one, two, three and breathe. My old life jacket would sit discarded on the beach, a safety net no longer required. I learned to always be aware, to have respect for the river and be on my guard. The Hudson could be as lovable as a sleeping newborn one minute and then as hateful as a junk yard dog the next, ready to bite at you with rolling white capped waves the size of an entry door, or to swallow you whole like a python with its vicious tides. But it also had an unspoken charm, a certain magic and its own life. It was as if it had its own song which I only could hear.

We would angle our swim northwest, diagonally against the current, towards the ancient lighthouse located almost in the river's middle, where it warned of the shallows behind it. The deserted two-story building sat desolate and lonely on a slightly canted circular stone foundation, having settled over the years. The concrete walkway that circled the building was guarded by a rusted and bent wrought iron fence. The siding was cedar shake with peeling white paint. A faded red mansard roof missing shingles sat on top. In the center of the roof rose a dirty glass light tower with a sagging circular catwalk around it. Sometimes a fog would roll in, looking like a bubbling witch's cauldron, obscuring everything except the glass tower with its automated light, rising out of the mist like a crystal steeple guiding the way.

Most times we would not make it to the building; instead we would stop and float with the tide treading water while we relished the solitude, beauty and wonder of the water. Usually we would float past the beach we left from and then have to swim vigorously against the tide to make it back. Mom taught me to always keep a reserve of energy in case of trouble, to never swim yourself into exhaustion. Many times, the tide would seem to have us firmly in its grasp. We would both reach deep down within ourselves and find another gear, a burst of energy and speed, and break free of its grip. Side-by-side we would power through the tide to shore. By the time we emerged onto the beach, we would both be out of breath. We would collapse on our beach towels, reveling in the warming summer sun. Then Mom would magically produce sweetened ice tea along with peanut butter and crackers from a brown paper bag and all would be great in my world. Occasionally, tankers or tugs would pass close by, hugging the deep channel edge, appearing so close it seemed we could reach out and touch them. We would have to scoop up our belongings and race up the shale path before the waves came crashing in. Standing in silence, we would watch and listen as the waves invaded the small cove, thundering off of the semicircle of rocks and cedars then roaring into each other until it seemed that the water was boiling. Once their energies cancelled each other out, the flat water would seep back into the river leaving a perfectly smooth beach, all signs that we had been there erased.

How I loved being there near the water, being in the water. How I loved swimming. Time stopped when I was swimming, the world a distant blur, a low hum of something heard but not recognized. I was at home in the water.

My reverie at the edge of the pool is broken as Billy and Tommy streak by me and cannon ball into the pool. The resulting splashes soak me from head to toe. Laughing, I follow suit and land between them, a water tsunami flowing up over the edge onto the white marble floor.

Pulling myself up onto the pool edge, I see Father Donovan stepping down from the main hall to the pool floor level smiling. He is carrying a cheap folding chair which he opens poolside and sits to watch us. He is older, in his early sixties, and has an air of quiet authority. He has a squarish build with a full head of sandy brown hair with only a rumor of encroaching gray. His blue eyes sparkle as he smiles, which he is wont to do most of the time. He also looks tired. I like Father Donovan. As does everyone else, or so it seems.

"Ten more minutes boys, then to the showers," he shouts as he tries to be heard over the roar of three energy charged boys. Shortly thereafter, we all reluctantly climb out of the pool as he is insistently tapping on the face of his Timex.

"Father, which way is the shower?" I inquire.

"The door is down there on the left, at the far end of the pool," he answers while pointing.

The three of us scoop up our clothes, shoes and gym bags and walk gingerly on the slippery floor followed by Father Donovan. Upon reaching a solid oak door, Billy turns the knob and pushes it open revealing a small changing area the size of a ping pong table with a wall bench along the left side. On the opposite end from where we just entered is another solid oak door. Opening it, I see a sight none of us had ever seen before.

In front of us is a room approximately twelve feet by twelve feet completely covered in light blue tile, including the floor and ceiling. Four can lights, one at each corner of the room, cast a dull glow over the area. In the middle of the room are three stainless steel pipes, one at the back end with the other two in front, extending vertically like a tripod with circular horizontal tubes sprouting like octopus tentacles every foot or so. There is a total of six of these level conduits spaced about a foot apart. They do not make a complete circle, but end at the two vertical pipes at each side of the entrance, allowing room enough to walk through. All of the horizontal pipes are full of holes punched on the inside half. The three vertical pipes all curve up towards the center ending in an oversized shower head.

"What do you think, boys?" Father Donovan asks.

"What is it?" inquires Billy.

"Watch," he replies as he walks to the right wall and pulls down a steel lever located there. Reaching below, he adjusts a temperature knob as the pipes hiss and whistle as air is pushed out of the small holes followed by a stream of gurgling, steaming water. The holes in the horizontal tubes are punched at varying angles so that the spray crisscrosses the inside space in every conceivable direction.

"Wow!" exclaims Billy.

"It's called a needle shower," offers the Father. "This one was custom built by the original owner to be oversized so that it could accommodate a wheel chair as well as an attendant. As a result, I think you three can easily get in there at the same time. Give it a go, boys! When you're done, put your wet suits in your bags so you don't saturate my car seats. Only five minutes though. I have to get you all home on time," he says as he exits the room.

"All right," yells Tommy as he drops his swim trunks and runs through the opening and into the spray followed by Billy and me.

The initial sensation I feel is that I am being inoculated by thousands of hypodermic needles at the same time, which is not at all pleasant. However, after a few seconds the warm needle-like jets of water feel great. Our laughing quickly subsides as we all realize that an open mouth quickly fills due to the hundreds of crisscrossing jets of water hitting us at the same time.

It is amazing how three boisterous boys can instantly become so soundless as we enjoy the sensation as hissing steam rises to the ceiling. In a matter of minutes, the air is thick with mist. I can no longer see the door and the ceiling lights look like distant stars winking at me.

Walking through the front entrance again, humidity cruelly slaps my face and strains my breathing. Father Donovan stands by his car, keys swinging in a circle around a finger. His Corvair crouches low to the ground like a predator. The sound of a distant lawn mower ruffles through the tree leaves as an unseen blue jay screeches in the distance.

"Are you ready, boys? Everyone in. Watch the seats as they are liable to be hot. Best to sit on your towels," he says as we all enter and settle into position. Father Donovan gets in and inserts the key that brings the cast aluminum engine to life with a roar.

"You might want to roll your windows down for the breeze," he offers. He doesn't have to tell us twice as we turn the handles as hastily as we can, lowering the windows.

The scorching car pulls around the parking circle and down the tree-lined drive, the hot air slowly drying our hair as I turn and look out the back window. The impressive white building with its two ground-to-roof porch columns looks like it is a lost cousin from Ancient Rome. As we drive away, I think to myself that I can't wait to return.

"Boys, as you know, each of your parents signed you up for seminary weekend which will be in Hartford County Connecticut." Hearing our sighs, he laughs and continues, "It is not what you think. The seminary is located on over a hundred acres with a beautiful lake and woods. Though the weekend's main purpose is to give you boys a first hand view of life in the priesthood, it is also meant to be a fun weekend where you will have time to swim, bike ride and hike. It is scheduled the second week in September and they have all given approval for you to go. What do you think?" he asks.

"How much of our time is free? I ask.

"Actually, the whole time is yours to do as you please. You will be given a tour to familiarize you with the seminary and grounds and then, other than scheduled meals, you are free to do as you please. Sound good?"

Looking at Billy, he shrugs and I say, "Sure, why not."

"Excellent. Your parents will get the necessary releases for you to miss school and Father Joye from our neighboring parish will be taking you. He will contact your parents with all the necessary information. I'm afraid the minimum age requirement is thirteen so you will not be able to go this year, Tommy. However, seminary weekend actually runs Thursday and Friday this year due to a schedule conflict on that particular weekend. That Thursday coincides with your turn for swim night here so you will still have that."

We both give Tommy our best sorry look as he turns and looks blankly out the window. It is as if he has not heard a word as the Corvair sashays down the country drive.

9.

September, 1964

Hartford County, Connecticut

Turning a hard left as the springs groan, Father Joye steers his rusting white Oldsmobile Eighty-Eight station wagon onto the brick paved driveway. Looking at him from the back seat, his balding head is as pink as a flamingo with tuffs of stubborn white hair hanging on at impossible angles. His square head on his equally square body always reminds me of a building and is the reason why Billy affectionately calls him 'Father Block'.

Expansive ash and elm trees line each side of the drive like sentries, whispering hints of yellow, red and orange, while sprawling lime lawns spill into the vastness on both sides. Looking out my window on the right side, I see a huge gray lake at the end of the recently mowed east lawn, a lone swan bobbing on the slightly choppy surface. Two faded white rowboats are tied to a small dock that juts out like an arm from a small sandy beach. There is another similar but empty dock on the other side.

Returning my gaze to the front of the car, I see a two-story granite seminary building looming in the distance like an ancient fortress. Ivy vines have clawed their way up the entire front side and half way up the huge red brick chimney that protrudes skyward out of a blue-gray slate roof. Leaded wavy windows twinkle in the sunlight and wink at us as the car winds along the meandering driveway until reaching a large oval parking area in front. In the middle is a white fountain that is shooting a geyser of water skyward like Old Faithful.

"Look at those flowers! I wonder what they are," Billy says.

"Those are golden colored Sawara Cypress mixed with pink and beige hydrangeas, both of which do well in fall weather," answers Father Joye. "My sister owns a nursery so I'm up on my botany."

Pulling the car to a stop by the front door, Father Joye climbs out followed by Billy and me, everyone is eager to stretch their legs and backs from the two-hour drive. It's almost noon and my stomach's groaning with hunger. The smell of freshly cut grass floats on the air.

"Whoa!" says Billy. "What a building!"

"It must be hundreds of years old!" I say.

As we stand marveling at the structure, Billy says, "Boy, it sure is humid for September," as he wipes the sweat from his forehead with the back of his hand.

"All right boys, get your belongings and let's go inside and get settled," commands Father Joye.

Retrieving our cases from the car, we follow him up bluestone steps to a massive oak front door. Just as Father Joye reaches for the bell, the door swings open and a dwarfish priest steps out and extends his hand. He is plump with a gray hair horseshoe crowned with a bald top, ashen hairs jutting out of his ears like sagebrush. He says, "You must be Father Joye. It is nice to finally meet you in person. I am Father Churchill with whom you spoke on the phone. And these are your boys?"

"Yes, Father. This is Billy and Danny," he says while pointing at each of us as our names are spoken.

"Welcome boys and thank you for coming. Usually we only have visiting priests here for retreat. In fact, we have had priests from your parish here several times this year and last fall, so it is a nice change to have you fellows here. We hope you will have an enlightened time with us. This is not a high-pressure sales pitch; rather, it is an opportunity for you to see how priests live and to spend some time in reflection. However, it is also to be a fun experience. I'm sure you spotted our lake on the drive in. We have row boats and of course swimming for you. We have quite the bike collection thanks to Father Coleman, as well as an extensive library which contains most of the classics ever written, along with theological books to which you are welcomed. I hope you will have time to read through some of these while you are here. Also, I think you will find the food here surprisingly delightful. In any event, grab your gear and I will show you to your room," he says.

Following him through a foyer, we enter an expansive great room that has a faint musty smell and is noticeably cooler than outside. Detecting indistinct cooking smells as well, my stomach grumbles even more. The wood wainscoting ceiling is two stories high with a huge brass chandelier hanging down on long silver chains. Along the right side an oak staircase clasps the wall and leads up to a landing before turning left and ascending to the second floor. Photographs of priests adorn the staircase wall, most likely past occupants of the seminary. An oak railing guards two sides of the upstairs hallway, its polished balusters reflecting the light from the chandelier below. The floor of the massive room is covered by a huge emerald-colored rug with white tassels on all sides. In the middle are several comfortable looking wood chairs with green fabric cushions, each one with a side table and a gold-colored banker's reading lamp. They are all arranged in a circular pattern around a massive glass coffee table that seems somewhat out of place.

"Boys," says Father Churchill. "You can go upstairs and put your belongings in the first room at the top of the landing. There are two beds in there and a private bathroom. You can unpack and relax for a while. We'll come get you shortly for lunch to be followed by a tour.

Taking his cue, we pick up our bags and shuffle upstairs. Billy arrives first and pushes open the door to our room. As he enters, I hear him say, "Holy crap, will you look at this! Priests sure know how to live."

Walking past him, I enter a huge room with a granite wall that has an oversized window with white mullions in the middle. The ceiling appears to be at least twelve feet or higher with a smaller version of the downstairs chandelier dangling from a single chain that appears too small for the job. Gleaming oak strips make up the floor and there are two beds at each side of the window. A closet door is set in the corner to the right of the entrance door. Two of the walls are curiously adorned with paintings of ancient sailing ships.

Wandering to the window, we look at a new view of what we have seen previously. From up here the lawns look even more expansive and the lake, guarded by a thick pine forest sprinkled with white birch trees, is larger than it seemed before. There is a rowboat on it now with a single person at the oars moving across the surface like a water bug, the lone swan no longer in sight. In the distance we can see the gently undulating green hills of the Connecticut landscape.

Billy walks over and opens the door to the bathroom and whistles. Following him, I stare at an oversized white iron tub elevated on four steel claws. The outside granite wall has a small window centered and the other walls are all oak wainscoting. A pedestal sink and toilet are tucked into the right corner of the room along with a free-standing black steel towel rack. A pile of fresh towels sits precariously on the edge of the sink like a platform diver ready to go.

Hearing a knock at the door, we turn to see Father Joye entering. "All settled boys?"

"Yes, Father," we reply.

"Good. Lunch will be served shortly so come downstairs in a few minutes. The dining room is to the left at the bottom of the stairs. After we eat, Father Churchill will conduct a tour."

"Follow me, boys. I gather you all had enough to eat at lunch?" asks Father Churchill as he commences the tour by walking back across the foyer from the dining room.

"I'll say!" replies Billy. "The sandwiches were fantastic, especially the bread."

"We bake all of our own bread here," Father Churchill says proudly.

"And the chocolate cake dessert! I feel ready to bust a seam," I say.

"Tell me about it," answers Father Churchill as he gently pats his belly. "Life here is good. This room here is our library," he says as he pushes open the door. Looking around, I see that the book cases go from the floor to the ceiling in the oval shaped room. A ladder on wheels extends three quarters of the way up to a black metal track that goes from one side of the entrance door all the way around the room to the other side. "As I said before, please feel free to use the library any time day or night during your stay."

Turning, he exits the library, goes left and pushes open the next door. We follow him in as he says, "This is the community living room. Here you can relax, read a book or a newspaper, write or anything else you want to do in relative quiet. The main difference between reading and relaxing in here as opposed to the library is that food and beverages are allowed. As you can see, we have many comfortable sofas and chairs at your disposal. We have group discussions in here every Friday night on various religious topics. I would encourage you two to participate. I think you will find it stimulating. It might give you further insight into how priests think and live."

Looking around, I see the décor is the same emerald green color as in the great room. On the walls are several more paintings of ancient sailing ships at sea. A large stone fireplace is centered on the right wall and probably accounts for the brick chimney I saw upon our arrival.

Exiting the room, Father Churchill says, "Next, I will show you the kitchen which is this way," as he turns left and walks to a hallway at the end of the great room. Upon entering, we go down several steps as the aroma of the kitchen saturates the air and the sounds of clanking pots and pans can be heard. He pushes open the door and we walk into an immaculately clean bunker-type room with shining white tile floors. There are duplicate ovens on the far wall and a huge gas cooktop located in the center of a massive island with an ancient butcher block countertop. Pots and pans of every imaginable size and shape hang from hooks over the island at the ready. On the left wall is a massive sink and drying countertop made of grayish slate and on the right wall are floor to ceiling shelves overflowing with food boxes and cans. Two priests are at work washing and drying the lunch plates and silverware, another is at the island preparing what looks to be tonight's dinner, to whom Father Churchill says, "Good day, Father Coleman."

"Good day to you, too," he answers.

Pointing to us he says, "These are the boys that came with Father Joye from New York. Billy and Danny, meet Father Coleman." He is tall and lean, yet muscular, and as he nods at us strands of his black hair fall across his forehead which he unconsciously swipes back with his hand.

"Pleased to meet you, Father," we both say.

"Likewise," he answers.

"Preparing tonight's meal?" asks Father Churchill.

"Indeed. We are going to have a Caesar salad along with my home-made lasagna with meat balls and for dessert, chocolate fudge cake with vanilla ice cream."

"Sound good boys?" asks Father Churchill.

"Yeah!" says Billy as I smile.

"It sure is hot and humid today. I assume you boys would like to go for a swim this afternoon?"

"Yes, Father!" says Billy as he then looks down in embarrassment for the outburst.

"Great. Let's plan on a 3 p.m. swim. Father Coleman here is our resident record holder for the across the lake and back swim if anyone feels like challenging him! But I warn you, he swam competitively at Michigan State," he says. Billy looks at me but I avert his gaze.

"Okay boys, the last stop on the tour will be the garden. So, follow me back the way we came," he says as he turns and exits the kitchen.

Walking out through a back door, I see an enormous garden with a chain link fence that must be eight feet high surrounding it. Following Father Churchill down stone steps, he pulls open a door in the fence which allows us entry. Closing the door behind him, he says, "The fence, as you can see, is a relatively new addition. The rabbits and deer were eating more vegetables than we picked so we had it installed last year. Being early fall, most of the vegetables have been picked but we still have an abundance of beautiful flowering shrubs, at least for a few more weeks."

Looking up and down the rows, I can see the stalks and stems of what has been picked. Several rows close to the side fence bear the remains of corn stalks. At the far end I can see a long wood trellis that has vines still bearing purplish grapes.

Following my eyes, Father Churchill says, "The grapes will be harvested in the next few weeks. We make them into jelly, juice and a little wine, but we don't advertise that," followed by a wry smile. "After the grapes are picked, we harvest the remaining vegetables and then till and fertilize the soil for next year's crop. We are one hundred per cent self-sufficient in providing all the vegetables we consume."

"Do you grow strawberries?" Billy asks.

"We certainly do, as well as blueberries, blackberries and raspberries. We have these all frozen. Would you like some strawberries with desert tonight?"

"Can I, I mean, we?"

"I'll see what I can do. In the meantime, the next hour or so is yours to do whatever you wish. I hope you can spend some time in reflective thought on the priesthood while you are here. You can meet Father Coleman down at the lake dock at three for a swim. You can either walk down across the lawn or feel free to use the bikes in the rack on the east side of the building. Any questions?"

"No, Father. Thank you," I reply.

"Yes, thank you Father," says Billy.

Watching Father Churchill walk away, Billy says, "So Danny, is it time for some thoughtful reflection or a bike ride!?

"Let's get our swimsuits on and go riding!" I exclaim.

"Sounds good," he replies as we turn to make our way back upstairs to our room.

Waiting outside for Billy in my swimsuit, I see that the buttery sun has begun its afternoon descent as a formation of geese noisily fly by overhead. Walking to the east side of the building, I turn the corner and see a bike rack stacked with eight identical black English racers, all with chrome fenders. Looking at them, I can't help but wonder where they came from.

"They aren't stolen," I hear from behind me. Turning, I see Father Coleman with a book in his hand. Smiling, he says, "Originally, we had only one beat up old bike. I took it to a shop in nearby Avon. Turns out the owner used to be on the swim team at UMass and we naturally hit it off. After many conversations of boasting about our personal times, we arranged a race across and back on the lake here. If I won, he would donate a new bike to the seminary. If he won, I would work for free for the equivalent of two weeks in his shop. That was eight years ago." Pointing to the bikes, he says, "As you can see, I have been doing very well!"

"Wow, you must be fast," I say.

Laughing, he replies, "I don't know about fast, but I guess I still have the endurance for the long race. In college, my race was the fifteen hundred meters. Do you swim Danny?"

"Now and again. Mostly in either the lake in my hometown or the Hudson River," I answer.

"The Hudson! If you have been swimming there you must be a strong swimmer."

"I do okay."

"Well, how about a little race across the lake and back this afternoon? I'll spot you a ten-yard head start."

"Sounds great, but I won't need the head start. But thank you anyway," I say as I see him arch an eyebrow.

"Well, that is very daring of you. I will see you down by the lake at three then, Danny," he says as he walks away while opening his book. At the same time, Billy comes walking around the corner.

Spying Father Coleman walking away, he asks, "What was that all about?"

"It seems like Father Coleman and I have a little race set for later on," I answer.

"Atta boy, Danny! Can you take him? I mean, he swam in college."

"Michigan State, yeah. He swam the fifteen hundred meters. I dunno if I can take him. I guess we will find out," I say as I pull a bike from the rack. Following suit, Billy pulls one out.

"Man, what a bike! It has ten gears! I've never ridden anything with more than three," says Billy.

"Okay, where to?" I ask.

"To the end of the road!" he yells.

"To the end of the world!" I shriek as we get a running start and then jump onto our bikes, the gears clicking as we each try to find the right one. Sliding down the brick pavement as easily as on our toboggans on Lenter's Hill, our bikes bounce over the uneven joints as a tepid wind warms our bodies. Laughing like hyenas, we approach a fork where the drive continues to the front entrance, to the left is an unpaved road. Without hesitation, or a spoken word, we both turn left onto the gravel path as our bikes bob on the rough surface. The ash and elm trees that line the main drive are no longer present; instead, a mix of white birch and pine trees line the road and the scent of sap is noticeable. As the road climbs in elevation, to my left I can see that we are alongside the lake. The road becomes steeper and I shift the gears to take on the hill. Nearing the crest of the hill, we both see a grass covered road to the right with a rusting chain lazily guarding it. In the center dangles a red and black sign that reads "Private Property".

"Why is that sign upside down?" asks Billy while pointing as he straddles his stopped bike.

Looking to my right, I see an inverted yellow, bent and creased metal sign with "POSTED" spelled out in large, black block lettering. Gazing around the forest, I see so many of these signs that they look as numerous as fireflies at night. Returning my gaze to the upside-down sign, I say, "See that rusted nail above the sign? My guess is that over the years the sign rusted around that nail and then a strong wind dislodged it, causing it to pivot around, ending upside down."

"I guess that could explain it. Let's go down the road."

"We only have about a half hour before we are to meet at the lake. Father Churchill said we'll have free time tomorrow morning before we leave, so why don't we explore it then?" I say.

"Okay. Race you to the lake," he says as he gets a running head start and mounts his bike. He is already almost out of sight by the time I get going.

As I begin the descent, I spot a path on my right and stop. It looks pretty narrow and steep but I figure I might beat Billy to the lake if I take it.

Turning my handlebars to the right, I start down. My bike immediately starts to vibrate and recoil over the rocks and gravel wash outs like a jet in turbulence. Hanging on for dear life, I squeeze the hand breaks constantly to slow my descent but it doesn't seem to be working. Just ahead I see the path makes a ninety degree turn to the right and then switchbacks the other way. Going too fast to make the turn, I launch over the side into the woods but remain upright. In front of me I see a downed tree and hit it before I can stop, hurling myself airborne and landing with a thud on the pine needle covered ground. Pushing myself up, I walk back to my bike which has a bent front rim and flat tire. "Oh, Christ," I say.

Picking the bike up, I have to carry the front wheel while the back wheel turns freely. Walking back to the path, I continue on down to the lake thinking *I am going to catch hell for this.*

"So, what happened here?" asks Father Coleman.

"Sorry I wrecked the bike, Father. I was coming down the path back there and couldn't make the turn," I say.

Laughing, he says, "Don't worry about it, Danny. I missed that hairpin turn the first time I went down that path too. That is a nasty corner. Leave the bike here on the beach and I'll have maintenance take it into town next week for repair. As you know, we have plenty of other bikes available."

"Thank you, Father."

"Are you still up for our little swim, Danny?"

"Sure thing, Father. I am okay, even if the bike isn't."

"Excellent! See the red buoy just off shore here? There is another one on the other side in about the same location. We will start here, go around that buoy and the first one to pass this one again wins. Billy, can you count down from five and yell go when we are in position?"

"You bet, Father."

"Okay, Danny, let's get in the water and warm up. It is a little later in the day than I would like, but we should be okay."

With that we both walk into the water and fall forward. As I go under, I notice the cool water is very clear and that I can see Father Coleman to my right. Coming back to the surface, I swim about twenty yards away to loosen up. He does likewise, then yells, "Ready, Danny? Come over here so Billy can start us." Slowly breast stroking back to his side by the buoy, I see him wave to Billy.

"Five, four, three, two, one and go!" hollers Billy.

Father Coleman instantly is under way using a very tight Australian crawl. He already has a five-yard lead by the time I get going. From the beach I hear Billy shouting encouragement as I begin my strokes. I'm caught swimming in Father Coleman's wake when I would prefer to be in smooth water. Veering slightly to the left, I swim at an angle away from him. Continuing until I pass through his wake, I then turn parallel to him. His lead is about seven yards, but I now have smooth water.

Concentrating on nothing but my routine, I start to slowly increase the speed of both my arm pulls and my leg kicks: one, two, three and breathe; one, two, three and breathe; one, two, three and breathe. Each time I tilt my head for air, I do it to the right. I don't see anything as I continue to swim at a steady pace. After a few head turns, I finally see the spray of water coming from Father Coleman's feet. With the next head turn I see his feet, on the next I see his legs, then his back and finally I see his head and arms. Taking a glance ahead, I see the buoy is very close, and I know that he will reach it first. As he makes his turn, I go under water.

Seeing his legs and arms churning the water like an eggbeater, and silver flashes as various fish head for the deep safety of the elodea and chara weeds, I circle the buoy rope and start back the other way coming up on his opposite side. He has gained a few yards when I went under water, but now I am on the side he doesn't turn to for breaths of air so he will not be able to see me until he figures out what I have done. By then it will be too late.

Reaching down for that other gear I always had, I slowly catch and then start to pull ahead of him. With each powerful stroke my body surges further and further in front. Having moved my head turn to the opposite side, I have been able to keep tabs on him. It appears that he thinks he is still leading me since he turned the buoy first. With my next stroke my wake finally reaches him and he turns his head towards me in utter surprise. By now, I am a good eight yards in front of him and am increasing the distance with each stroke. I don't let up until I pass the buoy and then turn on my back and slowly swim towards shore while barely breathing hard at all.

As I stand, Billy comes splashing into the water and tackles me, pushing me under while laughing. I come to the surface to hear him say, "Danny, I have seen you swim a lot but that was incredible!"

Over his shoulder, I see Father Coleman wading slowly towards me. As he does, he extends his hand and says, "Well done, Danny! Well done! That was amazing. That was a nice little trick you pulled around the buoy. I thought you were behind me until it was too late. How did you ever think to do that?"

"I really don't know, Father. That sort of thing seems to come naturally to me when I'm in the water."

"Well, I sincerely hope that you plan on swimming competitively in college someday. I still have some contacts at Michigan State, and I'm sure they would be thrilled to have you there. When the time comes, I would be more than happy to write a letter of recommendation for you."

"That is very kind of you, Father, but I have never been involved in competitive swimming. Our school doesn't even have a swim team and, besides, college seems like a long way off now. It is something, though, that I have always dreamed of doing."

"Promise me you will keep it in the back of your mind. You have a special talent and with the right supervision and training you could be very special in this sport. Okay boys, enough for today. Let's head back and get cleaned up for dinner."

Today is a beautiful day for our trip back home. The humidity has dropped off, the temperature cooling to be more seasonable. Last night after dinner we were given the soft pitch for the priesthood, which was set up by various previous comments about how good a priest's life is. Granted the building and grounds are beautiful, the rooms roomy and comfortable, and the food fantastic. I just don't think either of us will ever have a real interest. There is too much life in front of us, too much yet to be explored and discovered.

We were given two hours for bike riding before we hit the road today and we have pedaled back up to the road with the chain across it that we saw yesterday.

"To the right by the upside-down sign is a spot where we can push our bikes around the chain," says Billy as I follow. Reaching the grass road on the other side, we mount our bikes and start to lazily pedal. As we progress, the evergreens slowly retreat and are replaced by a white birch forest, their barks peeling like cresting ocean waves, their sweet aroma soaking the air. Vines with a circumference the size of my arm grope up out of the ground like the gnarled fingers of a giant witch, wrapping around the tree trunks like bronzed snakes, ultimately disappearing into a thick overhead canopy. Many trees are obviously dead, having been choked by the assault, and lifeless limbs are scattered on the forest floor like on a battlefield. Ahead I can see that the road opens up to an overgrown field spotted with locust, weeds and dandelions. Numerous deer are grazing at the far end and they all lift their heads and ears in unison as we approach.

I yell "Hey!" and the deer disappear into the forest in the blink of an eye.

"I have to pee," says Billy as he alights from his bike. Lowering it to the road, he walks off into the birch forest.

Standing in the middle of the road looking out at the field, it reminds me of those on the trail up Peekamoose Mountain in the Catskills.

Just then I hear Billy scream. Dropping my bike, I dash into the woods with my heart racing. Coming upon Billy, he's pointing to the ground saying, "Is that what I think it is?"

"Holy crap! It's a body!" I shout.

"Let's get the hell out of here!" yells Billy.

Looking down, I see the back of a skull with most of the skin missing. What remains is brown and wrinkled like old shoe leather with a few pathetic hairs sticking out indifferently. The back is covered by what looks to be the remains of a bluish sweatshirt, now rotting, with bony fingers jutting out of each sleeve like pencils. The bottom half has no clothes and most of the skin and muscle is gone, probably eaten by scavenging animals.

"Hold on, Billy," I say. "We can't just run from here. We need to mark the roadside where we came in so we can be sure to find this spot and then go get help."

After walking back to the road, we gather several downed limbs and clearly mark the spot.

"Christ," says Billy. "I nearly stumbled over it. Those remains look like a kid, don't they? How the hell did a kid get way up here by himself? He must have been terrified if he was lost. What an awful thought, to die alone in the middle of nowhere. This is sickening."

"Maybe," I say, "He wasn't by himself. Come on Billy, let's go back and get some help."

We are sitting in the library when a state trooper the size of a Mack truck walks in with Father Joye. He is very tall and looks intimidating in his crisp gray shirt and royal blue tie set off by gold brass buttons with multiple chevrons on his sleeves. "Boys, this is Officer Camp who would like to ask you a few questions," Father Joye says.

"Hi, boys. I know this is a traumatic thing, discovering a body. I appreciate the fact that you thought enough to mark the spot. You would be amazed how many times people find something and then cannot locate it again. Anyway, I have a few brief questions if you are up to them. Then you and Father Joye can be on your way home," he says as he pulls a small notebook and pen from his pocket.

"Sure, officer. I think we can answer any questions you have," I say.

"Good," he says while consulting his note pad. "Which one of you is Billy?"

"That's me," says Billy half-raising one arm.

"As I understand it, Billy, you are the one who found the body?"

"Yes, sir. I had to, well, go pee and I happened to walk into the woods where it was."

"Did either of you touch anything?"

"No, sir. I did not and I know neither did Danny. We just left and marked the road before returning here."

"Excellent. Again, I appreciate you both having the common sense not to disturb a crime scene."

"A crime scene?" I ask.

"Well, we must treat it as such until we find evidence to the contrary. That's it for my questions, boys. Thank you again for all that you did. We will take it from here," he says as he returns his notebook and pen to his pocket, turns and walks out of the room.

"Okay, boys, why don't you go get your things from your room and I will meet you out by the car. I think we have all had enough excitement for the day and it will be good to get you all home," says Father Joye.

As we climb the stairs to our bedroom Billy says, "I think I'm going to have nightmares about this."

"I know what you mean," I say. "If there is really a God, how does he let something like this happen?"

"What do you mean?"

"What I mean is, this whole weekend we have heard nothing but how powerful and loving God is and how priests are his body here. Same thing at home in church. We hear it every time. If God is so powerful and loving, how the hell could he let this happen to a small kid? It makes me start to wonder if there really is a God, you know? It makes no sense."

"I don't think you should be talking like that, Danny. Especially here."

"Yeah, well let's get our bags. I'm more than ready to leave this place."

10.

October, 1964

Dutchess County, New York

The bell rings indicating the end of the school day. I grab my books and start walking down the school hallway. Kids push, shove and jostle for position much like their parents on the way to work. Passing the business office, I happen to glance in and see Tommy sitting forlornly in a chair by the principal's door. Just then, the door opens and he disappears through it with his head hung low.

"Did you hear?" Billy says, startling me.

"Hear what?" I ask.

"Tommy evidently punched a kid during class and then mouthed off to the teacher again. The whole school is talking about it. That's why he is in there. I wonder what his problem is?"

"I wish I knew. I tried to talk to him after the last incident when he was sent to the principal's office but he just told me nothing was wrong. Obviously, there is and it seems to be getting worse. I really don't know what to do. I just hope he snaps out of it, and soon," I say.

"You coming to our soccer game later?" Billy asks.

"Sure thing, wouldn't miss it. Both Jo and I will be there. Good luck!"

"Thanks, but we don't need luck. You can put this game in the win column, now," he says with his usual confidence.

Sitting down on the cold bleachers with Jo by my side, I have a perfect view of the soccer field. A cool breeze chases leaves across the ground amongst the competitors, dressed in red and gold jerseys, as a dazzling fall sun warms our faces. Feeling Jo slide over close to me, she then puts her arm around my back. A contented smile comes to my face just as Billy scores a goal and his teammates mob him, the fans in the bleachers all stand and clap.

Looking to the south end of the field, I spot Tommy sitting alone on a sawhorse in front of the equipment shed, its rough sawn board and batten siding appearing to shine in the sunlight. The overhead door is up revealing rows of equipment for the various school sports-field hockey sticks, track hurdles, soccer balls, baseball bats and basketballs. Behind him, the branches on a wreathe of maple trees oscillate in the breeze freeing colored leaves that drift lethargically to the ground.

Raising a hand, I wave to Tommy but he is looking in another direction. Following his gaze, I see Sandy heading directly towards him. Nudging Jo, I nod in their direction.

Gasping, she says, "Oh no, not again!"

Grabbing her hand, I say, "Come on Jo, let's go."

Sprinting down the bleacher steps, our shoes clanking on the wooden seats, we jump to the black cinder track that circles the soccer field. Seeing Sandy in front of Tommy, I start running literally dragging Jo along. Getting closer, I can hear the shouts back and forth between them.

Suddenly, Tommy pushes Sandy and walks into the equipment shed, emerging seconds later with a bat in his hands. Before I can yell for him to stop, I helplessly watch him swing. It seems as if everything shifts into slow motion as Sandy makes a quick one-two punch first to Tommy's right eye and then to his jaw just before the bat lands flush on the side of his head. He spins around and falls, as blood gushes from his wound. Jo screams in horror as Tommy steps forward raising the bat high over and in back of his head preparing to take another swing at the now helpless Sandy.

"Tommy! No! Stop!" I yell.

Jo and I sit in the dimly lit hospital waiting room as nurses rush by in the outside corridor, each on some mission of urgent importance. The room smells of mysterious medicines and disinfectants. The walls have faded to an innocuous beige and on each wall are framed drawings of flowers. A lone window looks out at the parking area and beyond.

Blindly leafing through an old issue of Life Magazine with a wrinkled image of a Russian schoolgirl named Natel Gugulashvili on the cover, I read that she is from a village called Vazisubani. She doesn't look at all like the threat my parents make out the Russians to be. While flipping another page, Tommy's mother rushes into the room looking wan and teary-eyed. Her short unkempt blond hair is as tangled as a plate of spaghetti with dark roots showing at the hairline. Shadowy mascara runs below both brown eyes in tiny dark streams. She looks thin and frail in her oversized coffee-colored sweater that has stains and fabric pulls all over it.

"Danny, how is he?" she asks hurrying up to me.

Standing, I reply, "I don't know, Mrs. Willott. We just got here and they won't tell us anything because we're not family."

Her eyes dart to Jo and then back to me as she asks, "Where is the nurse's station?"

"Out the door to the left, I think," Jo says. Turning her head in what seems like slow motion, she gazes at Jo with empty eyes, gives an imperceptible nod, then turns and hastens out into the hallway, almost running into Billy as he enters. She doesn't seem to see him.

"What is going on with Tommy, guys?" he asks.

"I don't know for sure," I respond. "All I know is that he took a baseball bat to Sandy's head. Before Tommy hit him, Sandy punched him squarely in the eye and then in the jaw. Other than that, all we know is that Sandy is in intensive care and Tommy is being treated down the hall."

"Holy crap! What has gotten into that kid? Ever since we returned from the seminary, he has become a raging maniac. I mean, he seems to have gotten into some type of fight almost every day since then, and now this!" Billy cries.

"I know. He has changed overnight and I am not sure why," I concur as two State Police Officers enter the room.

"Any of you related to Tommy Willott?" the taller of the two asks. He stands well over six foot four, his tan felt Stetson shades his face giving him a threatening look. His expression is as flat as a piece of tile and his gray uniform is crisp, highlighted by a black stripe down each leg. I vaguely recall my father telling me once that this was in reembrace of fallen comrades.

"No, sir," Billy responds. "His mother just went to the nurse's station. It's down the hall to the left."

"Thank you," he coolly says as he walks out the door. The silent trooper follows.

Walking over to the window, I pull back the dusty curtain and see the black and white patrol car parked by the entrance, the yellow license plate redirecting the late afternoon sun. The bubble warning light sits like a lonesome island on the black roof. In the distance I can hear the wail of an approaching ambulance as people below walk nonchalantly to and from the parking lot.

"This doesn't look good for Tommy," Billy says voicing the concerns that we each hold for him. Sitting in silence, the clamor of the hospital engulfs us.

A few hours later, Mrs. Willott walks by with the two troopers behind. She stops, turns and takes a step into the waiting room. "You might as well go home. Tommy is staying the night and you can't see him," she states in a monotone voice.

"Is he okay?" I ask.

She gives a weary smile and says, "For now, yes. The punches he took severely injured his right eye and broke his jaw, which had to be wired shut. The doctors have given him medication for the pain but we will not be able to tell the severity of the injuries for several more days. So, please, go home. Thank you for coming. I will let Tommy know you were all here for him." With that, she turns around and disappears along with the troopers.

"Jesus almighty," swears Billy.

Without replying, I walk to the window and again pull back the dusty curtain. The three of them emerge and I see one of the troopers opening the back door for Mrs. Willott. He puts his hand on her head as she goes through the white door and sits. He closes it, pulls off his hat and enters the front passenger door. The other trooper stops to talk to an ambulance attendant, perhaps the one who brought Tommy here. He nods and walks to the driver's door, pulls off his hat and gets behind the wheel. In a few moments the car lurches forward and drives down the entranceway to the highway, slows and then turns right into the flow of traffic back to the awaiting world.

Looking at the threatening sky I say, "I just don't get it. This whole thing doesn't make any sense. Tommy is one of the smartest kids I have ever met and no part of this is smart. It isn't Tommy."

It has been eight straight days of cloudy skies and cold rain since we visited the hospital. During that time, we've learned that Sandy fractured his skull and was concussed but has since been removed from intensive care. The doctors say he is lucky to be alive and are unsure at this point if there will be any long-term issues.

Tommy was released after a two-day hospital stay. None of us has been able to see him, but I'm on my way to his house now to try again. Walking down the rough street surface, the low evening sun peaks out from behind a cloud, glints and then disappears. Red, orange and yellow leaves are dropping here and there, guided to the ground by the wind.

Rounding the corner on Oak Street, I view Tommy's house, which has been in a constant state of severe disrepair ever since I have known him. Loose plastic flaps on a covered broken window as a crow wails a plea somewhere in the trees high above me. Paint is peeling off the siding, the windows are filthy, and the lawn littered with bare spots and weeds. Rhododendron bushes that are planted too close to the foundation sport dead limbs with shriveled oval leaves. Several shingles are missing from the front side of the roof, the remaining ones are wrinkled by age and weather. The gutter is bent and overflowing.

In the drive, I spot the profile of a Mustang convertible, the white paint shining like a pearl. Walking diagonally across the street, I go up the driveway and onto the chipped and canted brick walkway. Nearing the house, the front door opens and Father Sipp emerges. Pulling the door closed, he starts down the rotting front steps before noticing me.

"Good afternoon, lad," he says.

"Hello Father. How is Tommy?" I inquire.

Stepping down to the uneven walk, he puts his arm around my shoulder and gives it a slight squeeze as he guides me back towards his car. "It is very sad, Danny. Very sad indeed. Tommy is recovering, but vision in his right eye, I'm afraid, may never fully recover. The doctors have told Mrs. Willott that in addition to possible vision issues, he may have muscle concerns with his eyelid over time. His jaw is wired shut to allow healing. Talking is hard for him, Danny. It's all very sad indeed, lad."

"Is he in trouble, Father?" I ask.

Stopping at his car, he removes his arm from my shoulder. Looking up at his narrow green eyes, the sun reflects off his shiny forehead like a mirror. "I am afraid so. The lad he hit, uh, what is his name?"

"Sandy. Sandy Stewart," I answer.

"Right. Mrs. Willott says Sandy's parents have pressed charges. There is a court hearing scheduled for next week. It looks like Tommy could be headed for reform school Danny. If there are any long-term physical problems from his attack then he could ultimately be looking at prison," he says.

Staring at him with uncomprehending eyes, tears flow down my cheeks. "But Father, Sandy always picked on Tommy. Everyone in school knows that. Even the teachers. He was constantly defending himself," I plead.

"Not this time, lad. I was told that you were a witness. Several of the players on the soccer field also saw what happened. You must know what they said is true, that Tommy hit him unprovoked. In any event, what is done is done. There are really no other options but one. And I have just given that alternative to Mrs. Willott.

"Father?" I utter.

"You best go home. Mrs. Willott doesn't want Tommy to have any visitors. Be on your way, lad," he declares. "I'm taking her now for a quick trip to the store just around the corner."

Just then I hear the front door open and out steps Mrs. Willott. Closing the door, she wobbles to the steps like a woman much older than she is, clawing at the railing for balance. Father Sipp goes back up the walk and meets her at the bottom of the stairs. Putting his arm around her, he helps her to and then into the car.

Turning, I walk down the drive and further up the street, leaves floating all around me like painted butterflies. Hearing the car start up, I watch Father Sipp back out of the drive, stop, and then proceed in the opposite direction with a wave of his hand. Mrs. Willott pulls a black scarf over her head.

Looking back towards the house, I notice Tommy in the upstairs window waving for me to come up. Looking both ways, I sprint back down the street, up the drive and onto the walk just as the front door opens. Tommy peers out but only leaves the door slightly ajar.

"Hi, Dane," he says weakly as wires lock his jaw closed.

Looking at his swollen black and blue face, I notice that his red streaked eye seems recessed, like an animal staring out of a low-ceiling cave. A yellowish-black bruise has expanded into his nose and across his right cheek making him look like a vanquished prize fighter. His mouth is a confused tangle of wires. He doesn't look at all like the friend I know.

"What happened?" I ask.

"Yove mea wif Sany?"

"What? I can't understand you. Talk slowly and try to enunciate if you can."

"Wif San. Dee?" he says again, slower but only slightly more clearly.

"With everything. Sandy, all the fights you have been getting into, the way you have been mouthing off to everyone, the way you have been avoiding your friends. Everything. What the hell happened, Tommy? What?" I ask.

"Lisen Dane, Mum b bat sewn. No hav lone to tal," he mumbles as I hear the distinct sound of Father Sipp's Mustang on the next street. "Dane yove hav to go. But, hav to tell yove," he says.

"What Tommy? What?" I ask.

"Yove to semary. Hae swim night," he says as the Mustang downshifts prior to making the turn back onto Oak Street. "Fathe, Dane, he hut me. Hut me raly bae."

"What do you mean? He hurt you?" I say as the Mustang makes the turn onto Oak Street.

Tommy mumbles in a panic, "Dane! Yove go ow bac dur! Nowe!" Pulling me into the house, he slams the door shut. We both run down the litter filled hallway that smells strangely like burnt toast as I hear the Mustang pull into the drive. Tommy eases open the back door and I go out and turn to face him.

"Tommy," I begin.

"No, Dane," he interrupts. "Go. Plese!" he finishes.

"But Tommy," I say again as he gently shuts the door. Hearing the lock click in place, I simultaneously hear the sound of shutting car doors. Turning, I run across the weed-choked and leaf covered lawn towards a battered gray wood fence. Jumping up, I grab the mossy top and hoist myself over, falling to the other side.

Out of breath, I look back at the wall that separates Tommy's world from mine. I think, *what does he mean that Father Donovan hurt him on swim night? How is that possible? Father Donovan doesn't seem like he could ever hurt anyone, much less a kid. What did he do to Tommy? Why didn't Tommy say anything to anyone? I just don't understand any of this. A priest hurt him? What the hell?*

Sitting here by the fence for the better part of an hour, I come to a decision. Standing, I walk back to the fence, leap up and grab the top, hoist myself up and over, and then drop on the other side. Looking at the house, all of the back lights are off.

Walking as quietly as I can, I go along the left side of the house, keeping low by the rhododendron bushes. Looking up, I can see Tommy's bedroom is dark. Stopping below the living room window, I push through the dead bush until I am under the window. Cautiously standing, I peer in through a broken slat in a cheap window covering.

Mrs. Willott is sitting up on the couch with her head tilted back, seemingly asleep. She is in her nightgown and a half empty bottle of vodka sits on the coffee table along with an empty glass. Smoke lazily rises from an unattended cigarette butt smoldering in a black ashtray.

In back of her is Father Sipp. He is looking into a mirror while he attaches his white clerical tab into his black collar. Evidently satisfied, he reaches over the back of the couch and pulls a blanket over her. Walking towards the front door, he picks his black overcoat up from a beat-up olive chair. Pulling it on, he glances back at Mrs. Willott as he opens the front door. His green eyes seem to be no more than slits as a seemingly wicked smile comes to his narrow mouth.

Seconds later, the Mustang starts and backs out of the drive. Then all is silent on the street.

Walking down Oak Street, I am confused and angry. I have been taught that priests are to be respected and loved, that they are God's voice to us. In a matter of hours, I hear that one priest has hurt one of my best friends and I have the sinking feeling that Father Sipp is up to no good. *What the hell is going on here?* I think to myself.

11.

October 1964

Dutchess County, New York

The fall sunshine warms my face as I hike up the twisting dirt trail to Mirror Lake. The ground is khaki brown, the color of the topical worsted uniforms I have seen in war photographs from Vietnam. It is a beautiful Indian summer day with an unseasonable temperature hovering around eighty degrees. The sky is the color of baby blue swiss topaz, air smooth as silk.

Hiking further up the path, the sounds from the county road below me fade like a memory. Fallen leaves carpet the path in bright lava reds, coral oranges and yellow ocher as they rustle under my footsteps. The tawny trees above sway back and forth in the slight breeze as if to an unheard melody. Their limbs seem to point at me accusingly as I trespass below them. The distant whistle from a laboring train engine sounds, echoes and then is gone.

Cresting a rise, I come to a small verdurous meadow that is covered in faded apricot-colored honeysuckle that look like miniature megaphones hung upside down. Both honey and bumble bees scurry from plant to plant, racing to beat the inevitable end of season withering.

Unexpectedly, I spot a huge black racer that's as big around as a kielbasa whorled up like an old discarded tire along the path edge. Its head is raised like a cobra ready to strike. Suddenly it lurches amongst the drooping honeysuckle and then all I can see are the plants moving left and right followed by what looks like a rodeo lasso being swung along the ground. It goes further into the honeysuckle then veers back towards the trail. What emerges is the black racer with a copperhead in its mouth. Twisting and turning over and over, the two snakes cross over and disappear back into the honeysuckle. Once again, I can see the plants moving this way and that as they roll amongst them. Suddenly all movement stops. Cautiously edging my way up, I look over and see the black racer has released the now still copperhead.

Crossing to the opposite side, I move on as the trail starts to climb again through a thick section of cedar trees, the smell reminding me of my mother's closet. Climbing up the last rock covered section, the foot path bisects a low fieldstone wall. Emerging onto a stark limestone ridge, I am looking down at the valley and Mirror Lake below. Over the top of the pines that surround it, I can see the surface slightly rippling in the waft.

Towering over the valley in back of the lake like a custodian is Lenter's Hill. Its face is a gold colored sloping meadow that cascades down to the edge of the lake, with maple, elm and birch trees on both sides. The array of multi-colored leaves seems to merge together as if viewed through a kaleidoscope. High above, a turkey vulture glides on a thermal, eyes combing the ground below for prey. It dips into a dive and briefly disappears beyond a row of white pines only to reappear seconds later with a stunned rabbit in its talons.

Walking down the slanting path, as I approach the pine trees, I can see Billy sitting on the old decaying dock, its one side stooped like an old man's shoulder. He is sitting with his hands behind him, face turned up to the soothing sun. The Beatle's 'All My Loving' drifts up mixed with static from his RCA Victor transistor radio.

Suddenly, I realize something is missing, incomplete, much like a chess set with a bishop absent or a deck of cards with the jack of hearts gone. A slight constriction occurs in my chest and I find myself gasping for air. Tommy. He is gone. But for how long? Days? Months? Years? Forever? It hits me how much I miss him and how much it hurts.

Staring down to the east side of the ridge, I can see in a field a distant tractor and wagon loaded up with golden bales of hay for winter storage. Two boys are walking behind the flatbed, one on each side, bending and then throwing the bales up as they come upon them. Billy is also looking at them and then catches me out of the corner of his eye. He turns and gives a seemingly half-hearted wave which I return. Upon my reaching the dock, he stands and unconsciously brushes off his pants.

"Hey," he says.

"Hey," I answer. "Great day or what?"

"Yeah. Heard anything about Tommy?"

Hesitating, I think of what I can say. What assurances can I give my friend? Thoughts run through my head like a runaway train but, in the end, nothing.

"No," I reply. "The house is vacant with no sign that anyone has returned. I guess he is gone for good."

Standing in an awkward silence, I glance up to the sky and see a v-shaped army of geese on their yearly journey southward. Off to the right side and a good distance behind is a lone goose. Is it sick? Injured? It seems to be falling further and further behind the group. Suddenly, it turns and starts downward away from the group. Watching as it descends in a lazy arc towards the lake, its wings spread wide like a Boeing 707 just before touchdown. It hits the water none too gracefully. Coming to a stop, the ripples it has caused head out in concentric circles. I can see blood on its left wing. It dips its head and looks at us as if imploring for help. Sometimes you just know.

"What was my best time?" I ask Billy as I strip off my shirt and bend down to untie my shoes and remove my socks.

"Are you kidding?" he questions. "The water has to be freezing."

"My time?" I ask again.

"Two minutes forty-five seconds."

Standing, I drop my jeans and step out of them. Walking to the end of the dock, I bend down and scoop up a handful of water. "Not too bad. Not bad at all," I say and strip off my Timex and hand it to him. "Give me a countdown," I say.

"You're crazy, you know."

With my toes on the dock edge, I bend at the waist with arms extended. Billy begins to count. "Five, four, three, two, one, go!"

With that, I launch off the end of the dock in a shallow dive, slicing into the water with almost no splash, like an Olympic diver. The cold water grips my body like a vise. Rising to the surface with my right arm angled at the elbow, I reach over and as far out in front of me as I can. One, two, three and breathe; one, two, three and breathe; one, two, three and breathe. I repeat the sequence over and over. I swim through the water like a fish, confident. I feel strong, at home. I think of all the happy times I have spent here with Tommy at this lake summers and up on Lenter's hill during winters. I spot Nag's boulder to my immediate left as I make my sequenced breath. Feeling the air cool as I enter the boulder's shade, I begin the turn invigorated. Kicking powerfully, the water rises in a rooster tail spray into the air behind me.

Emerging into the sunlight on the other side, I complete the one hundred and eighty degree turn and am now swimming towards the dock. My frustration about Tommy pours into my muscles like adrenaline. I think again about what has happened to him. I remember him as I last saw him, bruised and broken. It breaks my heart once again.

Billy is jumping up and down while waving his arms towards himself, encouraging me to go faster. One, two, three and breathe; one, two, three and breathe; one, two, three and breathe. My arms and legs start to burn. On every third stroke I breathe while sneaking a glance at the dock. I have true tunnel vision; it is all I can focus on and see. One, two, three and breathe; one, two, three and breathe; one, two, three and breathe. His shouts grow louder and louder until I reach out and touch the dock.

Pushing back, I float on my back not even breathing hard when I realize something. For the first time in my life I didn't really enjoy this swim. *Why is that*, I wonder. Then I understand it is because of Tommy and what happened to him. Whatever it was, it seems it happened on swim night at the convent and I guess as a result I will always associate swimming with that. *How can I ever enjoy it again*, I think?

After a few minutes, I breast stroke back to the dock. Billy's hands come down and lock under each arm, pulling me up onto the dock and depositing me into a sitting position.

"Holy crap! Two minutes and thirty-four freaking seconds," he shouts while holding the Timex up close to his face in disbelief. "How is that possible? You haven't come close to the old time in months and you beat it by eleven seconds? How?"

"Easy," I reply. "For Tommy." Billy nods in understanding. Having kept what Tommy told me a secret, I decide it is time Billy knew what I know. "You know, he tried to tell me what happened to him but with his jaw wired shut he was very difficult to understand. But what I heard and do understand is that he was talking about Father Donovan. He said Father Donovan did something that hurt him really bad at swim night."

"How is that possible? A priest?"

"I'm starting to believe that priests aren't the hands of God after all, as we have been told. They are just men, no different than any other man. They aren't just good. They are good and evil, like everyone else. This whole religious thing is starting to seem like a fairy tale. I mean, what kind of God lets that happen to the kid whose body we found at the seminary? What kind of God lets a priest hurt a little kid? I mean, come on."

"Like they say, God works in mysterious ways. You are just upset. You shouldn't be saying things like that."

"What, is a lightning bolt going to come out of nowhere and strike me down?"

"Well, we can't possibly understand God's intentions."

"Yeah, how convenient. Every time something can't be explained, the church says that," I say with a disgusted tone.

Seemingly uncomfortable with the discussion, Billy changes the topic by asking, "What are we going to do?"

Running my hand back and forth over my head, I concentrate on an inchoate idea and say, "This is what we are going to do. We can't bring back Tommy. But we sure as hell can cause some pain and suffering to Father Donovan for hurting him."

"What do you mean?" Billy questions.

"Let's gather our stuff, and I will explain as we walk to town."

Walking up the path, I see that the farmer and his helpers are gone from the field, having called it a day.

"Listen," I begin, "Some night at the weekly swim we are going to act. Pay attention to what I am saying. Memorize your part. And no matter what happens, stick to the story, okay? It may not be for a few weeks, but when the time is right, I will let you know. Stay ready. And this stays between you and me only, Billy. Jo is not to know. And we can never tell anyone else either. Pinky swear for Tommy," I finish as I extend my finger.

"Absolutely," says Billy.

We intertwine our fingers and shout "For Tommy!" as we extend our arms up to the sky until our fingers disengage. I notice the turkey vulture is back, making slow, lazy loops on the fall thermal looking for more prey. Looking down at the lake, I see on its surface a lone goose. The flock is long gone. It is alone with its fate, abandoned forever.

"Okay. Here is the plan…"

12.

November, 1964

Dutchess County, New York

It is a cool late November morning, the sun an indistinct blur behind the dirty window pane of a gloomy gray sky. Barren tree limbs undulate in the wind as if taunting us, leaves swirling around our feet. The two of us walk down the rough pavement on Oak Street, stopping in front of Tommy's decrepit yellow house. It looks forlorn, lonely even, like it is waiting without hope for the occupants to return. A lone crow sits on a tilted overflowing gutter, eyeing us suspiciously. Suddenly it caws and takes off into the somber sky. The opaque plastic sheet that once covered a broken window upstairs is now gone. The only trace left behind is a small tattered piece of plastic circling a rusty nail that sits in the middle like an island. The rest of the windows are dirty black, streaked like mascara running down a grieving mother's cheek. The olive-green paint on the trim and front door is peeling like it can't wait to break free and be gone from this place.

The house is a reflection of Tommy's life within its walls. His mother was obviously poor, his clothes and house bearing testament to this. He rarely brought lunch to school and never had any money. I often shared my lunch with him and my mom was good enough to pack enough food for the both of us. His mother's problem with alcohol had been evident for a long time, and was a constant source of fodder for the useless people in town who gossiped. Tommy always put on a brave face, but on a few occasions, he would let his guard down and let me know how bad things really were at home. My heart went out to him but, unfortunately, there was not much I could do which left me feeling helpless. Sighing, I realize that even when Tommy lived here, this was never a home only a house.

"I wonder where he is," says Billy.

"Don't know," I reply without thinking. "I guess we may never know. Funny, though, that in some way I feel his presence by his absence."

"Yeah, I think I know what you mean. I suppose, though, that we will never see him again. I hope his life gets better."

"I hope so too. You know today is the day, right?" I ask. Billy nods without speaking.

"Remember the story, the plan and stick to it no matter what. I know we don't know exactly what the Father did to Tommy, but we know it was bad. I wish you could have seen the look in Tommy's eyes when he told me that he was hurt. I think it was not only pain he experienced, but also shame. What we are going to do is just a prank, but I think we both feel the need to do something, anything, for Tommy," I say. "Even if the Father ends up feeling only a minor portion of the pain he inflicted on Tommy and his life it will be worth it, satisfying to our need for retribution," I finish.

We stand silently for a few more minutes staring at the barren house, each with our own thoughts. Turning, we start walking down Oak Street as I hear the distant caw of a crow.

Turning left onto Market Street by the A & P, we walk down the sidewalk whose concrete slabs are uneven and canted like playing cards randomly dropped, pushed up over the years by the roots of the elm trees that line it. Crossing over the state highway at the traffic light, we walk down the street past the Western Auto and the Five and Ten Cent store that hides in its shadow. Crossing the street in front of the Sugar Bowl, we walk further down the sidewalk to the diner. Looking in through the front window, I see old Bus and three ancient men gossiping over their early morning coffee. The smell of grease and bacon is in the air. Further along we pass Lawson's Lumber Yard and then turn the corner by the school that sits across from Saint Vitonus.

In the rectory drive sits Father Donovan's Corvair hugging the blacktop as tightly as a cat climbing a tree. We casually glance at it as we walk by, then turn through the gate in the chain link fence for another day at school.

Sitting on the cold bluestone steps outside the school in the early evening chill, I am waiting for Billy. The sky is gray as a battleship and the schoolyard is empty, all of the other carefree kids having long gone home. Across the street the Corvair sits silently, inert, dangerous like a loaded gun.

Hearing footsteps, I turn as Billy comes back through the gate carrying two duffel bags.

"Hey, Danny," he says.

"Hey. You ready?"

"I am."

"You know this needs to be done, right?"

"Yeah, I do. I had my doubts but I have thought a lot about this and I agree with you. I just wouldn't feel right, and I'm not sure I could live with myself, if we didn't do this for Tommy."

"All right, then."

"Here is your duffel bag with your swim gear. Your mom told me to tell you that she will pick you up later at my house. She and your Dad are going out for dinner."

"Thanks, Billy," I reply. "Looking at my watch I say, "Six forty-three. Let's do this."

Walking out of the school yard into the street, we see Father Donovan coming down the rectory steps with his car keys swinging on a finger. He notices us and gives a wave. An overloaded dump truck noisily passes by on Market Street, the driver downshifting and grinding a gear before it engages. Small pieces of topsoil fall off of each side and hit the road like cluster bombs, small brown clouds forming and then just as quickly disappearing.

"Evening, boys," says Father Donovan.

"Hi, Father," we both say.

"Right on time again I see. Well, let's not dally. Hop in and we will get going," he says.

Climbing into the front passenger seat, I pull it forward while Billy scoots into the back. Father Donavan clicks his lap belt and motions for us to do the same. Turning on the radio and the headlights while backing into the street, he stops and moves the automatic gear shift on the dash into drive and heads out onto Market Street as the Kingsmen belt out 'Louie, Louie'."

Turning left, we pass the same buildings as earlier but in reverse; the school, Lawson's Lumber Yard, the diner, the Sugar Bowl, the Five and Ten Cent store and Western Auto. Father Donovan slows the car as we approach the red light but as it turns green, he accelerates and heads out of town past the A&P and up the hill. Looking to my right as we pass Oak Street, I see Tommy's old house sitting empty in the dark, as alone as the first star of evening.

As we drive up the blue stone drive, I see hazy images of piles of leaves out on the lawn illuminated by a crescent moon. Some of them have red embers glowing from an earlier burning that appear to be judgmental eyes staring at me accusingly for what we are about to do. Father Donovan pulls the Corvair half way around the circular turnaround as the blue stone crunches, stops and shuts off the engine.

Looking out at a small maple tree lit up by the front entrance light, it has a single red leaf stubbornly clinging to a branch, moving back and forth precariously in the breeze.

"Okay boys, you have ninety minutes. Enjoy yourselves, but be safe," he says.

"We will, Father" I answer as we follow him up the steps past two gigantic white columns, across a black and white diamond pattern granite tile and into the mansion's foyer. The huge crystal chandelier illuminates the whole room from its suspended perch under the high rotunda ceiling. Its many lights sparkling, brightening the black and white diamond pattern floor tiles. Turning left, we head towards the pool area. Father Donovan goes straight to where two nuns are sitting reading in comfortable looking sofa chairs. It is time for his coffee and conversation and I can smell the fresh brewed aroma in the air. I catch myself wondering if it might be A&P Red Circle Coffee.

Crossing the foyer, I take the one step down into the pool area onto white marble tile followed by Billy. Walking the full length of the pool, I pull open the heavy oak door and enter the small changing room that separates the needle shower from the pool area. As we change, I say "Okay. We both know the plan. This is it. Remember everything we have proposed to do and, no matter what, stick to it," to which Billy nods. We quickly finish changing into our swimming trunks and then walk back into the pool area.

We start running from just below the step down from the foyer and cannonball into the pool, yelling and laughing as much as we can. We repeat the process over and over and over again, running back to the same spot by the step and standing there for a few seconds to give time for water to drip off of our suits and bodies. In short order a sizeable pool of water appears.

Nodding to Billy who is in the pool, he suddenly starts yelling, "Help! Help! I have cramps! Help!" as he flails his arms up and down against the water in a frantic slapping motion.

Facing the foyer, I yell, "Father Donovan! Father Donovan! Come quick! Billy is drowning!" I finish as I hear Billy's yelling and slapping continuing behind me. Father Donovan hesitates for a split second like a car starved for gas, then suddenly stands up as his coffee cup goes flying through the air, splintering on the floor. He runs right at me, seemingly gaining speed with each stride. His arms and knees are pumping as he approaches me and Billy's continuing screaming. As his first leather shoe lands below the one step, his sole hits the wet marble and he immediately loses his balance and falls backwards. First one and then the other leg extends upwards at impossible angles. He lands hard on his shoulders, his head snapping back onto the inflexible floor producing a sickening thud like a watermelon dropped off of a rooftop. Then all I hear is silence.

Billy pulls himself up out of the pool and walks over, standing beside me. Father Donovan is not moving. I bend down on one knee and put my ear below his nose. Silence. I put my hand on his chest. No movement.

Billy says from behind me, "My God! Look!" Standing, I stare down at a scarlet river flowing out from under his head, mixing with the water which disperses it into a complex pattern like a rubicund Rorschach test.

"Christ, we've killed him!" he says after which we both stand in a stunned silence.

Abruptly, the air is filled with a scream so deafening that I feel it could have shattered the windows all around us. Looking over, I see one of the nuns standing at the edge of the foyer with her hands now over her mouth.

"Sister! Please call an ambulance! Now!" I demand. She pauses for a few seconds and then turns to call for help.

"What are we going to do? We'll go to jail for this!" shouts Billy.

"Billy! Calm down, now!" I insist. "Listen, get a hold of yourself. This changes nothing. We have to stick to the plan. The police will be coming shortly and they are going to want statements from each of us, most likely separately. Stick to the plan. Do not add or make up anything other than what we discussed."

"Okay."

"Quickly now, let's go over our story one more time. Billy, what do you think caused your cramps?" I ask.

"Is this necessary, Danny?"

"Yes!" I emphatically yell. "It is necessary! Stop wasting precious time! Billy, what do you think caused your cramps?"

"I, uh, I ate four Malo Cups at home just before going to the rectory for the ride here," he responds.

"Is that it?" I ask.

"Uh, no, I also drank a bottle of birch beer soda. The clear one," he replies.

"Did you do what I asked at your house?" I inquire.

"Shit Danny, of course I did. What the hell do you think?" I sense the beginning of panic similar to what he exhibited in the mine.

"Calm down, Billy. We have to stay composed. We just need to be sure that everything is covered. Now explain how you were able to get out of the pool" I inquire.

"My cramps seemed to lessen and I was able to slowly breaststroke to the side where I was able to pull myself out of the pool which is when I saw Father Donovan lying on the floor," he says.

"Good, good. And I was just starting my run when I saw you were in trouble and yelling you had cramps, so I immediately turned and called for Father Donovan. Like I said, he came running, slipped and hit his head."

In the distance I hear the wail of sirens, probably both the ambulance and the police. Two other Sisters step down into the pool area and bend down to examine Father Donovan. A large nun with a puffy face and sad eyes like black marbles takes his arm in her hand and feels for a pulse. After a few seconds she lowers his arm and makes a negative nod of her head to the other sister who blesses herself.

As if suddenly aware of our presence, the large nun says, "Boys, why don't you go dry off and change out of your swim suits. I imagine the police will want to talk to you. Go!" she commands.

Nodding an acknowledgement, we walk down the length of the pool past the glistening bluish water to the changing room. Pushing the door open, it suddenly feels twice as heavy as it did before. As the door slams shut Billy is suddenly panicky and says, "Danny, we have to tell what really happened! We can't keep quiet about this! Christ, why did we do this?"

Grabbing him by the shoulders, I slam him into the tiled wall, his head making a thud as it hits it. I recognize the fear in his voice as it is the same as it was in the mine.

"What the hell, Danny?" he says in a shocked voice.

"Listen, Billy. Get ahold of yourself! We didn't kill him on purpose! Remember that! Do you want to be put in a reformatory school until you are eighteen? Do you want to possibly go to jail? Imagine what it would do to your family. We keep to the plan. Nothing has changed. You got that?" I ask as I see tears tracing down his cheeks. Embarrassed, he quickly wipes them away, takes a deep breath, and then seems to regain his composure.

He nods so I release my grip. "Remember, this was all for Tommy. Don't ever lose sight of the fact that Father Donovan hurt him. We don't know, we may never know, exactly what he did to Tommy. What we do know is that he hurt him bad enough that he changed into a person we did not know. Hurt him bad enough that he and his Mom had to move away. Neither of us planned for our prank to cause him to die but, as they say, what is done is done. We can't change that. Now, let's get dressed and go talk to the police," I say as I reach my arm out with an extended pinky. Slowly Billy does likewise, our fingers intertwine as we silently raise our arms until we are once again free from each other.

Coming out of the changing room, I see two state troopers and two ambulance personnel who I recognize as volunteers from the local fire company. They are dressed in light blue shirts and dark slacks, one of them has a fresh blood stain on his sleeve. The body has already been covered by a sheet and placed on a wheeled gurney. The sheeted corpse looks like it is waiting for a magician to come and say 'abracadabra', move his hands over it, and make it disappear. The two volunteers begin wheeling the gurney out, lifting the front end then the back over the step and into the foyer. A wheel squeaks forlornly as they head for the front door.

One of the troopers turns to us and I recognize him as the same one we talked to in the hospital the day Tommy got into the fight with Sandy. His tan felt Stetson is still on his head, still shading his face. He has whisker stubble which gives him an even more threatening look.

"Boys, can I have a word please?" he asks. "We need to take a statement from each of you. Sergeant Moran will talk to you in the foyer," he says pointing to Billy. "And I will talk to you here," he says to me. "My name is Sergeant Durkin."

Watching Billy and Sergeant Moran walk out into the foyer, I hear him say to me, "What is your name, son?"

"Danny. Danny Fosse," I answer.

"And your address?"

"39 Parsons Street. It is just off of Market Street in town."

"Okay, Danny. I know this is a difficult time, but tell me in your own words what happened here?" he says as he pulls out a small note pad and pen.

"Well, Father Donovan was out in the foyer having coffee. The two of us were running from here to the pool to see who could cannon-ball the furthest. We were just doing it over and over, having a good time. Then I heard Billy cry that he had cramps and saw him splashing about. I was standing about here so I turned and yelled to Father Donovan that Billy was drowning. He came running and slipped on the wet floor. He hit his head and didn't move after that," I say. Outside I hear the engine of the ambulance as it starts down the driveway. The siren is not on.

"I see. What about Billy?"

"Sorry?" I ask.

"You said Billy was drowning. The Father fell. How did Billy get safely out of the pool?"

"Well, he said afterwards that the severe cramping he had subsided just enough for him to make it to the side of the pool where he was able to pull himself out."

"I see," he says as he makes a note on his pad. "Stay here," he says as he steps up into the foyer. Turning around, I look down at the spot where Father Donovan fell and see an irregularly shaped pool of blood already starting to darken. Wiping a tear from my eye, I suddenly feel overcome by what has happened. Like the last time I was in Lenter's Mine, I begin shaking involuntarily, but this time not from cold but from raw fear. I hear Sergeant Durkin call to me "Danny, please come up here."

Walking into the foyer, I see Billy sitting in a chair. The two troopers are conferring by the front door. Approaching him, I can see alarm in his downcast eyes. He looks like a wild animal caught in a trap that it is unable to free itself from. Turning as I hear footsteps. Sergeant Durkin is walking towards us.

"Boys, I am going to take you home if that is all right," he says.

"Um, Father Donovan was going to take us both to Billy's house. My parents are out for dinner and they were going to pick me up there later on," I say.

"Okay, we have the address from Billy's statement, so come with me boys. I'll have the Sister call ahead to Billy's mom to let her know what happened and to inform her that I am bringing you home," he says.

Following him somberly, we both wear furtive expressions like we are part of a funeral procession. Exiting through the front door, we are blinded by the lights still whirling on top of the car as he holds the back door open. Billy slides in followed by me. Slamming the door shut like the closing of a prison gate, he walks around the front of the car, removes his hat and climbs in behind the wheel. He fastens his seat belt and turns off his deck lights while saying, "Fasten your lap belts, fellows."

The scanner belts out static and conversations between the dispatcher and other patrol cars as he eases the shift lever into gear. As he completes the turn to head down the drive, the headlights dart across the lawn and shine on the piles of leaves, the embers glowing and then dimming in the breeze like multiple red eyed snakes glaring at us.

Driving into town in silence, the only sounds are static and the radio dispatcher. The trooper turns onto South Street and makes the left-hand turn into Billy's driveway. Billy's mom is waiting on the porch clutching an unbuttoned red and black checked hunting jacket across her ample chest, her dyed blond hair matted to her head, while Billy's older sister Jennifer lurks in the background.

As we get out of the car, she rushes down the steps shouting, "Billy! Billy! Are you okay?"

Looking embarrassed, he says, "Sure, Mom. I'm fine" as she engulfs him with a hug. Looking over his shoulder she asks, "Danny, you okay?" I nod an affirmative.

Mrs. King looks at the trooper and says, "Thank you sir for bringing them here. Is there anything more you need?"

"Well miss, if it is not too much trouble, I sure could use a glass of water," he says. I look at Billy and see his eyes widen.

"Oh, certainly. Please follow me," she says as she starts back up the steps with her one arm still around Billy holding him close. She pulls open the storm door, which I grab, and then pushes in the front door while saying, "Jennifer, honey, would you mind going to your room?"

Giving her mother a perturbed grimace, she silently turns and heads up the stairs.

Sergeant Durkin removes his hat as we all follow Mrs. King down the narrow hall into the green kitchen as worn oak floor boards squeak like scurrying mice. She motions for all of us to sit at a wobbly metal table in the center of the room. Taking a water container out of the Philco refrigerator, she pours three glasses and distributes them amongst us.

"Would you like something to eat?" she asks.

"Well miss, not to impose but I do have a blood sugar issue and sure could use a small piece of that banana on your counter," he says.

"Well, most certainly," she says as she goes and picks it up and then hands it to him.

"Thank you, miss."

She then retrieves two Malo Cups and gives us each one saying, "Here boys, I'm sure you two must be starved."

The silence in the room is roaring in my ears as he slowly eats his banana between sips of water. I hear the slow-motion tick, tick, tick from the wall clock. Finally finishing, he stands and takes a last drink and asks, "Garbage?"

"Over there next to the refrigerator," says Mrs. King pointing the way.

"Thanks again, miss," he says as he walks over and steps on the floor level pedal opening the top of the container. As the lid slowly pops open, sitting on top in plain view are several Malo Cup wrinkled wrappers and an empty, clear birch beer bottle.

Dropping in the peel, he then turns and says while smiling, "You boys take care, hear?"

"Yes, sir," we respond as we sit with hangdog faces.

With that, he places his Stetson back on and heads down the hall and out the front door, the latch clicking noisily in place as it closes, while invisible dogs bark somewhere out back.

13.

December 1964

Dutchess County, New York

The first snowflakes of the season tumble randomly from the sky like dice, the weather worn headstones in the cemetery already covered with a light sugary frosting. The whole gamut of social strata is represented here from the altar tombs of the wealthy to the bevel markers of the poor. Here, death is an indiscriminate host. What you were, and what you did or did not accomplish in life, is meaningless. Worked your whole life just for money? How's that working out for you, now? Dead is dead inside these gates. During their lives people waste so much time and effort on the meaningless, the superficial, forgetting the finality of both time and death.

I turn to look at the approaching vehicles. The headlights of the cortege twinkle at me through the trees. The shadowy hearse pulls up parallel to the grave site and parks. The black Cadillac Coupe de Ville following likewise pulls to stop, after which the doors all open as the pall bearers emerge. As the balance of the long procession pulls in nose to end, the sounds of engines being shut off and car doors opening and closing fill the air like sporadic clapping.

Feeling an arm on my shoulder, I turn to see Billy who gestures a hello. Facing back, I spot Jo and her dad in the crowd. She gives a slight smile to me which I return.

Watching the end of the hearse swing open, the burnished mahogany casket slides out on rollers onto the waiting bier. The pall bearers, three per side, wait in position as the mourners make their way to the grave site while Father Joye stands solemnly at the head of the casket.

With everyone in place, he makes the sign of the cross and says a prayer I cannot hear. Finishing, he signals the pall bearers who grab the casket by its brass handrails and raise it up off the bier before slowly making their way towards us. Reaching the end of the burial site, they all turn until they are lined up, then make their way up until the casket is directly above the open burial vault. Bending, they place it upon the green straps of the lowering device. Standing again, they walk back in the direction they came from to be out of the way of the ceremony.

There is an awkward silence as mourners shift back and forth on their feet as someone sneezes. Every breath omits a little cloud of condensation in the cold air like everyone is smoking. The pungent smell of freshly dug earth hovers in the air, a distant horn of a tanker on the Hudson forlornly ricochets through the town like a pinball.

Taking a step forward to the end of the casket, Father Joye says, "My brothers and sisters, Jesus says, 'Come to me, all you who labor and are overburdened, and I will give you rest. Shoulder my yoke and learn from me, for I am gentle and humble of heart, and you will find rest for your souls. Yes, my yoke is easy and my burden light.'" Bending, he reaches for the aspergillum, pulls it out of a silver bucket, and proceeds to walk around the perimeter of the casket while sprinkling holy water which splashes against the wood and then trickles down the sides like tears.

Finishing, he replaces it in the bucket and says, "Into your hands, O Lord, we humbly entrust our brother, Father Donovan. In this life you embraced him with your tender love; deliver him now from every evil and bid him enter eternal rest. The old order has passed away; welcome him then into paradise, where there will be no sorrow, no weeping or pain, but the fullness of peace and joy with your Son and the Holy Spirit, for ever and ever."

"Amen," everyone says while making the sign of the cross.

"Eternal rest grant unto him O Lord."

"And may perpetual light shine upon him," all respond.

"May his soul and the souls of all the faithful departed, through Mercy of God, rest in peace."

"Amen," the mourners say while again making the sign of the cross.

Father Joye nods to Ed Black, the funeral director, who moves forward and disengages a lock causing the casket to start slowly lowering into the ground like a miner's elevator descending into a deep pit. Turning to face the grievers, he says, "That concludes our grave side service. Father Joye has one more thing he would like to say to you all. Father?" he says.

"Father Donovan was a dear friend to me, the community and the church. He will be sorely missed. Again, thank you all for coming and you are all invited to the rectory for refreshments."

With that everyone starts to walk to their cars. Turning, I face Billy as Jo and her dad walk over.

"Hi, Mr. Nelson. Hi, Jo," I say.

"Hi," says Billy.

"Hello, Danny and Billy. You two doing okay?" Mr. Nelson asks. "If you guys ever need someone other than your parents to talk to about what happened, you can call me anytime."

"Thank you, sir," I say. "That is very kind of you."

With that he says, "Well, Jo, we best be going."

"See you guys in school," she says with a smile as she follows her father towards their car.

Billy and I walk through the graves and up a slippery incline to the back of the church as the snow intensifies. Upon reaching the walkway at the back of the church, I look back as forlorn cars make their way up the road leaving only the open wound in the earth and a snow-covered mound of dirt. A backhoe starts, making its way slowly from the edge of the woods towards the grave site looking like a giant yellow scorpion in search of prey. It spooks a covey of partridges that scurry into the woods.

"You okay?" I ask.

"Yeah, okay," says Billy but his eyes say otherwise.

"Look Billy, I know this secret is something that will probably haunt each of us for the rest of our lives."

"Tell me about it. I have regret and remorse over what happened every single day, and sometimes I have a hard time sleeping thinking about it."

"I know. What we did may have started out as an innocent prank to get revenge for Tommy but we can't change what actually happened. It will undoubtedly be better for us with the passage of time. Father Donovan is gone, but as far as I am concerned, I am sorry for the way this happened but good riddance just the same."

"Yeah, I guess," says Billy. "Well, I have to get home."

"Me too, I'll see you later."

Watching as he shuffles around the side of the church, he disappears into the snowy afternoon. Hearing an approaching noise, I look up into the hoary sky and see a flock of geese flying in tight formation like a grouping of B-52 bombers. The honking grows louder and louder sounding like cabs on a congested Broadway during theater time. Following their flight path, the snow eventually blurs my vision until I can neither see nor hear them any longer. It is snowing so hard it is like being inside a ping pong ball, white being the only thing visible.

14.

December, 1967

Dutchess County, New York

Bulky snowflakes wander down from the obscure sky like remnants of some celestial pillow fight. Being a windless night, they fall straight down like tiny bleached missiles. Pulling my car to the curb, snow crunches underneath the tires sounding like stepping on peanut shells.

Both sides of the street are littered with cars, most that I recognize. The house where this party is being held is home to a kid that I barely know. When parents are away, word of a party spreads like wildfire in the dry California hills. The muffled sounds of music and laughter filter out from the inside. The kid will undoubtedly regret this in the morning, I suspect.

Upon opening my car door, the full cacophony is ratcheted up several octaves. Footprints in the fallen snow crisscross the road in every direction, looking like the trek of some lost explorer. The snow is increasing in intensity, and as I look up the lone street light looks like a small full moon behind a white wax curtain.

Walking across the street, I nod to a few casual acquaintances that I pass then head up the walkway to the front entrance. Before I get to it, the front door swings open and a kid I have never seen before races to the railing, leans over and spills his insides out as the Stones' 'Mother's Little Helper' booms out into the night. *This is going to be a great New Year's Eve party* I think to myself.

Grabbing the icy door handle, I sidestep his legs as I pull it open to enter a smoke-filled room with low lighting. It takes my eyes several seconds to adjust, as if I were in some cave, thick smoke already making them sting and water. Glancing around the room, I see the usual suspects making out on various pieces of furniture and on the floor as if they were alone. In the kitchen area I spot Billy amongst a group of our friends.

Spotting me, he is obviously intoxicated as he screams, "Hey, Danny! Over here pal! How about a beer?" as he hands me an ice cold can of Schaefer's. He has his left arm tightly around his new girlfriend Cheri, who looks at me with a bored, please rescue me look.

Smiling at her, I say, "Thanks, Billy. You been here long?"

"Bout tree hours," he slurs.

"I can see that. Have you seen Jo?"

"Nope."

"Well, I have to hit the head," I say as I look for a place to set my beer down on the crowded countertop which is strewn with half empty cans, bottles, overflowing ash trays and the remains of dips and chips in several bowls. I see a long, fresh scratch in the countertop with the potential villain knife stuck into a block of cheese like Excalibur. An unguarded bottle of half empty Vodka sits in the middle looking as out of place at this party as I now feel.

"Second door down the hall on the left," says Cheri.

"Thanks," I say as she winks at me. *Oh brother*, I think. Walking down the hall, I grab the knob and twist it only to find that it is locked. A feminine voice from inside yells, "It's occupied," this followed by other females laughing. *Why is it that girls go to the bathroom in packs,* I wonder while turning and walking back down the hall to the hazy kitchen.

Ambling to the back door, I stride down the back steps to the snow-covered lawn where I see footprints going off into the back woods in several different directions with return prints evident. Walking back to the first white pine to relieve myself, I look deep into the dark woods and can't shake the feeling that something is happening, something is changing. Lately, Billy and I have been spending more and more time with our girlfriends rather than with each other. Is it jealousy I feel? No, I don't think so. I think it is the realization that as we grow older the world is slowly splitting us apart as if driving a wedge between us, like frozen water splitting a rock crevice. Tommy has been gone for over three years and I feel Billy is slowly leaving me also. We were all inseparable as ice tightly packed within an iceberg. Now, I feel like there has been a spring thaw and the ice is calving. We are each slowly pulling away from the whole and falling separately into the sea, each drifting in our own direction. *One, two, three, friends forever*, I wonder.

Sighing, I finish and turn to walk back to the party. Entering the out-of-focus kitchen, I kick my feet together to knock off the snow as I hear Billy say, "Hey, Danny, it is Jo on the line," as he waves the phone at me.

Walking over, I grab it and push it to one ear while holding my hand tightly over the other in an attempt to hear.

"Hi, Jo. I thought you were coming to the party?" I say.

"Hey, Danny. I really don't feel up to it tonight. Would you like to come over? I'm house sitting for the Wilsons tonight. They're away for the weekend and asked me to watch the house."

Looking at the drunken Billy and the make out artists around the living room I quickly reply, "Sure, that would be great. Where do you want to meet?"

"Just walk out to Market Street and go towards town. I will meet you somewhere on the street. I'll leave in about five minutes."

"Great. See you soon," I say as I hang the phone on the wall cradle, the coiled cord twisting itself into impossible knots.

"Hey, Billy I'm going," I say as I extend my hand. "Happy New Year, pal."

Shaking it, he says, "Come on Danny, stay until midnight. It is only fifteen minutes away. This might be our last New Year's Eve together since we graduate this spring."

"Thanks, pal, but I told Jo I would meet her. Have fun," I say.

Going back out through the front door, I carefully sidestep the remnants from the sick kid. Glancing across the street, I see that my car has a light covering of light, puffy snow on it. Deciding to walk, I head down Charles Street, turn left and then right at the intersection with Market Street. As I walk, I think about what Billy said. What if he is right, that this is the last New Year's Eve we will ever spend together? The thought makes me sad.

As I get further down the isolated street, the only sound is the drone of electrical transformers which sound like hovering hummingbirds. Walking on the snow, it crunches under my feet, the shrubs and bushes in the yards appearing like they have been covered with white sheets like furniture in an abandoned house. Pushing my ungloved hands a little further into my jacket pockets, I seek warmth that isn't there.

Strolling into town, I notice that I am feeling very tired. I am the only moving thing on the street with the exception of the falling snow, which stings my cheeks like electrical sparks. Tire tracks that were made earlier are almost filled. Looking down the long street to downtown, the lights on each side make it look like an airport landing strip. Thinking of Billy and Tommy, I suddenly feel very alone in the world.

A few blocks ahead I see someone walk out of a side street by Saint Vitonus, moving in my direction. I instantly recognize the coat, hat and gait, which triggers a smile. Silently we walk towards each other as the features of her face come into focus set off by a broad smile. The only sounds are our feet crunching the snow and the hum of the transformers. Her auburn hair hangs in matted strands across her forehead and cheek, her bright eyes seem as lustrous as pearls.

"Hey, Jo," I say as I reach up and push back her damp hair. She doesn't answer but rather puts her arms around me. She pulls me so close to her that we are looking into each other's eyes, mine down to hers, hers up to mine. I feel my knees actually go weak as I gaze into her blue-gray eyes, the color of a winter sky, as a flush of anticipation rattles around my entire being. She raises her right arm up until her hand tenderly cups the back of my head like a mother holding a newborn, not too firm, not too gentle, but something in between. I see her slightly tilt her head and close her eyes as she pushes herself up onto her toes and kisses me. Her lips feel soft as warm butter as I smell her perfume. Is it Channel Number Five? I can never remember, but I do know that whenever I smell it, I will think of her, think of this night, think of this kiss.

Suddenly, the church bells start ringing and sporadic noises launch around the town signaling the start of the New Year. Pulling slightly away from her, I bring a hand to her cold cheek and say, "Happy New Year, Jo."

Smiling, she pulls me close again and puts her right hand again lightly behind my head. Staring into my eyes, hers moving back and forth as she looks at one, then the other, and back again. Then she stands up on her toes again and kisses me neither hard nor soft but something in between. I kiss her softly back with thoughts of Billy and Tommy being the furthest thing from my mind. I guess I may have just broken free of the iceberg myself.

Pulling away, her face only inches away from mine, she softly says, "I love you, Danny Fosse. I really do."

Hearing this for the first time, I gaze at her as my whole being warms. I am overcome with a rush of uncontrollable feelings like a runaway train; joy, excitement, wonderment, anticipation. I feel something deep inside stir like an animal awakening from a long winter hibernation. It starts bubbling up from deep inside me as I smile peacefully, joyfully. Looking deep into her lovely eyes, I say, "I love you too, Jo. With all of my heart."

Smiling, she takes my cold hand and we wordlessly start to walk.

In the distance, somewhere west across the Hudson, I can hear the faint sound of celebratory fireworks whispering secrets somewhere deep in the Catskills. Then, all is silent again. I don't hear the sound of our footsteps crunching on the snow. Or the overhead hum of the transformers. Just something that is in between, a delightful combination of the two.

I awaken to the sun peeking through the skeleton of a maple tree, warming my face, the smell of fresh brewed coffee hovering in the air.

Looking out the window, I see the snow stopped overnight and has yielded to an azure blue sky. Standing up, I rub my eyes as I walk to the kitchen.

"Good morning sleepy head, and Happy New Year," Jo says as she looks up from the papers scattered around the table.

"Same to you. Coffee smells great," I say.

"Help yourself. The cups are in the cupboard above the stove."

Moving to the table with a full mug, I ask, "What's with all the papers?" Sipping the coffee, I smile with satisfaction.

"Application papers, or did you forget? We both have to get these in the mail this week if we want to be considered for early out of state acceptance. I also have to arrange for my transcript to be sent to each one from community college."

Sitting down, I pick up a pile of applications to various colleges. What happens if one of us doesn't get admitted?"

Giving me an annoyed look, she says, "We have discussed this, Danny. That is something neither one of us can control. We both have excellent grades so I doubt that will be of concern. If it does happen, we will deal with it then. For now, let's not worry about it, okay?"

"There is one other thing I have been meaning to talk with you about."

"What is that?" she says with a concerned look in her eyes.

"My father's business is in trouble. A bigger company from Poughkeepsie has started soliciting business in this area and his revenues are way down as a result. He doesn't know that I know this, but he took a second mortgage on the house to pay for equipment and wages. I don't know how I could ever ask him to pay for college at this time."

"I'm so sorry to hear that. Is there anything I can do to help?

Smiling, I say, "Thanks, but no. I appreciate the offer. I will be working more nights and weekends to try to help him. I wanted you to know this because it could impact my plans to attend college."

"We'll get through this, Danny. Let's put our applications in and see what happens between now and September. That is a long way off. I have a feeling deep inside that this is going to be a great year. Okay?"

Taking another sip of coffee, I nod. "You know, Jo, I hope you understand how much I appreciate you. Especially your waiting for me to graduate high school before applying. I know you have not been happy attending community college when you could have been at a four-year university the last year and a half. You could be entering your junior year in college this fall if you had applied right after high school. I just don't want to be the reason again why you didn't go to college."

Smiling, she reaches across the table and takes my hand. Looking into her eyes, I see no further words are necessary.

15.

April 1968

Dutchess County, New York

Sitting in a chair on our front porch, I am sipping coffee when I hear a car door close.

Looking up, I see a man coming up our sidewalk whom I have never seen before. He is tall with a slim athletic build, a full head of fire red hair with seemingly as many freckles dotting his face as there are craters on the moon.

"Can I help you, sir? I ask.

"Are you Danny Fosse?"

"Yes. And you are?"

Walking towards me with his hand extended, he says, "My name is Roy Sigloch. I am an assistant to the swim team coach at Syracuse."

Grabbing his hand, we shake and I ask, "Why are you looking for me, coach?"

"Mind if I sit down?" he asks. "I have been driving all day."

"Help yourself," I say while pointing to an Adirondack chair.

After sitting, he says, "Where to start? I have a brother who is one of the coaches for the men's swim team at Michigan State. He used to swim competitively there when he was in college. One of his teammates was a guy named Ed Coleman. Does that name mean anything to you?"

"I can't say that it does."

"Anyway, you might know him as Father Coleman? He is a permanent teacher at a Catholic seminary in Connecticut just outside of Hartford."

At the mere mention of the name the memories of the day Billy and I found the body come flooding back to me. The shock, the fear, the confusion, and the anger.

"Yes, I remember Father Coleman. Why is that of interest to you?"

"Well, Father Coleman has been an active supporter of the Michigan State swim teams over the years. When he visited last month, he pulled my brother aside and told him a story of how a fourteen-year-old boy trounced him in a swim race at the seminary a few years back. My brother gave me a call to see if I could convince you to try out. This may sound strange, but we would like you to come to Syracuse for a work out. We have a regulation size pool and state of the art timing equipment. More importantly, we have one of the best communication schools in the country which gives us access to the best state of the art video equipment available. The Michigan State coaches want to see film of you. We would pay your expenses, of course. I would report back what I see to my brother, send him the videotape and, who knows, you might get at least a partial scholarship offer, if not a full one, depending upon how you do. Just a three-hour drive and you could potentially be rewarded with a scholarship. What do you think?"

Thinking to myself, *this could solve all of my financial concerns about having my parents pay for my college.* "Why not. When do you want me there?"

With a campus map in hand, I walk across the Quad past Hendricks Chapel as a stiff wind slaps at my face. A Canadian low pressure is bearing down on the city and severe thunderstorms have been predicated to follow the current light rain. Thank goodness it isn't winter or this system would wind up the snow making machine that is lake effect snow.

Looking over at Crouse College, the brown tower glistens as it towers over the city below. The lights on top of the Carrier building are flashing down in red indicating that the temperature is dropping.

Walking up the steps to Archbold, I pull open the door as a gust of wind attempts to slam it shut. I manage to squeeze through it just before it almost pins my gym bag. It closes with a loud metallic bang. Wiping the rain off of my coat and jeans, I see the sign for the Webster pool to my left. Striding down the corridor, I stop at a huge trophy case. In the center sits the Heisman Trophy won by Ernie Davis. On one side sits a group picture of the nineteen fifty-nine championship team. On the other side are pictures of Jim Brown playing lacrosse and football and a guy named Dave Bing playing basketball.

Walking down the tiled hall to a glass door, I look inside and see the pool is vacant. Pushing the door open, I step inside to the strong aroma of chlorine and see six marked flow through lanes for racing. The ceiling to floor windows instantly reminds me of those at the pool that I swam in when I was an altar boy. To my right I see a gallery for spectators with a sign that says capacity of six hundred. The lanes are marked above with black and red triangular flags which denote the swimming paths.

Moving down the length of the pool, my footsteps echo in the empty hall like a yell into a canyon as I look into the crystal-clear water and marvel at its transparency. I feel a sudden, long forgotten pull to the water. Images flash through my mind at the speed of light: swimming with my mother in the Hudson, one, two, three and breathe; jumping into the convent pool with my friends and circling around Nag's Boulder in Mirror Lake.

"What do you think?" I hear from behind me.

Turning, I see coach Sigloch. "Pretty impressive," I say.

"Did you have any trouble getting here?"

"No, not at all. I made it from home in slightly over three hours."

"Are you planning on staying overnight?"

"No, when we're done, I am heading home. I have to be at work tomorrow."

"On a Sunday?"

"It's a long story," I say.

"All right, then maybe we should get on with this. The locker room is over there," he says while pointing the way. "Why don't you change and come back when you are set. First, I will weigh you in and then I'll have you swim to one end and back which is fifty meters. It is our standard testing length."

"Okay. I'll be right back."

"Great. I'll set up the video camera while your changing."

Stepping up onto the starting block, I look down the marked lane to the other end. I feel as if the water is teasing me, daring me to dive in. Shaking my arms and hands at my side, I twist my neck and head from side to side. Looking again at the windows, I see the wind continues assaulting the panes with rain pellets. Bending down, I grab the starting block end with my fingers and freeze in position, readying for my dive.

Holding a stop watch, coach Sigloch counts down, "Three, two, one, go!"

Instantly, I am off and hit the water in a shallow dive. Surfacing, I melt into my routine. One, two, three and breathe. Over and over. Shortly I reach the other end where I roll, pushing off the wall with my feet. Surfacing, I draw on everything I have. I can actually feel myself increasing in speed as I effortlessly cut through the water. Approaching the starting block, I make a final surge and touch the wall.

Pushing away, I float on my back, breathing harder than usual for this length of swim. Looking up, I see coach Sigloch standing over me, smiling. "How are you feeling?" he asks.

"Fine, coach. Why?"

"Would you mind resting a bit and doing that again?"

"Sure, no problem."

Emerging from the pool after my second trial, I grab a towel and start drying off. My legs burn and I feel totally exhausted. As coach Sigloch walks over to me, I ask, "How did I do?"

"Let's put it this way, if I wasn't such an honest man, I would offer you a full scholarship to Syracuse here on the spot. And I'm not even the head coach. I was on the team here in college and I have been associated with this program in one capacity or another for over ten years. You just posted not just the best time I have ever seen in the fifty meters, but you blew the old time away. That is why I had you do it twice. I thought there was a clock problem with your first run. There wasn't. You have a special talent, Danny. And a bright future. You can expect a call from Michigan State, I'm certain. One way or another, paying for college is not going to be an issue for you."

"Thanks, coach. You have no idea how glad I am to hear that."

"One thing, though. Although you have a swimmer's build, you should try to put on some weight before you get into collegiate swimming. I show you at one hundred fifty-two pounds. Is that your normal weight?"

"Well, I think I may be down a few pounds. I have been working with my father at his blacktopping business and it is extremely hard work."

"Nevertheless, you should try to beef yourself up some. Extending his hand, he says, "Thank you for coming. You have a safe drive home. If you will excuse me, I have a phone call to make."

Having just told Jo the news, I see tears come to her eyes as she jumps on me, hands around my neck and legs around my waist. "I knew it! I knew it!" she cries.

Setting her back down, I put both of my hands on her face and smile. "I guess you were right on New Year's Eve. This looks like it is going to be a great year. What say we go tell my parents the news? I'm sure this will make their day."

16.

September 1968

Dutchess County, New York

Pulling my parents baby blue Torino station wagon into the gravel parking lot of Loren's Bar & Grill, I recognize several of the cars as belonging to my high school friends and acquaintances. It's Labor Day weekend, the end of graduation summer, and I realize this could very well be the last time I ever see some of them. The others I might see now and then, here and there, but what we have in common now will have been long gone like the leaves of a frozen winter tree.

Getting out of the car, I hear the muted hum of the chaos within the bar followed by a shout. "Hey, Danny!" calls Agnos. Smiling, I walk over to him, our earlier clashes on the football field a cloudy memory. Extending his hand, he gives me a wide smile as he says "Congratulations! I hear you and Jo were both accepted at Michigan State, and you got a full swimming scholarship. How the hell you ever pulled that off with our school not even having a swim team, I will never know! Anyway, it is fantastic and I wish you both nothing but the best of luck. So, when are you leaving?"

"Yeah, thanks pal, it is great. I'm heading to the Adirondacks tomorrow for a two-day hike and when I get back, we'll make our plans to leave. So, I hear you are going to apply to be a state trooper?"

"Yeah. I turn twenty-one this February. Seems flunking a few grades decreased my time frame from graduation to being eligible! Anyway, I will apply on my birthday and hopefully be accepted. And look here," he says as he pulls his upper lip up, "I finally got a permanent implant for that tooth you knocked out!" he says.

"Hah, good for you, Agnos! It must be nice to know what you

want. Best of luck to you, buddy," I say as I slap him on the back. "You see Billy?" I ask.

"Inside," he says as he motions with his head towards the door. Nodding, I turn and push through the first door and then through the second as he follows me in. The bar room is packed, cigarette smoke suspended in the air like Los Angeles smog as clinking of glasses, loud chatter and the clacking of billiard balls fuse into a loud whirring noise like a blender. The bar smells of cigarette smoke, cheap perfume and stale beer. Looking around, I spot Billy sitting alone in a booth by the juke box. 'Hey Jude' blasts out of the cheap speakers with a hollow tone as half the bar drunkenly sings along badly out of tune. An ancient unlit neon sign above his head advertises oyster stew for twenty-five cents a bowl.

Walking over, I sit down across from my friend on a worn red vinyl seat that squeaks.

"Hey, Danny. Where's Jo?"

"She and her dad went to see her aunt in Vermont for a few days."

"Is she excited about Michigan State?"

"Yeah, I'll say. She has had enough of community college and can't wait to get away."

"What will you have?" he asks as he stands to make his way to the bar.

"Can of Schaefers would be great."

Abruptly, I feel an unfriendly hand smack down solidly on my shoulder. Turning quickly, I am gazing up into the bloodshot eyes of Sandy. He has his left arm around his girlfriend Debbie, mostly for support, and his right hand held out towards me. I'm not sure if his wobbly stance is just from the alcohol or the lasting effect from Tommy whacking him with a bat. I suspect it is a combination of the two.

"Danny, I know we had our share of run ins over the years, but I just want to say that I have no hard feelings towards you. I just wanted you to know," he says as I look up into his red veined eyes.

Staring at his extended hand for a few uncomfortable seconds, I reach out and take it in mine saying, "What the hell."

Nodding, he turns and he and Debbie melt into the crowd as Billy returns, setting the beers on the table.

"What was that all about?" he asks.

"Auld lang syne," I say. "Forget about it. So, when you called me earlier today you said that you have something to tell me?"

"I guess so. As you know, I haven't decided on college for sure. With the war draft set to start this December, and with no sure college deferment, I thought it best if I enlist in the Army now and at least give myself some better options than were I to be drafted."

I am quiet, thinking. After a long pause, I say, "I don't know, Billy. Why enlist? You certainly have other options than college. Plus, you might get a high draft number and not have to go at all."

"To tell the truth, I just have to get out of this town, Danny. I don't know about you, but I think every day about what we did to Father Donovan. It haunts me. It's a shadow that follows me no matter where I go. It makes me sick. I also have not gotten over how I temporarily panicked when we got caught in Lenter's Mine as well as at the pool the night Father Donovan died. Maybe it didn't show, but I was seconds from losing it in there. I am still embarrassed about it. For the first time in my life, it makes me question my courage. I think I just need a change of scenery for my sanity."

My attention is diverted by the sound of a glass shattering and then chairs over turning. Standing, I see Sandy and Agnos swinging at each other. Walt the bartender grabs a pool stick and orders them to break it up and get out.

Turning back to Billy, I say, "The more things change…" to which Billy smiles. "You have a few months until the draft. Why don't you give yourself some time to think about this? There is no need to rush this type of decision, is there?" I ask.

"Well, Danny, I enlisted this week at the Dutchess County recruiting office in Poughkeepsie."

"Jesus Christ, Billy!" I say in exasperation. "What the hell! Why did you do that? You'll go to Fort Dix and then be shipped off to Vietnam." I drain my beer and slam the empty down on the table making a loud crack.

"Danny, calm down. The good news is that by enlisting I am eligible to take the exam to be accepted to Officer's School. I would then be going to Fort Polk in Louisiana after basic training."

"Yeah, but you have no guarantee. Either way, odds are short that you will be Vietnam bound. How long is your training?" I ask.

"Nine weeks in basic, then if I get into Officer's School it is another eight and a half weeks for the advanced infantry training."

"And did they tell you what percentage of the guys given advanced infantry training go to Vietnam?"

"Well, no."

"Billy, assuming that you do qualify for Fort Polk, if they spend the time and money to give you advanced infantry training don't you think they would then be more likely to send you to a war zone? I mean, wake up!" I scream.

"Come on, Danny. Take it easy."

"Christ, you want another round?"

"Sure."

Rising, I walk over to the bar as the Beatles' 'Hello Goodbye' thunders from the tinny juke box. Seeing Walt look in my direction, I wave my hand over the two empties and mouth "Another round."

Walt sets the beer down and I hand over a twenty. Waiting for change, I look over at Billy. *Just a kid,* I think. Walking back to the booth, I hand Billy his beer and sit down.

Sitting silently for a few minutes, I say, "Billy, do you even know why we are fighting this war?"

Looking surprised, he says, "Of course. To keep communism from spreading."

"So, you really believe the government crap that if we don't make a stand in Vietnam that the Viet Cong will be paddling up the Hudson? Come on, for Christ's sake. Use your head!"

"Okay, then why are we fighting?"

Sighing, I say, "It's simple. As with everything, it is all about money. And where there is money, corruption follows. It is good for the economy. Defense contractors love a good, long, prolonged war, especially one with aimless intent like this one. The checkbook is open wide, the green road lined with endless profit. The fat, corrupt government politicians love it because they get to wave the red, white and blue and act like they are doing something for once. The only ones who don't love this are the kids being slaughtered and the families receiving the boxes with their remains in them."

"Well, I believe in the government. I don't think they would deceive us. I feel like I am a patriot. I believe in this country, and in God, and that both are worth fighting for and, if need be, dying for. I really believe it is my duty to do this."

"Look around you, Billy. This country is a simmering pot about to boil over. There are more and more anti-war protests every day. This war is not only corrupt, it is despicable. Sentiments are changing. This has become a very unpopular war."

"You are entitled to your opinion. However, what is done is done and I am going into the army next month. I hope you will come to support my decision. It would mean a lot to me, buddy."

Staring Billy in the eye for several seconds, I extend my hand. "Best of luck, pal. I will be hoping that you are well wherever you go."

"You and me both," he says with a laugh.

"Another round?"

"Sure, thanks."

I order another round from Walt who deposits the bottles on the bar with a thud. Picking them up, I leave a buck on the damp bar. I look back to Billy sitting alone at the table as 'Hello Goodbye' ends.

Oh no indeed, I think.

17.

September 1968

Essex County, New York

Standing at the bald rock summit of Mount Skylight, I take in the panoramic view of the high peaks in early fall. This is the fourth highest peak in New York and from where I'm standing you can view over thirty other high peaks. The leaves have yet to turn but they are all signaling change by a dulling of their various shades of green. The late afternoon sun refracts on the top of the cloudy sky illuminating it with almost every color in the spectrum.

Taking a sip of water from my canteen, I screw the top back on and let it drop to my side on its leather strap. Earlier today, I left my car parked at the trailhead on Route 73 between Keene and St. Huberts. Making good time, I completed the eighteen-mile hike in about six hours, leaving me here at the peak completely exhausted. Hiking all the time, I am used to these arduous and back-breaking hikes but I don't ever remember it affecting me this much. I am also surprised how out of breath I am. I decide I better rest a little longer than planned.

Enjoying the view, I think about why I came. I want to not only challenge myself, yes, but I also want to spend some alone time to sort my future out.

Last month I received a full swimming scholarship to Michigan State based on my performance at Syracuse this past spring. Jo has also been accepted into their teaching program and is so excited to finally be off to a four-year college. On the one hand, I am thrilled with the opportunity to finally swim competitively and to go to college with Jo is something we both have talked and dreamed about for years. On the other hand, my father's business has not improved and the financial stress it is causing is more and more evident every day. He seems to have aged ten years this past year. To replace me, he would have to pay a much higher wage which he simply can't afford to do. If I go to college, I will be leaving him at the worst possible time. How can I do that when my parents have been so good to me? And if I put off college to stay, then Jo will either have to go alone or forego attending for the second time. I have a tough decision to make and, as of this moment, I haven't a clue as to what I will do.

The sun assaults the horizon and I feel like I may be lingering here too long. I check my compass and get my bearings. My intent is to hike back down the trail to the base, then veer off about a quarter mile and set up camp for the evening. It's later than I want it to be, so I'm considering bushwhacking a more direct route down to save time but am concerned with my lack of energy. After considerable deliberation, I start down off trail in a northwest direction since this is the sun side.

The underbrush is thicker than I anticipated and I fear I will lose sunlight before reaching the base. Seeing a clearing to my left, I push aside the leatherleaf and red elderberry shrubs in my path and emerge onto a gently sloping rock face that has random patches of moss. Looking down, I calculate I can save considerable time by going this route. Starting down, loose rocks move under each step. Some tumble down the rock face bouncing like they are on a trampoline.

Reaching a flat shelf, I see that I am only about twenty or so feet from the bottom and I feel there will still be enough sunlight to comfortably make camp. Feeling very fatigued now, I briefly rest while taking another drink of water. A chill is creeping as the sun gets lower and I start to shiver.

Stepping off of a ledge, my footing loosens a whole area of rock which begins spalling down the mountain side causing me to lose my balance and fall backwards. Trying to break my fall, I put out a hand but I can't stop the back of my head from bouncing off of a rock with a soft sickening thud. Suddenly I am no longer present. I sense my body sliding in slow motion but I do not hear or feel anything. It feels like I'm floating like a feather in the air and it seems like forever before gently coming to rest. It's like my entire being has been injected with Novocain and I have been placed in some type of sensory deprivation chamber. I try to yell but can't. I try to open my eyes but can't.

A hazy white light begins to emerge. It becomes brighter and whiter than any light I have ever seen. I am not sure what it is, but it keeps becoming brighter and brighter. Everything else fades out of existence-everything but the light. Then, as suddenly as it appeared, it starts to fade, first to a muted white then to a dull gray. Then it disappears and so do I.

Waking to an unknown smell of something cooking, I open my eyes and stare up at a log ceiling as a hammer hits my head. The pain radiates from the back throughout, my eyes feeling like they will explode. Putting my hand to the back of my head, I feel a large bandage.

"Welcome back," I hear a voice say.

Painfully turning my head to the right, I see an old man in a rocking chair whittling on a small tree branch. His white hair and matching long beard topple from his head and face like a waterfall, set off by sharp royal blue eyes. His body is shaped like an eggplant that was left on the vine long beyond picking time, and even though he is sitting I sense he is bent over under the weight of age.

"Where am I?" I ask.

"Between Heart Lake and Keene, not far from Lake Placid."

"God, my head is killing me. Do you have any aspirin?"

"Yes, but no. Yes, I do have aspirin, but no you can't have any. You suffered a mild concussion and aspirin, or any anti-inflammatory, is a no-no."

Surveying him skeptically I say, "What are you, some kind of doctor?"

Laughing, he says, "No, I am not some kind of doctor, I am a doctor. Or former doctor, I should say. I used to be a thoracic surgeon in Boston. Dee Purdy, good to meet you."

"Is the 'D' an initial for something?"

"It is not a letter, but D-e-e. That is my birth name."

"Pleased to meet you. My name is, ah, oh yeah, Danny Fosse."

"Don't worry about the slight memory issues. You're lucky that your concussion is very slight, the cut on your head not very deep. I examined you and I think with a day or two of rest you will be fine. You hungry?"

"I am a little, but I also feel a little nauseous right now."

"That's a common side effect of a concussion. Just get some rest and you can eat and drink when you wake up."

"Thanks again, Dee. I think I will take your advice and sleep some more," I say as I roll over and shut my eyes.

Waking again, I notice that it is dark outside. Rolling over onto my right side, I see Dee still whittling in his rocking chair. What previously was a branch is now a smaller stick about ten inches in length. He is pushing his blade away from his body as wood shavings roll up like breaking waves and then float to the floor like small butterflies. Looking up, he sees me and says, "Feeling any better?"

Pushing myself up into a sitting position, I say, "A little. Thank you."

"I bet you are hungry now, huh?"

"You bet!"

"How is your nausea?"

"It seems to have passed."

"Excellent. You go take a shower and freshen up while I finish preparing dinner. The shower is down that hall on the right, your pack is on the bed in the first room to the left."

"Thanks, Dee. A shower sounds great," I say as he walks over to tend to a boiling pot on the stove. Surveying the room, it is an open area, one small window on each wall, containing a living room, kitchen and a cobblestone fireplace that has an enticing fire dancing in it. On the log walls are various mounted heads of deer, a moose and a bear.

The bear has a green beret canted on its head and the moose has a cigar in its mouth.

Smiling, I get up and walk down the hallway entering a bedroom which has a very low ceiling. Grabbing my pack, I fish out clean clothes, a shave kit bag and head to the bathroom. Upon entering, I close the door and look into the mirror with surprise. My face has cuts and lacerations all over it and one eye is a yellowish black. Likewise, my arms and legs are all scraped and cut. Turning on the hot water, I splash my face and, after an initial burning sensation, it starts to feel good.

Returning to the living area after a hot shave and shower, I am feeling invigorated. As I enter the room Dee motions to the kitchen table which has several steaming dishes set upon it.

Sitting down, I say, "This looks great, Dee! What is it?"

Laughing, he says, "Squirrel stew with carrots and beans and my homemade garlic bread. I also brew my own beer, but no alcohol for you until you recover from that bump on the head. Instead, how about some tea?"

"Sounds good."

Sitting, Dee says, "Don't be bashful Danny, dig in."

As I spoon the stew into my bowl I ask, "So Dee, how in the world did you ever find me?"

Handing me a cup of tea, he fills his bowl, sets the stew pot down and says, "I guess it was your lucky day. Once a week or so I hike over to Heart Lake to do some fishing. My normal route was too muddy because of all the recent rain, so I hiked over to the Skylight Mountain trail and followed it to the base. Then I bushwhacked around the perimeter intending to hook up again with my normal trail when I saw you laying there unconscious. I was able to carry you back over my shoulder but had to leave your pack behind since the combined weight was too much for me. After I got you settled, I went back and retrieved your pack. You're very lucky that you didn't get more seriously hurt. You might have never been found since that side of the mountain has very few hikers due to the craggy terrain and heavy underbrush."

I shudder at the thought of what could have happened if Dee had not come along when he did. I think to myself *you could have easily died out there.* I feel like I have dodged a bullet for the second time in my life, the first being in Lenter's Mine.

"Bread?" he asks as he passes the loaf.

Grabbing it, I say, "Thanks. So how did you ever go from being a doctor in Boston to living in a cabin in the wilderness?"

Chuckling he says, "It's a long story. My grandfather Reggie originally built this place after he bought the thirty-odd acres it sits on. He raised my father and his brother here and never ventured any further than the local stores. I remember sitting with him one day when I was a kid. He was whittling on the front porch and I asked him why he never went anywhere. He laughed and said, 'Why would I want to go anyplace else when everything I need is right here? Tomorrow the sun will come up or it will not come up. If it does come up, it will either be clear or cloudy, wet or dry, still or windy, warm or cold. And if I wake up tomorrow, then that is all I need to know and all that I need.' He told me to always remember that you will be dead a long time so enjoy every second you have. 'What is, is, what will be, will be. So be it,'" he used to say.

"That is certainly a refreshing way in which to view life."

"What makes you say that?

"I like the simplistic honesty of what he said to you. It seems to me that most people work themselves to death for something they expect tomorrow, never really appreciating today for what it is, a gift. I like that he seemed to realize that everything he needed, and wanted, was right at hand, that the grass isn't always greener elsewhere."

"That's my grandfather, alright. So, what brings you here to the Adirondacks, Danny?"

"Oh, I came up here to get away from all of the distractions at home and to think."

"Problems?"

Laughing, I say, "I don't know if I would think of them as problems, probably more as decisions to be made."

"Welcome to life Danny. Everyone has difficult circumstances, difficult decisions to make. As a doctor, I often dealt with terminally ill patients. Many, many times I would see both terror and courage in their eyes when they would finally muster up the strength to ask me when they were going to die. And you know what my response was?"

"I couldn't possibly guess."

"Not today. That became our motto around these types of patients, simple words that emphasized the importance of carrying on today, of giving it everything you have left. Our other motto was dare to dream, dreams do come true. This gave them hope, something to cling to, like a life preserver tossed to a drowning man, something to look forward to, like tomorrow. Listen, I can't tell you what to do, but I can say you should follow what is in your heart, dare to dream and give whatever you decide to do your all. You can't go wrong doing that."

"Sounds like good advice, Dee. I'll remember that. So, what led you back here?"

"Well, I used to live and work in downtown Boston. I was wealthy beyond my wildest dreams and lived that way. Then one day, I had just completed an eleven-hour surgery and was coming off a week of eighteen-hour work days. I pulled off my scrubs and went to the men's room to throw water on my face. Looking at myself in the mirror, it finally hit me. I asked myself what the hell I was doing with my life. It was then that I realized that I was working myself to death and that life was passing me by like it does so many other people. So, I did what I just advised you, I followed my heart and my grandfather's advice. That was that and I have been here ever since and have never regretted it, not for one minute. So be it. Now pass me the stew pot, will you?"

Standing in the warming trailhead parking lot the next afternoon, after a restful long night's sleep, I extend my hand and say, "Thanks again for everything, Dee. You literally saved my life."

"My pleasure, Danny. Best of luck in making your decision."

Pulling my keys out of my pocket, I turn and open the back door of my car and throw my pack in while saying, "And who knows, Dee, maybe we will meet up again someday here on the trails." Rotating around, all I see is dense underbrush and a towering pine forest that have seemingly swallowed Dee whole.

Knocking on Jo's door, I hear footsteps approaching and then it opens. Mr. Nelson is before me saying, "Good evening, Danny. What happened to you, are you all right?"

"Fine, sir. Just took a little tumble while hiking this weekend. Nothing serious."

"You look like you have lost some weight. Are you sure you are okay?"

"I'm fine. It must be all the hard work I am putting in with my father this summer. Is Jo in?"

"She is sitting on the back porch. Come on in, you know the way," he says as he pulls the door full open.

"Thank you." Walking down the narrow hallway decorated with green floral print wallpaper, I pass through the kitchen that smells of baking bread and push open the back door to the porch.

Looking up from a book she is reading, Jo says, "Hey stranger, welcome home. What happened to your face?"

Smiling, I walk over and bend down to kiss her. "Just a little hiking mishap. It looks worse than it is. What are you reading?"

Closing the book, she holds the cover up showing '*Moby Dick*'.

"Rather difficult read, isn't it?"

"The language is dense, but it is well-written and totally worth the effort."

Pulling a chair up in front of her, I sit. Taking the book from her, I set it on an end table and take both of her hands in mine saying, "Jo, I have made a couple of decisions."

"Yes?"

"First off, I am not going to attend Michigan State this fall. I can't leave in good conscience with Dad struggling in his business. He really can't afford the going wage to hire someone to replace me. I have talked to the coaches at State and they said they would hold my scholarship for when I can come. I can attend college anytime, and I feel this is much more important right now. However, it isn't fair to ask you not to go so I want you to go without me. I feel awful about this decision, believe me."

Staring at me for several seconds, I'm not sure what she is thinking when she says, "You disappoint me. Haven't you figured out yet that we are in this together? If you have to wait, I can too. It won't be the first time, remember. We are still both young and have plenty of time ahead for college."

"You never cease to amaze me. You are really one of a kind. I love you. I mean, I really love you and want to spend the rest of my life with you."

"Is that a proposal, Danny?" she says laughing.

"You know what I mean, Jo. I'm serious. I really don't want to hold you back but, to be perfectly honest, in my heart of hearts I think if we enter into a long-distance relationship we will drift apart. I don't want that to happen. But you also need to follow your heart. If you think you should go to college, then you have my full support."

"I think we both need to do what is in our hearts. As I have always said, we will get through this. And, Danny," she says as she leans forward to kiss me, "You are in my heart."

Smiling, I pull her close smelling her perfume. Kissing her, I am suddenly back on a snowy street on New Year's Eve.

18.

August 1969

Dutchess County, New York

Finishing tying a Windsor knot in my dark blue tie, I pull it snug. Reaching for my black suit jacket, I pull it on and stare at myself in the dresser mirror. As I unconsciously wipe lint off of my sleeve, I notice that the jacket seems slightly large. The face in the mirror is drastically different from the boy of only five years ago. The braces that held my teeth prisoner for so long are finally gone after serving only four years of the initially imposed six-year sentence. The crew cut has been replaced by shoulder length dirty brown hair but the frame is still that of a runner, with eyes that appear old and tired beyond my years. From downstairs I hear Sly and the Family Stone's 'Hot Fun in the Summertime' drifting up and I smile.

Looking at the old black and white photograph tucked into the upper corner of the dusty mirror, I reach and pull it free. It is a photo I had taken, I remember, in the summer of nineteen sixty-four. In the background is Lenter's Hill, high and green as an Irish countryside, in the foreground are Billy, Jo and Tommy standing on the old canted dock on Mirror Lake, arms around each other and wearing the carefree innocent smiles of youth. It seems back then we had time between the seconds and were somehow able to dodge the grains of sand drifting through the hour glass. Now there doesn't seem to be enough time. It's hard to believe that was only five years ago.

"Danny, breakfast is ready," I hear my mother yell. Tucking the photo back in place, I start down to the kitchen, past the portrayal of The Last Supper, as the aroma of freshly brewed coffee smacks me. Leaning over the banister, I see Mom scrambling eggs on the gas flame, bacon and home fried potatoes simmering on the other burner. There by the percolator is a can of Red Circle Coffee. My mother looks up from the eggs and follows my gaze. "Bet you never thought you'd see that in this kitchen? We have to treat ourselves once in a while," she jokes.

Smiling, I go to the bottom of the stairs and turn into the kitchen as our collie Buck jumps off of the Chesterfield and greats me enthusiastically, wagging his tail as always. Giving him a quick pat on the head as I walk by, I grab a cup and fill it. Exaggerating sniffing the aroma, I watch Mom shake her spatula at me as she says, "All right comic, sit down and let me feed you so you're not late."

"Thanks, Mom," I say taking a seat, placing a napkin in my lap as she scrapes eggs from the cast iron skillet onto my plate, the metal on metal sounding like an anchor being lowered. She magically returns in seconds with the bacon, home fries and dry rye toast.

"It looks great, Mom. Thanks," I say as Buck barks to go outside. Mom walks over and opens the storm door a crack through which he squeezes like toothpaste out of the tube. Looking out the window, I see his black and white coat fly by in a blur in full chase of a gray squirrel. The squirrel feints right, left, then right again before leaping onto the trunk of an oak tree, sticking like glue. He darts up to safety on the first branch, looking down at the barking, frustrated dog. His cheeks are puffed with nuts and it looks like he will machine gun them down at Buck any second while he continues turning in exasperated circles like a black and white tornado.

Smiling, I reach for another sip of coffee and then take a forkful of eggs as Dad comes in through the back door. His face seems to be in a perpetual scowl these days, like he has much on his mind, much to do, disguising his dry sense of humor. His once full head of dark hair is already thinning, but his arms are still taut with muscles from years of labor. There is no one in the world I respect more.

"Morning, Dad," I say as I raise my cup in greeting.

"Good morning, son," he says. "You just get home?"

Laughing, I say, "Pretty close. Ran into a few old friends at the tavern and we, well, got talking about the old days and about…" I say, stopping before finishing.

"Yeah, I know Danny. This is a tough one to swallow," he says.

"It is a damn waste and a damn shame. The politicians in Washington have no morals. Their job description must necessitate being a complete moron," Mom says over the stove. "Do you want to ride with us to the service Danny?"

"Thanks Mom, but I think I'll walk over and get Jo first. We'll see you there," I say as I reach for the bacon and another piece of toast while Buck continues to circle the tree like he is caught in a whirlpool.

It is not even nine o'clock yet, the temperature already in the eighties on its way to the low nineties with almost a hundred percent humidity. It is a typical miserable August day in upstate New York. The mold spores will be attacking everyone with allergies.

Walking with my jacket over my shoulder, hand in hand with Jo, sweat beads form on my forehead. Looking up, I see the sun ready to emerge from a gloomy sky which will dial up the temperature like a sauna control. Wiping my forehead with my hand, we turn the corner across from Saint Vitonus and walk out onto Market Street.

On my right is Black's Funeral Home, the line already out the door and half way down the sidewalk. Beginning to walk down the edge of the street towards the end of the line, I feel a soft hand on my elbow. Turning around, I see Jennifer King dressed all in black with eyes as red as an ocean sunset.

"Jennifer, I don't know what to say. I, I…" I stammer into silence.

Giving me a slight smile, she wraps her arm around mine and says, "Come with me, you two. You are family." We walk past the waiting queue and up the steps. As we pass, people silently nod to her, sprinkled with a few, "I'm so sorry."

Entering the main viewing room, I see a flag-draped casket with two framed photographs on top. On both sides are identical flags with a blue replica of the War Office Seal on a white field, below it a scarlet scroll with the inscription 'United States Army.' Even though the room is air conditioned, I find myself sweating more than I was outside in the blistering heat, my shirt clawing at my lower back like a cat. Jennifer leads us to the first row of chairs where her mother and father are sitting. Spying us, Mr. King stands and extends his hand and says, "Danny, Jo, thank you for coming."

"Mr. King, we are so, so sorry. Billy was so very special to us."

"And you both to him, Danny."

Releasing his hand, I take a step over to Mrs. King who looks up at me like a lost puppy dog, her eyes puffy and doleful, her makeup running in tiny black rivulets. Bending down, I take her two gloved hands in mine and say, "I will miss him every day for the rest of my life," to which she gives a sad nod.

Looking to the back of the room, the line snakes in from outside and wraps around the perimeter of the room counter clockwise. It advances towards the casket in a snail slow, stop and go procession. Gazing towards the front of the line, I see Agnos who gestures to us. Walking over, he extends his hand and says, "Danny, you and Jo get here in line with us," as he steps back opening a spot for us behind his girlfriend Holly. Directly behind him I see a handsome man my age, but his good looks somehow make him look years younger even with the zig-zag scar on his left cheek. His chestnut hair is close cropped in the military style, and his hazel eyes radiate friendliness. He is dressed in a crisp green military service uniform, two rolls of medals pinned to his chest, hat tucked under his arm. One pant leg has a sharp crease to the cuff; the other is pinned up on the backside of the knee. As I enter the line he leans slightly forward on his crutches and gives me a nod and a smile which I return.

"Thanks Agnos, I appreciate it," I say as he gives me a slight affirmation. The line begins to move forward at the pace of an inchworm. Finally, we are in the front of the line and after Holly blessed herself and moved away from the casket, we walk forward and enter the prayer kneeler.

Looking up at the photographs on top of the casket, I see one of Billy in his army fatigues, a helicopter in the background. Smiling at seeing his face again, I am amazed at how grown up he looks. Then I realize, however, that he is, or was, only a nineteen-year-old kid.

Looking to the other frame, I see a photo of Billy, Tommy and me from a fall Saturday football game. We are all covered from head to toe with mud. Billy and I are standing in the back and Tommy's kneeling in front of us, a football in his hands. We both have a hand on Tommy's shoulders. A tear wells up in my eye and I hear Jo gently sobbing. Quickly, I wipe my tear away with a sleeve. Standing, I place my right hand on the casket and whisper, "One, two, three friend's forever, Billy. Friends forever," as Jo continues sobbing.

Taking her hand, we walk around the perimeter of the chairs, out the door and down the stairs to the street to make our way back home.

Today seems even hotter than yesterday, and after the almost hour-long funeral service, which was like being in a baking oven, Jo and I stride outside and come face-to-face again with the solider on crutches. As he is smoking his cigarette, the smoke curls up into his face causing him to squint one eye. Smiling, he extends his hand saying, "Danny, my name is Zens. Robert Zens. Pleased to finally meet you."

Taking his hand, I say, "The pleasure is mine. This is Jo. You seem to know me but I can't say that I recognize you."

Nodding to Jo, he takes another drag on his Camel, drops it and grinds it out with his good leg. Smiling, he takes a hand off of one crutch and rubs it up and down his damaged cheek saying, "Well, believe me, I feel like I have known you my whole life. Listen, can I give you two a ride to the cemetery? I was in the same unit as Billy and there are a few things I promised him I would tell you if this ever happened."

"Sure Robert, sure thing. You have a car?" I ask.

Laughing, he says, "You mean can I drive with one leg?" I blush. "I'm joking, Danny, only joking. Fortunately, I still have my right leg which is all I need to drive an automatic. I have my parent's car across the street, the blue Pontiac Firebird 350 with the Connecticut plates," he says pointing at it. "Call me Bob."

"I'll meet you two at the cemetery. I told Dad I would ride there with him," Jo says.

"It was a pleasure meeting you, Jo," Bob says as she smiles and walks away.

As mourners pour out of the stifling church like ants from an ant-hill, we begin to walk across the street. Looking at my expression, Bob reads my mind saying, "Yeah, I am pretty fast on these! Practice, as they say, makes perfect."

Smiling, I think *I like Bob*. Arriving at his car, he unlocks the door and sits down. He raises his crutches over his shoulder and pushes them into the back seat making a wood on wood clacking sound. Unlocking the door for me, I sit and buckle my seat belt. He does likewise, then turns the key, firing up the V-8 engine with a roar. Checking his rear-view mirror, he eases the car out into Market Street. "You will have to give me directions to the cemetery," he says.

"Keep going to the light and then straight through it. The cemetery is at Saint Peter's in the next town, about a twenty-minute ride," I say as I look at the houses down Oak Street as we pass, Tommy's yellow house being just a quick blur as we climb the hill going out of town. The car hugs the next curve like a lover and then the road straightens out on the flats between the two towns.

Watching out my side window, I see fields with corn stalk stumps that seem to go on forever, reminding me of when we visited Arlington National Cemetery on my high school senior trip. Black dots are scattered about the field as crows stand watch. The song on the radio changes to the Buffalo Springfield's 'For What It's Worth' as we continue down the flats.

"I hear you are quite the swimmer. Billy used to joke that you should have been born with gills you were so at home in the water," Bob says as he pulls another Camel from his shirt pocket and pushes in the cigarette lighter.

"Billy exaggerated a lot," I laugh. "Truth be told, I don't swim that much anymore, Bob. How did you get hooked up with Billy?"

Smiling as he reaches for the lighter, he holds the cherry red hot coil to the cigarette end and gives a pull that makes it glow like a coal furnace. Blowing out a ring of smoke, he replaces the lighter and says, "I met your friend at Officer's Training in Fort Polk in Louisiana. We hit it off right from the start. We graduated together and were deployed to Vietnam shortly thereafter. After a few months there, we both moved into the Airborne Infantry. Let's just say, I have a lot of respect for Billy. He was brave, loyal to the men around him and patriotic to a fault."

"I'm not surprised at all," I say smiling proudly at the memory of him.

Taking another drag on his cigarette, he says, "Danny, what I'm about to tell you never leaves this car, okay? I could be court marshalled for disclosing even the most general of what I am about to tell you. But a promise is a promise, and Billy made me swear that if he were ever killed in action that I would let you, and only you, know what really happened."

"Sure, Bob. It will never leave this car," I promise. Glancing out the window, I see the tops of the Catskill peaks with Overlook in the foreground, Indian and Plattekill off to the north beckoning.

"Your friend did not die in Vietnam," he says.

"What? How is that possible?" I ask incredulously.

Placing his cigarette in the ash tray, he blows out a long thin line of smoke like the contrails from a Stratofortress bomber. "Billy died in Laos," he says.

"Laos?" I say, not entirely sure I know where that is. "What was he doing there?"

"The United States has been secretly, and illegally, cluster bombing both Laos and Cambodia for years. The North Vietnamese have supply routes through there. Neither the North Vietnamese nor the United States are supposed to be there, so no one says anything about it. But the war has spread. It has been kept a secret for obvious reasons. With more and more people calling for the U.S. to get out of the war, and with all the anti-war protests, well, this information would not be well received," he says.

"Unbelievable. I thought this war was dirty, so this really doesn't surprise me. It just goes to show what I always believed, that you can't trust our government at all." Looking back out the window, the trees fly by in a green blur as I ask, "How did he die?"

"You need to understand that our unit was one of four helicopter groups based at the Da Nang Air Base. Our mission was rapid deployment search and rescue in both Laos and Cambodia. Each group would be rotated once every four weeks for a week stay at a secret airbase only six miles from the border of Laos. In the eyes of the military, we did not exist. We were called the Ghost Unit. We were segregated from the rest of the base and we went on, and returned from, missions with no one knowing where we went or what we did.

"There was a B-52 bomber that had engine problems and the crew was forced to parachute into Laos. We received radio contact from them when they reached the ground. They were in a very rugged mountain area and were surrounded by Viet Cong. They had very limited arms with them, basically defenseless. They radioed coordinates of an area where we could land. We were airborne in our Huey within ninety seconds of receiving the call. Accompanying us was a Bell AH-1 Huey/Cobra. Understand, Danny, that these were two well-armed copters. The Heuy/Cobra had a turret mounted forty-millimeter grenade launcher and twenty-millimeter cannon pods. Our Heuy had a nose mounted grenade launcher and side mounted machine guns and rockets. We were prepared, or so we thought.

"We flew at tree top level for about fifteen minutes before reaching the site. Our pilot, a guy named Mike Derre, was the best I ever flew with. He zig-zagged between the trees until he spotted the opening. I didn't think we could fit in with a shoe horn but somehow, someway, he got us down with a very violent landing. The Huey/Cobra circled, ready to provide cover support. As soon as we touched down, Billy and I were out the door, setting up a perimeter around the chopper. The other member of our team, a guy called Jack McGloin, manned the machine gun on the chopper.

"At first it was eerily quiet, just the sound of rotor blades whirling around. Then we spotted three airmen emerging from the trees. One was wounded and the other two were half-carrying, half-dragging him along. From behind them came the deafening sound of gun fire and suddenly mortar rounds started exploding all around us. At that moment the Huey/Cobra above us started pounding the tree line behind the airmen with ordinance.

"Our orders were to stay put and not advance from our perimeter, but Billy took off for the airmen. Jack and I provided cover fire along with the copter above as explosions rocked the ground around us. Upon reaching the men, he picked up the wounded man and motioned for the other two to get to the chopper. They both came running by me with a look of complete terror in their eyes, like they were being chased by the devil himself. From my vantage point I saw them get on board the chopper just as a mortar shell ripped through the back part of the fuselage and out the other side, exploding in the ground some distance away. Fortunately, they were not hurt and the chopper was still operational at that point.

"Meanwhile, as Billy approached my position a swarm of Viet Cong, looking like hornets emerging from a poked nest, came out of the wood line with their AK-47's blazing. I mean hundreds of them. I stood firing my M-14 and Jack was hammering them with the chopper gun as the Huey/Cobra fired cannon shells and launched grenades at them from above. Each time a Viet Cong was hit by the shells or grenades, all that would be left was a red mist. Before long, the whole tree line was a continuous crimson vapor. Then there was so much smoke you couldn't see ten feet in front of you.

"Anyway, Billy reached me with the wounded man in tow. I grabbed him and the two of us ran with him to the open door and tossed him in. We then went to our knees and fired back everything we had. Mike increased the blade revolutions to ready for a rapid take off as we then made for the door. Billy got in and as I was getting ready to jump in my leg buckled. Everything went slow motion. I remember the look on Billy's face as he screamed and reached out to grab and pull me into the chopper as it started to rapidly take off. The next thing I knew I was waking up in the base hospital with most of my left leg gone."

Pulling to the stop sign in town, Bob looks at me for an indication of which way to go. Pointing, I say, "Go straight and then take the next left which will take us right to the church."

Nodding, he slowly accelerates past the town memorial and through a close row of houses that crowd both sides of the road like strap hangers on a rush hour subway. On the radio, Three Dog Night begin to sing 'Easy to be Hard.'

"Anyway," he continues, "When I awoke, I was at the air base hospital being prepared to be evac'd to an offshore carrier. Jack, our gunner, came to my hospital bed and told me what had happened. As we took off AK-47 fire came up through the bottom of the chopper where Billy was seated. He was killed instantly. It also ruptured a fuel line which is why we made a controlled crash landing a few miles from the remote air base. The airman we had picked up all survived and Jack pulled both me and Mike out before the chopper exploded. Billy's body was still inside. After explaining what had happened, Jack gave these to me," he says as reaches into his shirt pocket and then holds out his hand.

Holding mine out palm up, I watch him drop a blackened and bent silver chain into it. Pulling it closer, I stare down at a twisted, scorched Saint Christopher medal.

"Billy told me the story of this and I promised if anything happened that I would see that it got back to you," he says.

Tearing up, I look at him smiling and say a simple word of, "Thanks." He pulls into the church parking lot and puts the transmission into park but leaves the engine and air conditioner running.

"This means more to me, more than you could ever know, Bob. Thank you." Looking out the window, I can see the Military Honor Guard standing at attention by the grave site, rifles butt down on the ground.

Smiling, he says, "I think I do understand, Danny. I really do."

"Bob, one question though. How long ago was he killed?"

Hesitating, he answers, "How did you know?"

"Your leg," I say. "And how good you are with crutches. If you were with him when he died, it had to be long enough ago for you to be treated for a severe wound and then shipped home for rehabilitation."

"Billy was right, you are smart! He died in March. We were in the Ghost Unit, but on paper we were assigned to actual combat units. When he was killed, it made for an uneasy situation in that the Army could not acknowledge he was killed in Laos. So, his remains were kept on base until the unit he was 'assigned' to was involved in a major battle with a large loss of life. That happened last month when that unit engaged the Viet Cong's 268th regiment. Billy was simply listed as killed in action in that battle, his casket was then flown home for burial along with the other soldiers. I spent the months after the mission at various Veteran Administration hospitals and was just released last month. And here we all are."

Shaking my head, I can only say, "Unbelievable," while rolling the medal in my hand.

"Hey Danny, what do you say we go pay our final respects to our friend?" he says.

Arriving back at Bob's car after the touching ceremony, we stand in awkward silence as the empty hearse crawls by.

"I hope this isn't out of line, given the gravity of the day, but are you doing anything this weekend?" he asks.

My mind is still numb from the ceremony. "Not that I can think of, why?"

"Two friends and I bought tickets for the Woodstock Festival for August 16th through the 17th not far from here over in Bethel, New York. They can't make it so I have extra tickets if you would like them. My parents have a cabin in that area which is fairly close to the concert site. I was thinking of going directly from here to fish and just relax for one day and then go over to the show. The tickets and cabin are for free, we just need to get food and drink. It might be just the thing we both need after this. What do you say?"

I think of Billy and his take life head on style. I think of his laugh, and all the good times we had as kids. And the tragedy we shared, and how our lives changed after it. I think, *if our positions were reversed, would he go? Damn straight he would, and he would be pissed if he knew I didn't go because of him. He would say, 'Get on with your life already man, would you.'*

"That sounds like a great idea, Bob. I think Billy would like that. Would it be okay if I asked Jo to come? I think this could be a good diversion for her also. She has taken this very, very hard."

"That would be great. Certainly, she can come. Let's dedicate the weekend to Billy. I agree that he would like that."

"Then it's agreed. Let's do it," I say while wiping the tears from my eyes as Barry McGuire's 'Eve of Destruction' comes pounding defiantly out of the radio.

19.

August, 1969

Sullivan County, New York

Bob pulls his Firebird onto a rugged dirt road the color of bloodshot eyes. The red clay is wet and muddy from the rain that's currently pouring down. Outside of my window, the bushes brush up against the doors like we're going through a car wash, making a scratching sound like a cat trying to get out of a door. Ahead I see an opening and glimpse water off to the side of a cabin as the car bursts from the brush and stops.

"I guess I need to get down here and trim the brush back from the road some! Grab everyone a cold beer and follow me," Bob says.

Reaching into the backseat, I lift the cooler lid and pull out three ice cold Rheingold's. Grabbing the can opener attached to the cooler by string, I open the cans and then exit the car followed by Jo. Trying to duck the rain drops, we run after him around the cabin's edge. In front of us is a small grayish lake with no other structures visible on it, other than a short wooden dock with old tires tied along each side, and a badly dented silver rowboat moored to it. The shoreline is covered with evergreens, dotted here and there with white birch that stand out like dandruff on a green sweater. The rain is falling so hard now that it looks like continuous lines are tethered from the water surface to the sky.

"Up here," Bob says as he races in a pogo stick hopping motion up the steps to the tin roofed porch with Jo and I in hot pursuit. His crutches pound each step like tom toms.

Shaking off the rain drops, I hand him and Jo each a beer and say, "Wow! What a beautiful spot!" as the rain drums methodically against the tin.

"Yeah, I always liked it here. This lake and cabin have been in our family for generations. My great, great grandfather named this Dragonfly Lake and it has stuck."

"Why Dragonfly Lake"? Jo asks.

Laughing, he says, "You'll see later on. You know, when I was in Vietnam and things would get really bad, I would travel back here in my mind. I would imagine myself sitting on the dock out there with a fishing line in one hand, a cooler of beer alongside me, the sun tanning my face. Probably seems silly, but the memories of this place helped me through some very tough times over there. Here, help yourselves to an Adirondack chair," he says motioning for us to sit. We do so as he pulls a chair over close to ours with a screech, then sits. Down by the lake, two squirrels chase each other at dizzying speeds before jumping onto the base of a birch tree, disappearing up the trunk.

"I don't see anything silly about that at all, Bob. Here's to memories," I say as I raise my can in a toast.

Bumping our cans against each other, he says, "To Billy," and then takes a long drink.

Sitting in thoughtful silence, we watch the rain pelt the lake's surface as a distant clap of thunder rumbles off in the distance. Shortly the rain starts to lessen and, in a few minutes, it is nothing more than an intermittent drizzle as the sun starts to filter through the thinning low clouds.

"Look at that!" he says, pointing to the left. Turning, we see a bright rainbow coming from high on the west and disappearing into the trees to the southeast. "See where that rainbow ends? That's just about where the concert will be. Come on guys, let's unload the car and put the food away. I don't know about you, but I'm hungry. Tomorrow we will wake up at 0500 hours to get out on the lake before sunrise. If you two don't mind cooking tonight, I will go out and get a can full of worms since the ground should be loaded after this rain. Then we will be ready to go in the morning."

"Sounds great!" we both say.

Waking to the smell of coffee and frying bacon, I stretch as I glance over at Jo who is still sleeping, looking as beautiful as ever. Gently pushing off the sheet and light bedcover, I swing my feet onto the cold timber floor. Standing, I quietly pull on my shorts and my favorite faded yellow tee shirt.

Walking into the kitchen, I see Bob standing at the stove with one hand stirring eggs and the other gripped to a crutch. Hearing me, he turns his head and says, "Help yourself to some coffee. The eggs will be ready in a few."

"Thanks," I say as I walk over to the counter and pour myself a cup out of the shiny silver percolator. The open can of Folger's Instant Roast sits nearby emanating its intoxicating aroma. Taking a sip, I smile with satisfaction.

"Take a seat," he says as he brings a cast iron skillet to the table and shovels out a generous portion of eggs, bacon and home fries. Scraping an equal portion on another plate, he then goes and deposits the skillet back on the stove with a metallic clank. Reaching to the side of the sink, he switches on a radio releasing Archie Bell and the Drells singing 'Tighten Up.' "Love that song," he says.

Just then the bedroom door opens, Jo walking out in an oversized, faded green Michigan State tee shirt saying, "You boys starting without me?"

Laughing, Bob says "Take a seat, Jo, and I'll bring you some coffee."

"That sounds great," she says.

After pouring her a cup and bringing a plate of food, he takes his seat saying, "Looks to be a cloudy day today, but it should be excellent fishing this morning," as he shovels food into his mouth. "Eat up. We want to be on the lake within the next fifteen minutes."

Smiling to myself, I like his organization and take control style. Plus, I have no issue with following his orders to eat up.

After throwing the dirty dishes into the sink on top of the frying pan, he says, "You guys grab the cooler and I will go get the poles and bait and will meet you down by the boat in a few. Oh, and Jo, would you grab the portable radio?"

"You got it," she replies as I finish my coffee.

Carrying the cooler and the radio, we head out the front door into the dim dawn. Spotting Bob coming from a shed on the north side of the building, he has the poles in one hand that is wrapped around a crutch handle. All of the other items are stuffed into the net which is held by his other hand which is also on a crutch handle. We all meet at the dock at the same time and follow him down it to the boat.

"Take the front seat, Danny. I'll row from the middle seat and, Jo, you can sit by the transom. You can set the cooler in the back and Jo you can put the radio on my seat." Handing us both life preservers as we climb in, he says, "Since I know you both can swim, those are for sitting on. These old aluminum seats aren't that comfortable."

"Thanks," we both say while placing them onto the seats before sitting. Watching as Bob loosens the tie line, he places his crutches on the bottom of the boat and nimbly hops in while maintaining his balance. Seeing me watching he says, "Practice makes..." to which we all laugh.

After settling in, he slides the oars out from underneath the seats which make a scratching sound and pushes the pins into the pin locks with a tinny bang. He then turns on the radio and the Rascals come on singing 'It's a Beautiful Morning.' Taking a crutch, he pushes it against the dock and the boat moves away. Replacing the crutch on the boat bottom, he dips the oars into the water, pulling hard on the right one a few times as we spin around until we are facing towards the middle of the lake.

"Here we go!" he says as he dips and pulls the oars over and over. The boat glides across the surface like a water bug until we reach the middle where he stops rowing. The boat slowly drifts to a halt as the Rascals finish up.

"Next up will be 'Slip Away' by Clarence Carter," the DJ says. "But first an update for all of you who will be heading upstate to Bethel for the Woodstock Festival. Evidently thousands upon thousands of people have already started to arrive today, the day before the show. State Police and event organizers are asking people to not come early as there are no facilities available. Also, only those with tickets will be admitted. The forecast is for a rainy weekend, but also for fun, so enjoy folks!" As he finishes, Clarence Carter starts to belt out his soulful song.

"How many people are they expecting at this show?" Jo asks.

Bob snags a worm on a hook as he says, "I'm not sure. I think I heard somewhere upwards of fifty thousand or so."

"You're kidding! How big a place is this?" I say.

"It is being held at Max's Dairy Farm, so they have lots of open alfalfa fields to accommodate that many people," he says as he hands me the baited line. "Here you go. Good luck! Sure, you don't want to try your hand at this, Jo?"

Laughing, she says, "Thanks, but no thanks, Bob. Fishing is not my thing. My job today is to keep the beer coming!"

"Good girl!"

Taking the pole, I shift sideways in my seat and give a hard, over-head cast which only goes about four feet before plummeting into the water with a whoosh.

"Not a fisherman, eh?"

"Only been a couple of times," I confess.

"Watch here. First off, we will sit back to back so we can side cast and not hook each other. Secondly, it is all in the wrist, just like throwing a Frisbee."

Reeling in my line, I move my right arm with the pole across my body and then move it back while snapping my wrist. I watch in fascination as the line flows out effortlessly as the reel whines like a small child followed by a small splash about twenty feet away, the yellow marker bobbing on the surface.

"Now that wasn't hard, was it?" he says. I hear him cast out of the opposite side of the boat, followed by a splash.

"What are we fishing for?" I ask.

"This lake is quite deep so mainly we are looking for lake trout, but you may hook into a perch now and then."

The radio belts out Cream's 'Sunshine of Your Love' as my yellow bob disappears and my line goes taut.

"Pull back! Pull back! Hook him!" yells Bob.

Pulling the pole back over my right shoulder, I feel the weight on the other end then nothing as the line goes slack."

"He got away. When you feel that first tug you have to pull back to set the hook, otherwise they won't stay on. Reel it in and I will put more bait on for you. Don't worry, you'll get the knack of it before long."

Bob no sooner baits my hook and I cast back when his line goes flying out. "Got one!" he shouts. I watch him expertly play the fish, letting him run and then reeling him in. Over and over he does this for about three or four minutes when he finally says, "He's getting tired. Get the net, Danny. We are having fresh trout for dinner tonight!"

The sun is setting in a slide show of scarlet and amber that reflect off of the lake as we sit in our Adirondack chairs by a glowing fire, the smell of frying fish in the air. We fished most of the day and I finally was able to hook a few small lake trout and a perch. Bob educated me on how to release them the correct way, how to not touch their gills or eyes, how to handle them with wet hands to minimize the chance of infection, how to hold them horizontally and, most importantly, how time was of the essence in returning them to the water. All in all, it was a most satisfying day.

"Guys, look out there," he says.

Gazing out onto the open lake, at first, I do not see a thing. Then, I spy a wavy movement just above the water surface like a hot road in the summertime.

"Come with me," he says as he stands, grabs his crutches and walks toward the dock. Hiking to the end with him, Jo and I see a rainbow of moving metallic colors: brown, black, orange, blue and green. Hundreds and hundreds of dragonflies are darting back and forth inches above the water surface, their double set of wings looking like World War I biplanes.

"Wow! What a sight!" Jo says.

"You asked how the lake got its name, now you know. Legend has it that the Indians that used to occupy this land centuries ago believed that the dragonfly was an escort to the afterlife. They said that is why it has two sets of wings. When a person dies, they would appear, give them one of their wings and together they would fly to the next world."

"I like that thought. I like it a lot," Jo says as we stand in silence for several minutes marveling at the sight. Then she says, "It's funny the different beliefs people have, isn't it?"

"It certainly is," I say. I think, *this certainly makes as much sense as all the other religions people blindly believe in. Maybe more so.*

Turning, Bob starts back to the shore and we both follow.

Opening another beer, I stare silently at the fire and think of Billy and Tommy. They should both be here enjoying this with us. Billy is gone forever, and Tommy may well be also. I miss them both, miss the good times we shared. I miss their laughs, their smiles, and even their wise cracks. All I have left of them is memories. I feel somewhat guilty enjoying this without them.

"Thinking of your friends?" Bob says.

"How did you know?"

"Easy. I used to see that same look on Billy's face almost every night. When you are in battle and engaged over there, in a way it is easier. It is the downtime that gets you, when you have time to think of home, family and friends. A lot of guys don't survive that in one way or another. But Billy would have. He was not only physically tough, but emotionally and mentally as well. You would have been proud of him."

"I am proud of him," I say as Jo gives my knee a slight squeeze.

After a few hushed minutes, Bob says, "I think the fish is ready."

Just as he is handing us our plates full of golden-brown trout, we hear a single dog day cicada making a sound like a shaking tambourine. Then, others join in, then more and more until the sound surrounds us building to a piercing crescendo. Then they stop as suddenly as they started, all is silent save the sound of the crackling fire.

Bright daylight streams in through the window and socks me in the eyes as I awake. Like yesterday, the smell of coffee and bacon wander in from the kitchen. Pushing back the covers, I sit up on the edge of the bed and notice that it is very humid.

Jo rolls over and says, "Good morning, handsome."

"Good morning to you too, beautiful," I reply as I bend down and kiss her.

Smiling, I stand and pull my clothes on as Jo slides out of bed wearing the same oversized tee shirt as yesterday. Giving her a hug, we walk together out of the bedroom and once again see Bob busy at the stove with the radio playing on low.

"Morning, guys. The coffee is ready," he says without turning around.

Grabbing our cups, we fill them and sit down at the table. The hum of Gary Puckett & The Union Gap playing 'Young Girl' glides through the air as Bob turns around with a full skillet and moves towards the table. After scooping out generous portions of his staple eggs, bacon and home fries he returns the pan to the sink. Refilling his cup, he takes a seat, saying, "There have been some interesting developments regarding the concert."

"How so?" I ask as I take a sip of coffee.

"Remember when you asked how many people they were expecting and I told you around fifty thousand or so? Well, it seems that about that many showed up yesterday! Already this morning both the Thruway and Route 17 are massive traffic jams. Estimates now are that hundreds of thousands of people will be showing up and there are nowhere near enough facilities to accommodate that type of crowd. I walked out to the end of the drive and even this road is loaded with cars parked and people walking. The show isn't even scheduled to start until later today."

"Unbelievable! Are we still going to go?" asks Jo.

"I'm game if you two are. The only thing is, we will have to walk. There is no way to get a car through this mess."

"Will you be able to do that? I mean with your leg and all?" I ask.

Laughing, he says, "You don't worry about me. After all, I have been through situations a whole lot tougher than this."

Smiling, I say, "Okay then, let's do it!"

"After breakfast, let's take it easy for the rest of the morning and plan on heading out around noon. The forecast is for rain later on, but we've got several raincoats in the closet here and I'm sure we can find one to fit each of you. We have several knapsacks here so we can each carry one. We need to travel light, so I suggest we each take a blanket and I will cut up a piece of plastic for each of us to put on the ground. Also, it probably will be a good idea to take an extra pair of socks as well as shorts and a shirt. As for food, since it is going to be so hot and wet, I suggest taking a jar of peanut butter from the refrigerator and I'll put crackers in a plastic bag. Finally, as many beers as each of us can carry!"

"Let's not forget the opener!" says Jo.

"Good point! Wouldn't that have been a disaster?!"

It is almost noon when we all head down the cabin steps. Pointing to about nine o'clock on the lake, Bob says, "There is a trail over there that cuts directly out onto West Shore Road. From there it is less than three miles to the site. Better put your raincoat on. The path is overgrown and the brush will most likely be wet."

Pulling on our raincoats, we watch Bob start in that direction as we catch up and walk alongside him in silence. Coming upon the trail, he turns left into it and is ingested by the underbrush, disappearing in seconds.

Pushing aside a limb with my hand, we follow. We have entered a fairly dense pine forest that surrounds Dragonfly Lake. It is so thick that it seems like twilight in here instead of midday. Watching Bob, he expertly navigates the rocks and roots on his crutches. Walking silently on the olive moss and tan pine needles covering the path, the only sound is the crutches squeaking under his weight.

Suddenly Bob stops, raising his hand he says, "Look over there." Off to our right about thirty yards away is a flock of wild turkeys. There are two toms strutting with their multicolored tails spread wide like a fan, red wattles brightly displayed, heads bobbing back and forth with the consistency and rhythm of a typewriter key. Behind them is a group of hens followed by about a dozen jakes and jennies. As we silently stand, they move across the path up in front of us and then are quickly out of sight, only their gobbling audible. Soon that too disappears.

"Wow! That was something!" I say. "I have never seen such a large grouping of young turkeys!"

"There is an abundance of them in this county. With the combination of evergreen woods and open fields they have flourished, though the hunters are making a noticeable dent in the population as of late," Bob explains.

Continuing our hike, about fifteen minutes later we begin to hear an unfamiliar distant din. As we continue on, it becomes louder and rowdier. Suddenly the trail emerges onto the side of West Shore Lake Road and all we see is chaos.

Parked cars line the sides of the road in both directions. As far as we can see, people are walking to the east. It looks like a massive tie dye and blue jean tsunami, and most everyone is happy, smiling and laughing. The fragrance of pot is weighty in the air, people carrying every imaginable item: coolers, blankets, plastic sheets and folding chairs. Some have dogs, some have very small children. Standing while watching in amazement, I see a young pregnant girl pass hand in hand with a boy. The road's surface has clumps of ruddy mud everywhere brought onto it from the road side by both people and cars. Someone has a radio blasting out 'Take a Letter Maria' and a crowd walking with them is singing along.

"Well, what do you think?" asks Bob.

"I'm speechless! I have never seen this many people!" says Jo.

"Just wait. I have a feeling that you are going to see a lot more!" Walking up to the road, we turn east and join the current of people.

After about an hour walk, we are swept into the concert field by a mass of humanity, with no tickets required. It has been announced that it is now a free concert. The field in front of us seems to be a sort of natural bowl with what appears to be the concert stage set in the middle at the bottom. Behind it is a small lake with people swimming in it. There are people everywhere and more seem to be coming in a continual flow. I have no idea where they're all going to go.

"This is going to be a problem," Bob says. "There's gotta be well over two hundred thousand people here already."

"Dude," says a rail thin teenager standing alongside us smoking a joint, his thin shoulder length hair looking like corn silk. "I just walked up from Route 17. It is a parking lot and I hear the Thruway is the same way. This is far out," he finishes as he takes a drag and walks away.

Rolling his eyes, Bob says, "See what I mean! I think we should strategize on where to go. I don't think we want to be caught in the middle of this mess if something happens. Plus, if we have to take a leak or something it could take hours to get clear of the crowd. What say we walk the perimeter? It looks like the music will start soon and once everyone gets settled in, we should have a better shot at moving around."

"Lead the way," I say. We'll follow."

Bob heads left through the ruck and is evidently planning on circling the venue in a clockwise direction. As we are pushing through the crowd, the loudspeakers crackle and I hear an introduction of Richie Havens followed by his signature guitar sound as he introduces 'Minstrel from Gault'. The crowd explodes in applause, excited not for the tune so much as for the beginning of the show.

"Woodstock is officially under way!" Bob yells in an attempt to be heard over the music and crowd noise. Nodding, we follow him until we finally emerge from the main crowd into a kind of people eddy circling around the shore of the perimeter.

Walking for a while, we hear Richie Havens finish another song, starting up again on 'Strawberry Fields Forever' as the crowd roars. We half-walk, half-slide down the muddy field to the south of the stage. Looking over, Richie Havens is still just a dot to my eyes.

"Follow me. I've been here before. I want to show you something," Bob says as we move to the edge of a woodland of maple and oak trees that ends at water. "Fillipini Pond. When I was younger, I met a few local kids in the area and we used to sneak through the fields to party and swim here."

Bob pushes into the brush and woods as we follow. Seeing that we are on a dirt path of sorts, it is obvious that it has not been used for some time. I hear splashing and laughter and, as we come to an opening onto the pond, we see dozens of people skinny dipping in broad daylight, in front of hundreds of thousands of people. People are swimming, bathing, kissing and one couple is unabashedly making love beneath a white pine, evidently oblivious to all of the commotion around them.

Jo nervously grins at them.

Laughing, Bob says, "Peace, love and dope, brother!" as he pushes on further up the path passing a red "Posted and Patrolled" sign.

The sounds from the pond fade, but the music seems to be getting louder as we hear the next band, Sweetwater, singing 'Motherless Child' to the evident delight of the clapping throng. Following Bob a few more hundred yards into the woods, he stops and points up saying, "After you two."

Looking up, we see wooden slats nailed to a huge oak tree. Higher up is a wooden platform. Seeing my questioning eyes, he says, "Deer stand. When we were kids and used to party here, this was a popular make out place. Climb on up."

Turning, I help Jo reach up and grab a slat as she starts to climb up effortlessly with me following. Finally reaching a hole in the platform, we find ourselves on a triangular shaped stand. Stepping out on it, I look down and see Bob's crutches leaning against the tree trunk as he climbs nimbly up using his strong arms to pull his good leg up to each slat.

Suddenly I feel very tired and faint. Jo asks, "Danny, you okay?"

Holding tightly to the railing as the woods spin, I say, "I'm okay, Jo. Just a little fatigue, probably from the walk," as I go down on one knee.

"Danny! Are you okay?" she yells as she kneels down putting an arm around me.

"Fine, Jo. Just a little dizzy. Give me a second, I'll be okay," I say before I pass out.

Upon waking on my back, I am looking up at Jo's very concerned face. "Thank God. Are you okay?

Smiling, I put my hand on her cheek and say, "It is nothing, Jo. Really, I am fine," as I grab the railing and pull myself up.

"It is something. You seem to be tired all the time now, Danny. You used to be able to do hikes like this with no problem. I'm worried about you. And what about your weight loss? It is obvious that you are much thinner than just a few months ago. Maybe you should go see your doctor?"

"Probably a result of all the hard work with my father. Working in the summer sun can really shed the pounds," I say while Jo looks totally unconvinced.

Bob's head pokes through the hole. Jo extends her hand, and pulls him up onto the platform. He grabs the railing and stands saying, "You okay, Danny?"

"Yeah, I'm fine. Just dizzy, no big deal. It has already passed."

Watching him, he says to us, "Take a look over there."

Turning around, we see a view like no other. Sprangled out in front of us is a hillside with so many people that they look like multi-colored ants on the side of an anthill. It is hard to see individual people, just a mass of colors that move like a vibration. Sweetwater is now singing 'Day Song' as the whole side of the hill moves slowly this way and that like a field of hay in the wind.

Smiling, I can't help but say, "This is unbelievable, Bob. I don't think I will ever forget this. Thanks!"

"Ditto, Bob! This is fantastic!" Jo screams.

"No need to thank me, guys. Billy is the one you need to thank. No matter how screwed up this war is, or how wrong, your friend still made the ultimate sacrifice for this," he says as he spreads both arms wide. "Just look at all of these people, at all of the freedom they're enjoying. Here they can do anything they want. In the end, that is all any of us really needs or wants. And Billy would tell you that that is worth fighting and dying for."

Looking out over the mass of humanity, I again smile and feel like Billy, and even Tommy, is somehow here with us. I can feel their presence just as assuredly as I can feel the music and Jo's arm around my waist.

Turning, I bend and give Jo a quick kiss on her cheek just as Bert Sommer starts singing 'Jennifer'.

20.

October, 1969

Dutchess County, New York

Walking down our icy front side walk, I turn left and head down Parsons Street as the early season winter storm air chills me to the bone. A town truck rumbles by spreading salt in concentric circles, its snow plow scratching the road with an unbearable screeching sound like fingers on a chalkboard, sparks flying. Tree limbs are bent over like old men under the weight of ice from last night's surprise storm.

In the distance, a lonesome siren wails as I turn the corner onto James Street. Looking both ways, I cross over and start up the walkway to number nine. Stamping my feet on the outside mat, I push open the door and am ushered in by a gust of cold air.

Shutting the door, I walk to the receptionist window and say, "Danny Fosse. I have a nine o'clock appointment with Dr. Pappo," to the red headed lady sitting there. Looking me over, she takes her pencil and moves it down the appointment book. Stopping on my name, she says, "Here you are. Take a seat Danny. The doctor will be with you shortly."

"Thank you," I say as I remove my jacket and hang it on a coat hook. Striding into the sitting area, I see only one other patient, a gray-haired lady with hair starched into position like an army helmet, glasses perched precariously on the end of her razor thin nose. Looking up from the magazine she is absently thumbing through, she gives me a smile, which I return. Walking to a chair against the opposite wall, I sit down looking at the print on the opposite wall of a Norman Rockwell painting of a boy standing on a chair, his pants half pulled down, the doctor in the background preparing a needle.

Reaching onto the table, I grab a copy of Sports Illustrated and begin flipping the pages not really seeing what I am looking at. Instead, my mind is preoccupied with worry about myself. It wasn't until after I fainted at Woodstock that I began to think back and start to piece together a troubling picture. I have slowly been losing my energy and even the smallest exertions have left me weak, breathless. Each incident in and of itself never seemed much to worry about at the time. But now, I can see that this has been a disturbing trend which I have ignored. Then there is the weight loss I have been experiencing over the last few months. Suddenly, I am overcome with a premonition that something could be seriously wrong as a door opens and a nurse in a white blouse and skirt, white stockings and white shoes says, "Danny Fosse. Follow me please."

Standing, I drop the magazine back onto the table and walk through the door. "Second door on the right," she tells me. Entering the room, I hear from behind me, "We should have your test results shortly, Mrs. Tadlock," after which the door closes with a loud click.

Looking around, the room looks just like his other patient rooms which I have been in several times over the years. It is painted beige, with a beige table top and stainless-steel sink under an oversized silver medicine cabinet. An x-ray viewing light is off to the right of the examination table. A lone small window looks out at a fence in the side yard on which sits a squirrel that appears to be watching me. Looking out the window, I am suddenly very emotional, fearful and on the verge of tears.

The door opens and Dr. Pappo strides in holding a chart under his arm. The bright ceiling light reflects off of his bald head and casts small shadows on his wrinkled face. Extending his hand, he says, "How are you doing, Danny?"

Shaking his hand, I say, "I guess you're the one with the answer to that question."

Smiling, he pulls up a chair facing mine. Opening his chart, he reads in silence then closes it saying, "I hate to have to tell you this, Danny, but the hematologist report shows that you have leukemia."

"Leukemia? I'm not really sure I know exactly what that means."

Sighing, he strokes one hand across one of his thick snow-white eyebrows saying, "Basically, you are losing the functionality of your red blood cells. These are the cells that transport oxygen to your body's cells and carbon dioxide to your lungs. The reason this is happening is that your body is producing too many white blood cells. When there are too many of these, they affect the functionality of the red blood cells. This is why you have been experiencing the fatigue you told me about. It probably also explains your weight loss."

"Is this fatal?" I ask with trepidation.

Putting a hand on my arm, he says, "Danny, this is not a death sentence. You will be given targeted chemotherapy. I have made arrangements for you to go to Manhattan to Sloan Kettering. I have talked to an Oncologist, Doctor Carter, who you will meet with. He has reviewed your test results and seems confident that after the initial treatments, you will be able to come home and travel back and forth for future treatments."

"What are the side-effects of this treatment?"

"The most common are nausea, constipation and hair loss. Again, these will pass once the treatment stops. The time period of the treatment will be determined by Doctor Carter. Here is his number," he says as he hands me a slip of paper. "I know this is tough news to take, Danny, but there is an excellent chance for remission and recovery. Do you have any questions?"

"A million," I say. "Why me? Did I bring this on myself?"

"Well, these things are usually a combination of genetics and environmental factors. The bottom line is, where the science stands today, we really don't know."

Standing, he says, "Well Danny, I would suggest you go home and talk this over with your family and the people closest to you. Again, if you ever have any questions or need to see me for treatments for any side-effects from this after you start, call me anytime. Good luck to you, Danny," he says while opening the door for me. `

Walking back down James Street, I am numb, in a daze, the reality of what I just learned now hitting me. I feel alone, exposed, vulnerable, mortal, like a high wire trapeze artist realizing he is losing his balance and there is no safety net below or a deep-sea diver on the ocean floor who realizes his tank is extremely low on air. *Someone help me,* I think.

Sitting in the rear seat of the taxi, I look out at the glass front of Sloan Kettering on New York Avenue. Opening the door, I step out of the car as does Dad and Jo. The driver pops open the trunk, Dad grabs my suitcase, sets it on the ground and pushes the trunk closed. After paying the fare, with tears in his eyes, he says, "I'll give you two a minute. I'll meet you inside."

"I think this is going to be tougher on him and Mom than it is for me," I say as Jo puts her arm around me.

Putting her head on my shoulder, I hear her gently sobbing. Pushing her arm down, I turn and face her saying, "Now, now. We talked about this. I need you to be strong for my parents, okay?"

"Sure, Danny, I'm sorry," she says wiping her tears with her hand. "Are you sure you are okay?"

"I'm just worried about Dad. His business is still struggling and it has been wearing on him. And now I will be heaping medical bills on him. Without me being able to help him, I'm afraid of what will happen. He really can't afford to hire help and he doesn't need this additional worry or expense at this time."

"We'll work it out. My dad has already talked to your father and he will be helping him out when he can nights and weekends. You just concentrate on getting better, you got that?"

"That is extremely thoughtful and generous of your father," I say as the words start to stick in my throat. "Please give him my heartfelt thanks."

"You can tell him yourself next time you see him."

Placing my hand on her cheek, I say, "I love you, Jo. You're the best thing that has ever happened to me. Thanks for everything. Are you ready?"

"Born ready. Let's go beat this, Danny," she says as she puts her arm back around me. Together as one, we walk slowly towards the front door as flocks of cabs honk around us like frenzied Canadian geese.

21.

June, 1970

Dutchess County, New York

Looking in the mirror after my mid-day nap, I am not sure I recognize the face that is reflected there after eight months of treatments at Sloan. Thinking back, I remember the battery of tests I was subjected to; the constant blood and urine tests, my body being poked and probed through every possible orifice. Then the constant bombardment of my body with chemotherapy treatments hitting me like artillery shells, leaving me weak, aching, nauseous and frightened as a bruised and bleeding fighter, not knowing if I can answer the bell for one more round.

My hair is long gone and I have red patches all over my scalp. My lips are chapped and bloody. I am down to one hundred and thirty-five pounds and my skin no longer seems tight, sagging like a bloodhound. Surprisingly, my eyebrows not only stayed but have become very dark. I joke with Jo that I look a little like Mr. Potato Head. Due to the weight loss, my clothes no longer fit. My whole body feels like a shadow, like it is someone else's.

Opening the medicine cabinet, I see my old butch stick. Laughing, I pick it up and remember my crew cut and how I used to wax it every morning. Putting it back on the shelf, I grab the white vial next to it, pop off the lid and pour out two blue pills that seem impossibly big to swallow.

Running water, I pop one into my mouth then bend down to scoop water in. I repeat with the second pill, then wipe my mouth on the towel. I have to take these four times a day to fight off any infections.

Looking again at my reflection, at least the good news is that Doctor Carter said I now appear to be in remission. I now will only have to go for monthly tests and treatment once a week, but that I can take. My appetite is slowly returning and I have started to gain a little weight, though nothing noticeable. Doctor Pappo has recently started me in physical rehab hoping that muscle tone will return to my ravaged body. Fatigue seems to be my constant companion.

Still, I have been able to continue working most days with Dad, excepting the days after treatment when I'm at my worse. Though I have little strength, I am able to drive the trucks and roller. It takes great effort, but I never let on to Dad that I feel anything but fine.

Walking down the stairs past the Last Supper portrait, I can smell the sweet aroma of coffee. Looking up from the stove, Mom says, "Good afternoon. How are you feeling?"

"I'll be better after a cup of coffee!"

"Help yourself, I just brewed a pot. Would you mind getting the mail while I finish cooking your lunch?"

Pouring a cup, I say, "No problem, Mom," as I walk to the front door. Stepping out onto the porch, I set my cup on a wobbly table next to a weathered Adirondack chair and saunter down the steps to the mailbox.

Reaching in, I pull out several catalogues and letters. Closing the box door, I stroll back up the walk while shuffling the letters. The last one I look at makes me stop dead in my tracks. Instantly I recognize the handwriting. The postage stamp mark is from Pennsylvania.

Settling into my chair, I rip open the envelope, pull out the letter and start to read.

Dear Danny:

I hope this letter finds you well. I am sorry I have not contacted you for so long, but Mom was always worrying about me being found and brought back for assaulting Sandy. I am also so very sorry about the loss of Billy. When I heard about him, I cried for days and still tear up whenever I think of him.

The real reason I wanted to reach out to you was to clarify what hap-

pened to me when you and Billy were away in Connecticut on seminary weekend. I know the last time we talked, when I rushed you out of the house, you could hardly understand me because of my jaw.

Anyway, as you know, we had our regular Thursday night swim scheduled. I almost didn't go that night but with Mom being the way she was, I decided I just wanted to get out of the house. I showed up at the rectory at the same time as always. I was there only a few minutes when Father Sipp pulled in with his Mustang. He told me that Father Donovan had taken ill and that it would be only him and me tonight. I remember being somewhat concerned but, hey, I was a kid and all I wanted was a swim, a hot shower and to be out of the house.

I had the whole pool to myself. I remember I was really enjoying my swim. When it was time, I walked into the changing room, removed my swim trunks, and went into the needle shower closing the door behind me. I don't know if you remember, Danny, but we had no hot water in my house. The only time I ever had a hot shower was in the school locker room. So, this was always a real treat for me. I remember turning the shower on and all the needle sprays of water coming out at once steaming hot. It didn't take long for the room to fill with a mist so thick that I couldn't see the walls.

I was standing in the middle of the hot, soothing shower and I couldn't even see the needle shower due to the steam when I heard a click. Funny, after all that happened, and after all of these years, it is that click of the door closing that I remember most vividly. I remember turning around and out of the steam Father Sipp appeared like a ghost.

All I remember is holding onto the circular bars of the shower. I opened my mouth to scream but all of the water sprays instantly filled my mouth so I couldn't. My hands burned but I couldn't let go. When it was over, I stood there holding the bars so tightly that my burning hands ached. When I turned around and faced the haze, I was alone. Afterwards, I was so ashamed that I didn't want to ever see anyone again, even you guys. I held everything inside and it would come out in violent rages. That is why I was always getting into fights.

You have to understand also that Father Sipp was taking advantage of my mother. He used to stop by on the pretense of helping her with her alcoholism but, in fact, he used to bring her liquor and then basically rape her. That is why I never wanted to go home when he was around. If he is still at Saint Vitonus, Danny, be careful of him.

When I told my mother what had happened, she confronted him and threatened to expose him. He offered her cash and help in resettling in a new town in Pennsylvania and he continued to send monthly payments up until the day she died. We never spent more than a few years in one town before moving. Father Sipp had told her that Sandy suffered permanent physical damage and has balance and memory issues. Mom was constantly afraid that the law would catch up with me for what I did to him.

I apologize for taking so long to contact you. With each passing year, I feel the threat of being found and returned to New York to face charges lessens, but I'm still afraid. In spite of that, I thought it was time for you to know the truth about what happened. I hope you are still with Jo and, if you are, send her my best.

Here is hoping that someday, soon, we can meet again.

Friends forever,

Tommy

P.S. Please forgive me, but I threw my Saint Christopher medal into the stream on the way out of the convent that night after the incident. I know Billy, you and I swore we would wear them forever. I am truly sorry, Danny. I hope you can understand and forgive me.

Putting the letter in my lap, I feel the blood draining out of my face and feel slightly faint as Mom steps out onto the porch. "Danny, did you get the mail?"

Looking at me, an alarmed look materializes on her face as she says, "Danny, are you okay? You look very pale. Maybe you should come inside and lay down on the couch for a while."

Gathering my senses, I say, "I'm okay, Mom. Just drank the coffee a little too fast, I think. I will be all right. Here's the mail."

Reaching out, she takes and says, "Let me know if you need anything, okay?"

"Okay, Mom." She nods, and walks back into the house.

I am literally in shock. It feels as if all the air has been sucked out of my lungs and I can't breathe. What does Tommy mean that Father Sipp is the one who hurt him? I was sure he told me that day at his house that he was hurt at swim night and Father Donovan is the one who took us to the convent. I remember fairly clearly what he told me because it upset me so at the time.

I am in total confusion when it suddenly hits me. *Oh God, no! Please God, no!* I think.

The truth strikes me like a lightning bolt as I lean back in my chair for support. With his mouth wired shut, it was difficult or impossible for Tommy to enunciate his thoughts clearly. When he said the Father hurt him at swim night, I naturally assumed it was Father Donovan. Billy and I accidentally killed an innocent man! Father Donovan was blameless, and our childish prank cost him his life. Emotions flow over me like a waterfall; sadness, regret, remorse, pity, shame, disgust but most of all, anger and guilt. Anger at Father Sipp for what he did and guilt for what Billy and I did.

Folding the letter, I stick in back into the envelope, pushing it deep into my pocket. I feel like running down the street as fast as I can while screaming at the top of my lungs. *I need to get out of here*, I think.

Walking into the hallway, I yell, "Mom, I'm going to the fair to see Jo. I'll be back soon."

"Okay, have fun, but be careful," she says from the kitchen.

Coming to a quick decision, I am not going to confide with Jo about this. Billy and I are the only ones who know what happened to poor Father Donovan, and Billy took his secret to the grave, as will I. I am, however, going to show her Tommy's letter and see what she thinks should be done about Father Sipp. Tommy was her friend also.

Turning the corner onto Millbury Street, ahead of me I see the bright lights of the town fair. Every year, the fair comes the second week of June for a four day stay. This year, Jo is working afternoons and evenings at the Saint Vitonus booth serving the hot roast beef sandwiches they sell.

Walking slowly towards the entrance, I can hear the harmonious sounds of music and laughter and smell the aromas of various cuisines.

Reaching for my wallet, I hand over a dollar for the entrance fee at the gate. Walking down the midway, I am struck by the contrast of all that is around me with the way I feel. To the right of me, the Ferris wheel spins in a blur of light as do my emotions. To my left, the Dive Bomber spins as rapidly as my thoughts as the screams of its occupants can clearly be heard over the din of the fair.

Strolling further along, I am accosted by various game vendors trying to entice me to shoot basketballs, fire guns and throw baseballs all in an effort to win a crappy ash tray or small stuffed doll. On the corner, sitting on a stool, is a man in a bright tie-dye tee shirt with his chestnut hair pulled back in a pony tail. He is playing a hurdy-gurdy, and a small crowd stands raptly in front of him, watching as he turns the crank rosin wheel which rubs the instruments strings sounding like a violin. Everyone is smiling but me.

Glancing ahead, I spot the sign for 'Roast Beef Sandwiches'. People are two deep waiting their turn. Moving closer, I spot Jo hurriedly handing out food, taking money and making change. As she hands back a customer change, she wipes her brow with the back of her hand and spies me in the crowd. Her eyes widen and a broad smile comes to her face. She motions with her hand to the side door and as I walk in that direction, I see her exchange a quick word with a woman who nods to her in response.

Leaning against a wall towards the back of the booth, I watch the crowd strolling by with vacant eyes. Just then, a door opens and Jo comes out.

"Hey, Danny! I didn't expect to see you here tonight." Evidently sensing something, she adds, "Are you okay?"

"I need to show you something. How long until you get off?"

Looking at her watch, she says, "It is almost four now. My afternoon shift ends in a half hour for dinner break for which I have an hour before I have to return."

"Okay. How about I wait for you here then we can go somewhere quiet?"

"You're scaring me. Is everything okay? Are you okay? You don't look well."

"It's not what you think, Jo. Don't worry. Go finish your shift and we'll talk later."

Leaning close, she kisses me softly on the lips. Pulling away, she says, "See you in a bit," and then disappears through the door, a concerned scowl on her beautiful face.

Sitting on coarse hay bales out back of the 4-H barn, Jo is reading Tommy's letter as I sit listening to the sounds, glancing at the sights of the fair. Observing her eyes as she reads, they seem to register confusion, sadness, horror and then disgust.

Finishing, she folds the letter and stuffs it back in the envelope as tears stream down her cheeks. "How could he? A priest? It's disgusting. Poor, poor Tommy...," she says as she chokes back her emotions and tears.

Taking the envelope, I deposit it into my pocket while saying, "What do you think I should do, Jo?"

"Go to the police, Danny! What else can you do? You have to before this pervert does this to some other kid!"

Pausing a few seconds before answering, I say, "Jo, I don't want to go to the police."

"Why the hell not, Danny?"

"Think, Jo. The only proof I have is Tommy's letter. The police won't act based solely on that. Plus, they will want to know where he is and talk to him and then he could be prosecuted on the outstanding assault charge filed by Sandy. Besides, this is personal." *More than you will ever know,* I think. "I want to be the one to take him down and I have just the way to do it."

"And how are you going to do that?"

"I'm going to confront him and see what happens. He certainly won't be expecting that and maybe I can trip him up enough so that he will admit to what he did."

"I don't know Danny, I don't trust him, he has always seemed a little creepy to me. This could be dangerous. You don't know how he will react or what he will do."

"It won't be dangerous where I am going to do this. There couldn't be a safer place."

"And where might that be?"

"At the church."

22.

June, 1970

Dutchess County, New York

Sitting in the dark in the last pew of Saint Vitonus, I look up at the Stations of the Cross that line the aisle on each side. Remembering from catechism classes, these are also known as the Ways of Sorrows which hits me as being ironic, given what has happened. I was brought up to believe that this church was a sacred place. Now it is just a building.

In the front of the church an elderly lady is silently praying in front of a lit candle, her cane propped up against the wainscoting, rosary beads in hand. Smelling the candles and incense, it takes me back to my first mass as an altar boy here with Billy and Tommy. I remember how nervous we were, how much in awe we were of being part of our first mass. That seems so, so long ago now.

A single woman sitting waiting for the confessional stands and enters it as the elderly lady grabs her cane. Gingerly, she stands and then shuffles toward the door with the clack-clack-clack of her cane echoing off of the vaulted ceiling. High above the altar, a crucified Jesus watches her leave.

Standing, I walk across the back of the empty church and head down the aisle, sitting where the woman sat minutes ago. The front door slams, indicating the woman with the cane is gone.

Minutes later, the woman leaves the confessional, walks to the front of the altar and genuflects while making the sign of the cross. Her footsteps slowly fade followed by the front door closing.

Standing, I enter the confessional. Kneeling, I look at the screen in front of me as a small door behind it is slid open like in a prohibition speakeasy, revealing only a silhouette in the dark.

"Welcome, my son," I hear from the dark.

"Bless you father, for you have sinned," I say.

"What, what did you say?" says a confused voice.

"I said you have sinned. I know what you did to Mrs. Willott and Tommy."

Looking through the screen, I see the silhouette rapidly rise followed by the curtain being ripped open. Just as I stand, the confessional's curtain is torn open.

Standing before me, Father Sipp's green eyes are bulging wide, his narrow mouth open with spittle and drool evident as he shouts, "I might have known, Danny Fosse. I knew you were trouble from the moment you returned from seminary."

"Save it, asshole," I say trying to anger him as I have planned. "I'm calling the police on you as soon as I leave here."

"And what, lad, exactly are you going to tell them?"

"For starters, that you got Mrs. Willott drunk and took advantage of her. Remember the last night before she and Tommy left town, when you and I talked on the walk? You then took her to the store. Well, I was standing in the street when Tommy motioned me into the house. He told me exactly what you did to him on swim night. I went out the back when you and Mrs. Willott returned, but I never left. I watched through the window," I say calling his bluff. "That is what I am going to tell the police."

"I don't think so, lad. And you know why?"

Suddenly I am timorous and remain silent.

"Because I know where Tommy is. Before she died, his mother and I were in constant correspondence because I was sending her money. I have saved all of the letters with the return addresses, stored them in my desk. In these letters, she says nothing that would lead the police to think anything was wrong. Quite the contrary, actually. Of course, I really don't need the letters. I could just tell the police where he is. But the letters serve to nicely contradict what you are saying. Might I remind you that the warrant is still open for Tommy for his assault with a deadly weapon? It might have been years ago and mostly forgotten about, but if you talk to the police then I will be forced to give them the letters and his address.

"You're bluffing," I say.

"Think so, lad? Follow me," he says as he walks assertively back through the sacristy towards the back door. I am frantic, my mind racing. *Maybe I should run*, I think. Holding the door open, he motions me through. Taking one step, I feel a blow to my head and fall to my knees. Dazed, I look at the wall to the side of the door and see the silhouette of his right arm raising and then start downward, then nothing.

Waking, I find myself leaning against a car window. Raising my head, a shooting pain erupts in the back like an explosion. Reaching a hand up, I feel wetness and swelling.

"Welcome back," I hear a voice say. Slowly looking to my left, I see Father Sipp pointing a gun at me. "Out of the car. Now!"

Opening the door, I shakily get out and push it shut. Looking back down the road, I see birch and maples trees closely leaning over the road edge as if trying to get a better view. Turning around, I spot a rusted chain that sags lazily across the road, secured in place by a badly tarnished lock. I recognize it immediately. We're standing at the end of the mining road.

"Seriously, you would shoot me if I ran away?"

"Try me, you little prick. Go ahead, run. It would make it a lot easier on me, that's for sure," he says as his eyes narrow like a striking snake. "I'd just drag you off into the woods and let the animals at you. By the time they found you, there would be nothing left. Certainly no one would ever suspect me. Go ahead, run."

"Then what are we doing here?"

Saying nothing, he walks to the trunk, opens it and pulls out a gym bag and tosses it at my feet while slamming the trunk closed. Watching, I see him lift his floor mat and toss the keys under it, then shut the door. "Pick that up. Let's go," he says motioning with the gun.

Bending, I pick up the bag, walk to the chain and step over it as a headache thumps like a well drill pounder. Together, we start to trek up the trail, me in front and he behind with his gun aimed at my back.

Standing nervously by the entrance to Lenter's Mine, I look longingly back out over the valley. The sky is a silky blue with scattered lazy puffs of cirrus clouds, the evening sun illuminating a pallet of verdant greens, reminding me of past similar, happier days. The rounded tops of the distant Catskills look to be a hazy mirage through the summer heat, like looking through copious cobwebs. A faint waxing gibbous moon can be seen sneakily rising in the sky. I wonder, *will this will be the last time I ever see it and this view?*

"That is far enough," he says. Watching him walk over to the mine entrance, I see the old *"Lenter's Limestone"* sign is still leaning against the entrance wall. There is a new stainless-steel hasp on the door with a shiny new padlock securing it to the Judas door. Pulling a key from his pocket, he unlocks the hasp. Looking into the woods, I briefly think of making a run for it amongst the trees.

"Go on. Try it," he hisses. Putting the key back into the lock, he tosses it to me and says, "Put that in the bag and get the flashlight out." Reaching down, I pull open the bag flaps, deposit the lock and key and pull out a red flashlight.

"Bring the bag and give me the light." After handing it to him, he says, "After you," as he pulls on the door. The warped bottom catches on the ground so he gives it a sharp jerk, allowing it to open.

Stepping inside, I instantly recognize the same cold dampness and musty smelling air as on my last visit. The rough walls and ceiling are jagged, still appearing as if they had been chewed, electrical metal conduits with broken light fixtures and cables run along the ceiling before disappearing into the darkness. The delicate transparent silk of spider webs is weaved from almost every available surface. Following the entrance tunnel, with the aid of the light shining from behind, I walk until I come to a ledge. Walking up beside me, Father Sipp shines his light downward.

On the floor in a crumpled heap are the remains of the elevator that Tommy was on when it collapsed years ago. The rusted and twisted steel framework looks like the remains of some prehistoric animal. A rusty sledgehammer, its head the color of butternut squash, its rotting handle a gloomy black, sits like an island next to an old motor. Six separate tunnels can be seen going in different directions, all dry as bone. On the floor edges, white stalagmites cast dancing shadows in his faint light. The corroded loading cart still sits tipped on its side like a dead animal, its rusted wheels an orangish-red.

"Reach into the bag and get the rope ladder out, then fasten it there," he says while shining the light onto the two rock anchors Jo had previously spotted. Kneeling, I yank open the bag and wrench out the rolled-up ladder. Tugging one end free, two carabiners bang on the rock floor like cymbals. Standing, I walk over to the anchors, fasten them to the ladder and let it drop. As it unfolds, each wood step clacks against the rock face sounding like a galloping horse.

"Again, after you," he says motioning with the gun.

Turning around, I drop a leg over the edge as I hang onto the top rung. Finding purchase, I drop my other leg to the same step and begin my descent.

Arriving at the bottom, I move back away from the wall. Father Sipp shines the light on me and says, "Get over there by the cart." Turning, I walk over to it and stand, watching him.

Putting the flashlight in his pocket so it is shining straight up, he inserts the gun into his waistband. Reaching into the bag, he pulls out a roll of duct tape and throws it down to me. "Catch. Don't try anything stupid, lad. I can have the gun in my hand in seconds."

As he is descending, escape is foremost in my mind. I think about running down the tunnel behind me, but remember it ends at a cliff above the subterranean lake. Also, I wouldn't get far before I would be in complete darkness and utterly blind. Anger fills me and I decide that if I don't make it out of here, then this son of a bitch won't either.

Moments later he is at the bottom and has both the flashlight and gun pointed at me.

"Give me the duct tape," he says as he hands me the flashlight.

Handing it over to him, he says, "Both arms out, please." Extending them, he wraps the tape around my wrist with several turns. Tearing it from the roll, he discards it on the floor.

"That way," he says as he takes the light back from me while motioning to the furthest tunnel to the right. As I walk towards it, I see his light play across the shale deposits and remember Tommy's warning about this tunnel. Heading into it, I sidestep pieces and small piles of rock that have dislodged from the ceiling. The light from behind me moves in a jerky motion, making my shadow move from left to right and then back again on the floor in front of me like a confused, trapped bird.

Emerging into a small chamber, I see two shafts at the far wall. The one on the left side is about five to six feet wide. There is about ten or so feet of shale and limestone to its right and then a second, slightly wider shaft.

"Over to the left," he says as I anxiously walk to the edge, turn sideways watching him approach.

Giving a smile that is pure evil, he shines the light down to the bottom and says, "Take a look."

Staring at him with murderous intent, I shift my gaze into the lighted shaft. At the bottom of the approximate twenty-foot-deep shaft is the roof of a collapsed mine cage on which it appears are small birch limbs scattered about. Focusing, I see that it is really the bones of two small skeletons. With horror I look back at him and say, "What the hell did you do, you pathetic pervert?"

Exploding in anger, he shouts, "Pervert! Those kids asked for it!" his face turning florid as white frothy spittle flies from his mouth, his eyes bulging like a frog. Moving away from the shaft, he motions me to the right shouting, "Get over there!"

Shuffling to the right, I stop in front of the second shaft. Thinking back to what Tommy had told us, this must be the ventilation shaft. He walks to the edge on the other side of the opening and shines his light down. "Look!" he screams, a miasma of breath hitting me, white foamy spittle pooling on his whiskered chin, with eyes feral, pupils as large as black olives.

Turning my head, I look down the shaft and can see no bottom. Looking back at him, he moves with side steps like a crab until he is only a foot or so in front of me with the tunnel we came in at his back. Raising the gun, he says, "You should have kept your mouth shut, lad. It didn't have to end this way."

Out of options, as far as I can tell. Images whirl around my mind like leaves caught in the whirlpool at Farley's Stream. Fond memories of tobogganing, swimming, and just hanging out with Billy and Tommy. Of all the time I have spent with Jo, of our future plans. And, of course, poor innocent Father Donovan. If I could have one moment in time back to do over, that night at the pool would be it. I feel sweat beading on my forehead and my hands are shaking. For the second time in my life I'm afraid I'm about to die, both times in this mine.

Then it hits me. Clearly. I really am about to die. All of the nerve endings in my body sizzle and spark like I have grabbed a downed high-tension wire. My feet are suddenly leaden, like boots that have walked through wet clay, my teeth ache like I have bitten down on aluminum foil, my heart is beating so fast that my whole being vibrates, my mouth dry as sand, sweat beads form on my forehead, wiggling down like miniature, moist worms. Curiously, my hearing seems acute, I feel I could hear a pin drop in the next county, when, in fact, I do hear something faint, like an unseen squirrel running through fall leaves far off in the woods.

Then, I see it.

A smile comes to my face. *Keep the bastard talking*, I think.

A connection is made in my mind for the first time. "Let me ask you something. You said earlier that you knew I was trouble from the moment I returned from seminary. I remember Father Churchill saying that it was nice to have us boys there for a change since he usually only has visiting priests. He mentioned that priests from our parish had been there several times the previous year. You killed that kid we found, didn't you?"

Twisting his face into a depraved smile, he says with the sibilant hiss of a snake, "Why not? Sure, I killed him. And it was fun. He never should have been found, but you had to go ahead and stumble on the body. Fortunately for me, no one ever suspects a priest. I am untouchable, I am God! That is what ultimately makes all of this so perfect. Is that what you wanted to hear?" he shouts slurring some of his words, his eyes seemingly bulging out of his head. *He's insane,* I think.

"And those bodies in the other shaft. Those are the two boys who went missing from Poughkeepsie?"

Narrowing his eyes, he says, "I'll give you one thing, lad, you are a smart son of a bitch. Yeah, those are the boys and they were most enjoyable. And there is nothing you, or anyone else, can ever do about it. I'm sorry about this, lad," he says as he straightens his arm so the gun is only inches from my face."

"Did you hear all of that, Jo?"

Hesitating, he smiles and says, "Nice try, lad. Nice try."

"Every word," comes booming out of the darkness behind him.

Reflexively, he slightly turns his head to look as he shines his light towards the back of the chamber. Using my taped hands as a club, I pull them over my left shoulder and then come down hard on his arm causing him to drop the gun which rattles on the floor as it slides to the edge of the shaft. I crash my body into him, sending us both to the floor as he drops the flashlight which spins wildly, stopping with its light shining towards the shaft.

"Danny!" I hear Jo yell, followed by her approaching footsteps clicking on the rock floor like castanets as her flashlight shines on us.

My hands still bound, I can't grab onto Father Sipp and suddenly I feel a foot in my groin, followed by excruciating pain radiating throughout my body like an electrical shock.

Feeling her hand on my shoulder, Jo helps me up while shouting at Father Sipp, "What the hell is wrong with you, you degenerate? You're pathetic and disgusting!" Looking at her eyes, they are wide as the night sky, filled with hate and anger, but not fear. With her blue bandana tied off in the back, the small auburn ponytail jutting out, I have never been so happy to see someone in my entire life.

We stand helplessly side by side facing him. Having retrieved the gun, he is now on the edge of the shaft with it pointed at us. His face is ruddy, saliva drooling out of his mouth like a rabid dog. His eyes are untamed, full of rage and furor like a sea tempest. He is definitely insane.

Getting an idea, I say, "How do we know that your gun is even loaded? I never saw you put any bullets in it. Being the incompetent ass that you are, you probably forgot. I mean look at how sad, feeble and ridiculous you are. You prey on innocent, little boys. You aren't even a real man."

As agitated as he now is, the words push him further into ferocity as he points the gun down the shaft and fires, the sound reverberating throughout the mine. "How is that? Convinced now, lad? The next is for your girlfriend. After you watch her die, it is your…"

Before he can finish, pieces of shale start breaking off of the ceiling from the concussive force of the gunshot as the whole chamber starts juddering. Like a spring shower, there is one piece, then another, then another until it is pouring to the floor. Pulling Jo close, I raise my taped hands over us just as there is a tremendous roar. We are looking at Father Sipp one second, and in the next he is gone, as the edge of the shaft collapses from underneath him. His scream echoes up from the abysmal shaft for a few seconds and then is muffled by tons of crumbling stone crashing down, burying him.

"Run!" I yell to Jo. She aims her flashlight as we dash out of the chamber and down the tunnel as pieces of shale spit all around us. Suddenly, Jo trips over a piece of rock and goes down hard. The light flies through the air, then, total darkness. We are blind in a rock storm.

"Danny, don't move!" she shouts. I hear a faint scraping sound as she scours the ground with her hands. Then I hear a metallic clack sound. Seconds later, the light comes on and I see Jo on the floor.

Grabbing her elbow, I help her up and we continue to run.

Emerging into the entry cavern, we stop at the base of the rope ladder panting. "Are you okay, Jo?"

"I think so."

"Look!" I shout as my eyes widen in horror as she shines the light back at the tunnel. A huge gray cloud of dust is blowing out of the tunnel like a sandstorm towards us.

"Give me your hands!" she yells as she grabs for the tape edge and quickly starts unwrapping it from my wrists. Pulling the last of if off, she shouts, "Up the ladder! Now!"

"No, Jo. You first!"

"Go Danny, don't argue. Who is the better climber? Now go!"

Looking at the approaching dust cloud, I grab a rung and climb as fast as I can. Reaching the top, I look down seeing Jo is halfway up, the flashlight beam from her back pocket moving with her hips like a searchlight. Seconds later the dust cloud catches her, enveloping her. She disappears from my view. Gone.

"Jo!" I scream. "Jo!"

Dropping to my knees, I peer into the darkness. Seconds later, I see a faint light that gets brighter and brighter. I see a hand come up out of the dust and grab a rung, followed by the other and then her upper body emerges. Reaching down, I grab her hand and help her up to the ledge.

Panting from exhaustion, I look at her dust covered face. She is coughing and hacking, bent over her knees. Finally, it subsides and she smiles. She pulls the flashlight out of her pocket, shining it below. Looking out over the top of the dust cloud, it seems to have leveled off as the rumbling from the tunnel diminishes. Then, suddenly, all is quiet.

"Let's get out of here, okay?" I say as I bend and reach into Father Sipp's bag, removing the lock with the key in it.

"Okay," she says. Smiling, she takes my hand and we walk down the entrance tunnel and out into the night air.

Outside, a bright first quarter moon is now high up illuminating the valley. Stars are shining radiantly in a shadowy sky. Turning the key, the lock pops open. Pushing the door shut, I pull the hasp over the hook and secure the lock, placing the key in my pocket.

Looking at Jo, her face and hair are covered with white limestone dust. She smiles at me and I think she has never looked so beautiful. "How in the world did you find me here? I ask.

"You told me you were going to confront Father Sipp at confession and I was worried about what might happen. I have never liked or trusted him. Since you told me that you didn't want me to go, I decided I would at least wait outside the church in case something happened. Seeing his Mustang go by with you leaning against the window with your eyes closed, I knew something was wrong. I followed his car and saw him pull into the old mining road. I pulled into the lot for the Lenter's Hill path and ran back down to the mining road.

"Seeing you two still in the car, I watched for some time. I was afraid to leave you to go get help. When you were still sitting there as dusk approached, I ran back to my car and got a flashlight out of the glovebox, but by the time I returned the car was empty. I figured that he was taking you to the mine.

"Once I got inside and on top of the ledge, I could hear your voices. Scrambling down the ladder, I followed the sound down the tunnel until I could see faint light on a wall. Shutting my light off, I carefully moved forward until I could see the two of you. You know what happened after that."

"That was quite a risk, Jo, but I owe you my life. If you hadn't come, no one would have ever found me or knew what happened to me. Thank you."

Gazing into my eyes, she puts one hand gently behind my head and the other around my waist as she pushes herself up on her toes and lightly kisses me. "No thanks needed, love. Are we going to go to the police now?"

"We can't do that, Jo. At least not right away. He has letters from Tommy's mother that has his address on them. I know that after all of this time, most likely no one is actively looking for Tommy. Just the same, I would feel better if those letters were never found. I don't want any chance to exist that someone could find out through them about what Father Sipp did to Tommy. I need to protect his privacy, his dignity if I can. I owe him that much."

"What are we going to do, then?"

"We are going to steal them. I have a plan, but we need time. First, we have to get rid of his car. We can't leave it here where it might be found. Let's get down to the road, I will drive his car and you follow me in yours," I say as an anonymous animal shrieks twice in succession from somewhere deep in the woods below.

"What if we get stopped? Can you even drive a car with a standard transmission?"

"We can take the back roads so I doubt we will have any trouble. As to driving a standard shift, my dad has been letting me drive his trucks on job sites since I was a kid, so that is not a problem. Anyway, we better get going, time is short."

Where are we going?"

"The river. Low tide is in forty minutes."

23.

June, 1970

Dutchess County, New York

The vivid luminous moon is now soaring in the sky, casting pale light on the ashen river. Waves undulate tenderly, making a gentle splash as they tickle and kiss the rocks on shore. Across the river, to the north, somber light winks from the lighthouse tower, the illuminated Catskills appearing backlit by the moon's rays.

Parking her car by the pavilion, Jo walks over to where I stand by the Mustang as a truncated screech from an owl echoes through the woods.

"Help me fold the vinyl top down," I say. Together we roll it back, strapping it to the rear deck.

"Let's go," I say as we both hop in.

Shifting into first, with the lights off I let the car creep up the access road over golden pine needles and Kelly-green moss soft as carpet. Moonlight sneaks through the branches of the tall, twisted pines in pencil sized shafts, lighting our way like we are in an enchanted forest in some nursery rhyme. Seeing the path that I am looking for just ahead, I turn the car off of the road as the springs squeak in dissent. Driving to the edge of the shale incline, I stop. Below us, the small cove reflects moonlight like a mirror underscoring the shale embankments, the small pebbles on the beach sparkling like gemstones.

"Ready?" I ask.

Smiling, Jo turns to look at me and says, "Born ready."

Laughing, I put the car in gear and it starts to trundle down the incline as the car bounces and the frame screeches. Reaching the beach, I look to our right and can see the tide is almost at complete low.

"The water here is now only a few feet deep out to the underwater cliff edge. You best get out here and I will get out of my clothes," I say as I prepare to climb out.

Turning to face me, Jo says, "Please be careful," and then exits the car.

Standing by the car, I strip down to my underwear and hand Jo my clothes. Getting back behind the wheel, I turn to the right crawling forward until the car is in the water. Driving forward, the river quickly engulfs it. Feeling the engine sputter, I accelerate slightly. Water is half way up the door when the front end suddenly moves downward, meaning it has slipped off the cliff's edge.

Quickly standing, I put one foot on top of the door and dive off just as the back end pops up, pushing the front further under water.

Making a few quick overhead strokes to put distance from the car, I turn and tread water watching the river flow over both the front and rear door tops. Sinking at a forty-five-degree angle, the only thing now visible is the rear deck. Seconds later it is gone in a pool of swirling water as a pair of gulls fly by screeching.

Swimming back towards the beach, I feel the shallow river bed as I cross over the cliff edge and stand. Wading to shore, Jo meets me with my clothes in her arm. "Here, dry off with your shirt," she says handing it to me.

Drying off, I realize for the first time that I am still wearing both Billy and my Saint Christopher medals. Pulling them off, I rub Billy's burnt and bent medal between my thumb and forefinger. Looking at Jo, I see sadness in her eyes then she gives me a knowing smile.

Nodding, I ball them up, cock my arm back across my chest and side toss them far out into the river.

Just like throwing a frisbee.

Hitting the surface, they skip once, make a small splash and disappear forever.

"What are we going to do about our filthy clothes?" I say. "They would be hard to explain."

"No problem. My dad is away on a business trip so we can go to my house and do a wash." Suddenly, Jo yells, "Oh no!"

"What?"

"Danny, I lost my mom's earring!"

"I am so sorry Jo. I know how much they mean to you."

"Danny," she says, a serious tone in her voice. "You don't understand. I lost it in the mine."

24.

June, 1970

Dutchess County, New York

Sirens wail as fire trucks, a police car and ambulance streak by us through the morning fog, hazy lights blinking like fireflies, heading out of town to some unseen emergency. Waiting for them to pass, Jo and I cross Market Street hand in hand. In front of us, the white asbestos siding on Saint Vitonus is blemished with gray dirt tinge, the stain glass windows dark and foreboding like eye sockets in a skull. Looking up, the top half of the black steeple disappears into heavy fog making it seem as if some giant, angry hand reached down and snapped it in half.

Strolling into the rectory drive, I whisper to Jo, "Ready?"

"Born ready."

Knocking on the screen door, it rattles like a drum cymbal. Inside, I can hear the shuffling of approaching feet, then the door is pulled open as Mrs. Armstrong says, "Hello Danny. Hello Jo. How can I help you?" Her grizzled hair is pulled up in a bun with a brown plastic chignon holding it in place. She is plump, with a round face, and is the spitting image of Aunt Bee on the Andy Griffith show.

"Is Father Sipp here?" I ask.

"No, not yet. Would you like to wait for him for a while?"

"If it is not an imposition," I say.

"Please, come in," she says while holding the door open.

"Thank you." Sniffing the air, it smells of baked goods and burnt candles.

"Please, have a seat in the living room while you wait. Would you like some tea?"

"That would be great," Jo says.

"For me, too."

"I'll be right back, make yourselves comfortable," she states as she heads for the kitchen.

Standing, I walk over to the fireplace mantle and pick up a photograph of Father Sipp. In it, he is surrounded by a group of boys in little league uniforms. He has both hands on the shoulders of the boy in front of him, a crooked smile on his evil face, his beady eyes narrow incisions like a turkey vulture.

Shaking my head, I replace it as I hear Mrs. Armstrong return saying, "All we have is Earl Gray, I hope that's okay?"

"My favorite," says Jo. As she places the tray on the coffee table, Jo says, "Could I use your bathroom?

"Sure, dear. It is on the right, just outside this room."

"Thank you," Jo says as she stands.

"Would you have another I might use?" I ask.

"Sure, Danny. There is one at the top of the stairs to the left."

"Thank you," I say as I head up the stairs. Finding the bathroom, I open the door and close it while standing on the outside. Walking quickly across the hall, I open a door and, looking in, guess it is Father Sipp's room.

Stepping into it, I see a roll top desk against the wall by the closet. Moving quickly to it, I pull out one of Jo's bandanas which I brought to guard against leaving fingerprints. Using it to grab the roll top handle, I slowly slide it up. Pulling the chain on a small lamp, the desktop is illuminated like a prison yard. Inside is a desk blotter on which several unopened envelopes sit along with a pencil sharpener, roll of tape and a cup full of pens. Two rows of small drawers are in the back.

Reaching into my pocket, I pull out a key and set it on the blotter. It has on it a small dirty, yellowed circular paper key tag on which I have printed "L. Mine." My father has everything labeled with these on his workbench, and I found this blank one sitting discarded in a dusty window sill.

Grasping a drawer handle, I pull it open and expose a confused tangle of paper clips. Shoving it shut, I pull open the adjacent one which is full of rubber bands and erasers. Grabbing the handle of the last top row drawer, I slide it out exposing a bundle of letters secured by a wide rubber band. Looking at the return address, I see Pittsburgh, PA. Pulling one out, I open it and scan the words verifying it is from Mrs. Willott.

Downstairs, I hear Jo flush the toilet followed by footsteps and then muted conversation.

Pushing the letter into the bundle, I stuff it into my shirt. Grasping the drawer, I start to push it shut when a photograph catches my eye. Reaching for it, I pull it out and am looking at a small boy who appears frightened. Staring at it, suddenly recognition comes bubbling to the surface of my mind as I see part of a rusted chain behind him and an upside down "POSTED" sign over his right shoulder. Feeling my heart racing and beads of perspiration on my forehead, I turn it over and there is a date on the back of September, nineteen sixty-three. Looking in the drawer, I see other pictures. They are all of boys, all similarly dated on the back. The top one is dated May, nineteen sixty-four. The one underneath, March, nineteen sixty-four. Suddenly it hits me, *Oh Christ.*

Wiping them clean, I return them and thrust the drawer shut. Getting an idea, I pull it back open, reach down, grab the key from the blotter, placing it on top of the photos. Pushing it shut, I pull the light chain and tug down the roll top. Moving to the door, I put the bandana in my pocket, cross the hall and go into the bathroom where I flush the toilet. Turning on the cold water, I splash it onto my face. Reaching for a hand towel, I dry off then head downstairs.

Sauntering back into the living room, I say, "Sorry. I guess breakfast didn't agree with me."

Smiling, Mrs. Armstrong says, "Danny, your tea has gone cold. Let me reheat it for you."

Looking at my watch, I say, "Thanks, Mrs. Armstrong, but I have to get going to help my dad at work today. Just tell Father Sipp when he returns that we were sorry we missed him."

"Is there any message?"

"I was just going to ask him if I could work this weekend at the church booth with Jo."

"I'll let him know when he's in."

Standing, we all walk to the door. As we exit, Mrs. Armstrong says, "Have a good day," just as the church bell tower bells start to clang.

Sitting on Jo's front porch with the letters in my lap, she asks, "What are we going to do now, Danny?" Several boys on skateboards come racing down the street amongst shrieks of laughter, turn the corner and disappear from sight as an old collie trails limping, trying in vain to keep up.

Thinking, I don't respond. Minutes later, I say, "What if we never contact the police?"

"What! Why would we do that?"

"Think about it, Jo. It won't be long until someone reports Father Sipp missing, most likely Mrs. Armstrong. At some point the police will go through the rectory to find clues as to what happened to him. It won't take them long to find the photos of the boys and the key I labeled. Then they'll go to the mine. When they enter, they'll find his gym bag and based on that they'll do a thorough search of the mine. I'm fairly certain that the collapse was only in and around the shaft Father Sipp fell into since we only saw small pieces falling from the ceiling on our run out of there. If that is the case, they will find the remains I saw there but not him."

"I don't know, Danny."

"Listen, this is perfect. The police will never look under the tons of debris in the second shaft. Why would they? It will be assumed that collapse happened a long time ago. Based on all of this, they'll most likely think Father Sipp skipped town and put out a warrant for his arrest. The families of the boys will get to bury their loved ones and we know Father Sipp will never be found. He never will hurt anyone again. It is perfect."

25.

August, 1970

Dutchess County, New York

Having hiked back up to the waterfalls, the mid-day sun shimmers on us as we sit on a blanket on a ledge overlooking the valley. Below us, the town seems in motion as cars move up and down the various streets, the sound of the falls thundering up through the trees. South of the town, high on its hill, the deserted old red brick schoolhouse glows in egg yolk colored sun rays, Farley's Stream glittering behind it. Jo has packed a picnic, and we sit in silence enjoying our turkey sandwiches and chips while sipping on cokes.

"Danny," she says, I have to tell you something." Noticing the sudden change in the tone of her voice, I turn towards her unexpectedly serious face.

"What is it? Is something wrong?"

Setting her soda down, she says, "My dad has been transferred. He will be leaving in a week or so."

"Transferred? To Where?"

"Italy. It is a three to four-year assignment, after which he will be moved to Atlanta," she says as she stifles a sob. "I'm going with him, Danny. His company will pay for the rest of my college, as well as graduate school, if I go with him. The local university offers a teaching program for working with kids with disabilities. You know that has always been something I wanted to do. It is a once in a lifetime opportunity that I just can't pass up. I'm so sorry. I know this is not what you want to hear, but I feel I have to do this. For myself."

Stunned, I find I cannot think of anything to say at first. I feel, for the first time in my life, that my heart is breaking. Gathering myself, I say, "You should go, Jo. I know that studying abroad has also always been your dream. And to have it paid for, well, it is a no brainer. You have already sacrificed too much. You have been going to the community college because of me, instead of pursuing the degree you really want at a four-year college. I am anchored here for now and I don't want to tie you down too. You have to go. I'm happy for you. I truly am."

"I know this sucks, Danny. I've been torn up about this ever since I found out about his transfer and the college tuition program."

Keeping my composure, I respond, "Wow. Look at the bright side, Jo, what an experience it will be for the both of you. Italy, wow. Just think, you will be able to visit your mom's relatives in France."

Looking at me, tears start to well up and then stream from her blue-gray eyes. Sobbing, she says, "Danny, I don't want to leave you. I love you. How am I going to survive this? You said one of the reasons you were glad that I didn't go to Michigan State without you was that you were afraid that a long-distance relationship would not work, remember?"

Pulling her close, she rests her head on my chest as I stroke her hair which has a slightly fruity smell. "I do, Jo, but we can write each other, occasionally talk on the phone."

Pushing away, she says, "It won't be the same and you know it. We are bound to drift apart after all that time," as tears once again start to drop. "I'm so afraid that what you said might be true. I'm afraid I will lose you."

Putting my hand on her cheek, I say, "You'll never lose me. Besides, I could come to visit," I say.

Smiling, she puts a hand to my cheek and says, "That is sweet, Danny. But think of the cost. Think of your dad's business. Think of your illness. Even though you have been in remission, you still need regular treatments. You can't travel abroad."

Far off the cliff, a pair of turkey vultures float on the hot thermals like kites, gliding in lazy circles as they scan the ground far below for prey.

"Then maybe you could come back to visit?"

"That is a strong possibility but it won't negate the fact that there will be so much distance, so much time, between us. It worries me. You know, in a strange way this might be good for me, other than not being able to see you." Looking at the town below, she says, "This place holds many good memories which have, unfortunately, been stained by the few bad. Maybe new scenery will help me to bury the demons that this place holds for me." Placing both hands on each side of my face, she pulls close as her eyes move back and forth looking at first one, then the other of my eyes. "Danny, do you really think we can survive this?"

"I do, Jo, I really do. I love you and could never, ever love anyone else as much."

Smiling, she moves her hands behind my head and slowly pulls me down to the blanket. Tenderly touching her, I feel passion and intimacy but, foremost, I feel love, a love I am sure will have a place in my heart for all eternity. With the roaring falls alongside us, the sun warmly watching us, we become one with the world and each other.

Standing on the platform at the train station, I hear the waves of the Hudson slapping on the rocks like a flat tire going down a road. Far out, a red and white tugboat lazily pushes an open barge, the rounded piles of crushed stone piled high like scoops of ice cream. In the distance, the avocado Catskills loom protectively.

A speaker above us crackles with static as the arrival of the two fifty-five to New York's Grand Central Station is announced. Looking up the tracks, I see a silver train emerge from a distant tunnel, slightly banking around the slowly curving tracks as it heads for the station.

Looking into her eyes, I can see tears welling up again. "Now, now. We talked about this," I say wiping her tears away.

"I know. I'm sorry. This is just so incredibly hard."

Smiling as I wipe another tear away, I hear the concussive sound as the train blows into the station, a small windstorm following it. It slows and, finally, stops with a squeal as the cars all slightly buck backwards.

A door creaks open, and a pudgy, ruddy faced conductor steps down saying, "Train to New York, board here," as he bends with difficulty, placing a small yellow step stool on the platform. "All aboard."

People rush past us to get in line as Jo hugs me so tightly I feel I might lose my breath. Looking over her shoulder, I see the last person in line board.

"You need to go, Jo."

Reaching up, she tenderly wipes a tear off of my cheek saying, "I will write you every week, I promise. I will love you forever, Danny," as she grabs her bag and walks over to the conductor. Holding her arm, he helps her up the steps. I watch as she climbs the three steps, turns right and disappears.

Seconds later, the train sounds its whistle and pulls forward with a slight jerk. Soon, it has gathered momentum and is racing towards its destination. The train tilts slightly to the left as it curves around a corner disappearing from sight. I no longer can hold back my emotions as I start to sob.

Walking down the platform, I climb the stairs and walk over the tracks and descend to the parking lot by the river. I walk up to the water's edge, the waves gently caressing the rocks, as tears trickle down my cheeks. I feel very much like I did at Billy's funeral, like my insides have been ripped out. I am dreading that I might not only be losing what is now my best friend, but the love of my life. I think, *is it possible I will never see her again?*

Pulling down Parsons Street, I see a state trooper car pulled to the curb in front of the house. Parking my car in the drive, I get out as the door opens and Paul Agnos steps out. "Hey, Danny. Can I talk to you for a minute?" His eyebrows are still as thick as hedgerows, and he looks as fit and strong as ever.

Feeling slightly confused, I say, "Sure, Paul. Come on in."

Holding the front door open for him, he removes his Stetson and walks in.

"Come into the living room and take a seat," I say. Walking in front of me, he settles onto the couch with his hat in his lap.

Sinking into a recliner across from him, I say, "So, what can I do for you?"

I'm sure you, like everyone else in this town, are aware of the Father Sipp investigation."

Feeling my skin going cold at the mention of the name, I reply, "Of course, only what I have read in the papers."

"Well, most of the reporting is accurate. His housekeeper, Mrs. Armstrong, reported him missing and we naturally searched the rectory and found dated pictures of young boys. One has been positively identified as being the remains you and Billy found at the Connecticut seminary. You should feel good about that, since that poor family finally will get closure as to what happened and a measure of peace."

"I'm glad we could help."

"Well, we also found a key which lead us to Lenter's Mine. Inside, we found a gym bag which Mrs. Armstrong positively identified as his. Both the Bureau of Criminal Investigation and state police did an extensive search in the mine, which also included divers going into an underground lake. I was part of that search team and we ultimately located the remains of two boys at the bottom of a mine shaft. We almost didn't go in there because it was evident that there had been some sort of collapse previously, but we were able to with no trouble or further downfall.

"Wow, that must have been a frightening experience."

"Indeed. Anyway, Danny there is just one thing I can't explain and I was hoping you might help me."

"Me? What could I possibly know about any of this?"

"What has bothered me from the beginning about this, is why would Father Sipp leave the rope ladder and gym bag in the mine when he knew they would be identified as his? Also, why would he leave the key for the lock on the mine door and incriminating pictures in his desk? If he was going to skip town, as he evidently has, then these things make absolutely no sense. Do you see my problem?" he asks.

At a loss for words, my mind races. "I see what you mean," is all I can say.

Reaching into his shirt pocket, he extends his arm and opens his hand revealing an earring shaped like a small gold rock ax. "I believe this is Jo's? It wasn't hard to recognize it since it seems she used to wear these almost every day in high school."

Seeing the jewelry, the blood runs from my face and I have to sit back in the chair.

"Danny, you need to tell me how this got in there and what really happened, you understand?"

Sighing, for the next ten minutes I detail what Father Sipp did to Tommy, his mother, how I confronted him, how he abducted me, how Jo followed us, about the gun he drew, the shot he fired, the shaft collapse, our disposal of the car, the trip to the rectory, the taking of the letters and the placing of his key back into his desk. Finishing the story, I am both emotionally and physically exhausted, so I lean my head against the chair backrest and stare up into nothingness.

Looking back down and over to Paul, I see that his face is ringed with concern as he rubs a hand over his whisker stubbled cheek.

"Danny, when I became a trooper, I took an oath, one I firmly believe in, to uphold the law. They taught me that the law is black and white, and blind, but justice is sometimes found in a gray area somewhere in between. What you did in removing those letters from Father Sipp's desk, and putting his key back there, is extremely serious. You were tampering with evidence in a murder investigation. And I won't even talk about what you did to his car. On the other hand, I don't see at this point what possible good could come out of disclosing what you just told me. Other than an arrest warrant that will stay open, my inclination is to leave this as it is. I know Tommy was dealt bum cards ever since he was a kid and, to be honest, there were times I wanted to whack Sandy across the back of his head myself. Even though he has physical issues from Tommy's attack, he seems to have gotten on with life fine. I can't see how justice would be served in dragging Tommy back here to face those old charges, though he probably would if the wrong person knew about this. Most of the prosecutors I know are sensible and straight shooters, but there are also a few asses with political ambitions who might see this as an opportunity for a splashy headline. As they say, sometimes it is best to let sleeping dogs lie.

"Also, just between you and me, we have had more than a few complaints against Father Sipp over the years but were never able to get anything to stick. Unfortunately, in the end, no one ever wants to believe a priest is capable of anything but good and that makes prosecution extremely difficult, if not impossible. Plus, it seems the Catholic Church was doing everything possible to protect him. Every time we made inquiries into complaints about him, they stone walled us at every turn. It was very frustrating. Then there is the possible danger of going back into the mine again. If an attempt was made to recover his body for a positive identification it could cause additional collapses. I don't see how that is worth risking additional lives for."

Standing, he extends his hand to me with Jo's broken earring in it saying, "Here, you should have this, Danny."

Taking it, I look him in the eye and say, "Thank you, Paul. You have no idea how much I appreciate what you are doing."

Smiling with a nod, he places his Stetson back on. "Oh, I almost forgot to tell you. The town has decided to seal the mine entrance with reinforced concrete. Anyway, you take good care of yourself, okay Danny?" he says as he walks to the front door and lets himself out.

Standing, I walk to the window and pull the lace curtain back just in time to see his black and white car back out of the driveway, stop and then roll down Parsons street until it is lost to sight.

225

26.

September, 1974

Dutchess County, New York

Parking the red ten-wheeler next to the curb on this cul-de-sac, I pull out the handle for the brakes which pop on with a loud gust of air like opening a giant soda can. Grabbing the two lunch boxes on the passenger seat, I open the door and step down onto the gas tank, then hop to the ground. Reaching up, I push the bottom of the door as it swings shut with a clank. Staring up at the door, I see *"Fosse Blacktopping"* spelled out in black cursive print.

Looking back up the long meandering drive, I see Dad sitting on a roller compacting the freshly laid blacktop, the smell of tar and diesel fuel overwhelm the air. His long-time laborer, Clint, rakes along the drive edge as steam rises from the surface like from a pot of boiling water. At the top of the drive sits a huge, newly constructed house with multiple towering steep slate roofs. The front entrance has two huge alabaster columns similar to those at the convent and the lawn similarly flows on each side of the drive into the distance. The mid-day sun sparkles through a sparse cloud cover and twinkles off the massive glass windows, reflecting in a blinding light.

Waving to Dad while pointing to the lunch boxes, he nods an acknowledgement. Walking under a maple, I sit and lean up against the trunk as I spot an elderly couple strolling my way, hand in hand, which causes me to smile.

Hearing the roller shut off, I turn to see Dad and Clint talking. Nodding, Clint walks to his black International pick up and is soon driving away with a wave. Looking back at Dad, as he walks towards me slapping the dust from his pants, I notice that even though he is only in his forties he already is slightly bent from years of manual labor.

He is slender and wiry, but still quick as wit, as agile as a ballerina with forearms that would make Popeye envious.

Settling on the ground next to me, he grabs a lunch box saying, "Let's see what Mom prepared for us today." Pulling out a foil encased sandwich, he unwraps it and then, with a satisfied grin, says, "Leftover meatloaf, my favorite."

Smiling, I likewise unwrap my sandwich, then unscrew the top of my thermos pouring out a steaming cup of coffee. Handing it to Dad, I fill mine and replace the top as he says "Thanks."

Sitting in silence for a few minutes, he turns to me and says, "Danny, I need to tell you something."

Fearing the worse, I say, "Sure Dad, what is it?"

"Mr. Coyne has been helping me negotiate the sale of the business for the last few months. I didn't want to say anything until it was a done deal but, last night after work, I signed the contract. An excavating company out of Poughkeepsie has purchased it and will be taking it over next week. Even though business is down, they wanted to purchase the recognized name and good will built up in the community over so many years. They indicate they see real potential in expansion in this part of the county. Mind you, it's not a fortune but it will solve all of our financial problems and leave Mom and I with money in the bank."

Caught completely off guard, I say, "Hey, congratulations Dad! That is terrific news."

Smiling, he says, "Danny, I want you to know how much I, and your mother, appreciate the sacrifices you have made in helping me out the last few years. Without your help, I would have gone under for sure. I feel guilty for having you work during your illness, for the low wage I paid you and for keeping you from pursuing your college dream. I want you to know, with the sale of the business we can afford Michigan State if you want to reapply. I know the swimming scholarship there is no longer available. In any case, it is time for you to pursue whatever your dreams are."

Thinking for a moment, I say, "I appreciate that, Dad. But I think I am going to go in a different direction. Since I have had a relapse and been back in this new treatment, I don't want to make any definitive plans. I guess I will know when the time is right."

Patting me on the shoulder, he says, "I'm sure you will, son. Also, Mom told me about the cash you have been giving her from your meager paychecks these past few years. Please, don't be angry with her for telling me. I must say, when she told me I was never prouder of you in my life. It took a real man to do that. Anyway, Mom will be depositing everything you have given us into your checking account. Also, we will be able to come current on all the past due medical bills. So, you see son, today is a great day for us all."

"I don't know how I can ever thank you and Mom for all you have done for me, for all the sacrifices you both have made."

"We both would do it all again in a heartbeat, believe me."

"What about Clint?" I ask.

"As part of the contract, the new owners have to guarantee to keep him on for at least a year. He is such a great worker that I have complete confidence that they will keep him on past that."

Taking another bite, I lean back against the tree with numerous random thoughts of what I will do swirling in my head. Sipping my coffee, I look at the truck that has been my second home for so many years and find, surprisingly, that I am going to miss it as well as working side by side with Dad. Truth be told, the work was a needed distraction for me, taking my mind off of the daily battle I was fighting inside. Having not really thought about it previously, though it was exhausting work I realize that I have numerous great memories working here, but probably the best is just having been able to spend so much time with Dad. That, I am certain, I will miss.

Relaxing in silence, we slowly finish our lunches as Clint returns. Pushing his foil wrapper back into the lunch box, Dad snaps it shut and stands as I do the same.

"Mom and I are going out tonight for a little dinner celebration but we shouldn't be too late. Remember, we have to get an early start tomorrow to finish this last job up."

"You and Mom deserve it. Enjoy. I'll be ready early tomorrow," I say as I hear the roller start up and see Clint slowly moving forward over the soft steaming blacktop. Glancing down the road, I see the backs of the elderly couple as they continue to shuffle along, hand in hand, seemingly going nowhere particular, and not caring in the least. I think of Jo, what could have been, all that we missed.

27.

September, 1974

Dutchess County, New York

Standing by the two open graves, I pull the collar of my coat up as the rain beats on the tent top like a tap dancer. The water streaming from the battleship gray sky slides off all sides of the roof making thin, translucent walls of water. Looking down, I watch as the caskets are simultaneously lowered to rest, side by side. A cool autumn breeze blows as Father Joye invokes a prayer in Latin. Walking around the grave's perimeter, he casually sprinkles holy water as if he were watering flowers.

Addressing the assembly, he says, "That concludes our service today. On behalf of Danny, he would like to thank all of you for coming today to pay respect to his parents."

With that, people turn and walk in a zig-zag motion, like moving chess pieces, amongst the gravestones, invisible under their umbrellas. Those without protection cautiously run on slick grass with hands held high over their heads. Shortly, the sound of doors opening and closing and engines starting flood the graveyard.

Glancing one final time at my parent's caskets, I feel right with my decision to have a Catholic mass and burial since they both were devout parishioners even though I hold the church in contempt, being responsible for Father Sipp's actions. If the police had complaints about him as Agnos told me, then the church had to also be aware, yet they continued to let him stay on. It was all I could do to stand quietly as Father Joye rambled on and on in a language no one understands. However, I had to let my parent's beliefs take precedence over my personal feelings.

Looking to my right, I see a sole man lingering under a small black umbrella. His gray hair and gray suit make him look older than his years, but his Irish green eyes sparkle with youth and vigor.

Walking over to him, I say, "Thank you for coming, Mr. Coyne. My parents were very fond of you, they would appreciate that you came."

"Think nothing of it, Danny, they were good people and what happened is a damn shame. You doing okay, son?" he asks.

"Yeah, okay, I guess. I don't think the full impact of this has registered with me yet."

"That is to be expected. All things get better with time. I know that sounds old and trite, but trust me, from my experience in these matters it is true. Listen Danny, we don't have to meet today like we planned. Why don't you take some time, then call me at your convenience?"

"Thank you, but it is okay. I would rather meet as scheduled and get this over with."

"If you say so. I'll see you in my office then at two o'clock." With that he shakes my hand. Stopping at the end of the two open graves, he blesses himself and then moves on to his car.

Standing alone, I say my private good byes to Mom and Dad with a lump in my throat, a knife in my heart. Turning, I walk away from my car and towards the far woods. Stopping at a small grave marker, I look down and read, "Billy T. King. U.S. Army. 1950-1969. R.I.P."

Hey, Billy, I think. *Missing you pal, sure wish you were here now. Seems like everyone I have loved is gone; Mom and Dad, Jo, Tommy and you. It is a terrible feeling, being alone, Billy, but I guess you know that from Vietnam. I miss everyone so much, but maybe you more because of what we shared. It is awful bearing the burden of what we did to Father Donovan alone. At least you and I could talk about it together. I miss that, Billy. I can't even bring myself to visit his grave, and it is only about a hundred yards from where I now stand, and where you rest. Well, got to go buddy. I'll visit you again soon. Friends forever.*

Wiping tears from bloodshot eyes, I turn and walk in total exhaustion towards my car. The grounds crew have begun taking down the tent, the green covering having been removed exposing piles of russet dirt running in small red rivers. Looking down the cemetery road, I spot a young girl in a bright yellow raincoat on an impossibly large bike pedaling furiously as a dog runs around her in large arcing circles, barking thunderously as the wheels spatter water.

Walking down Market Street, I pass the more than familiar buildings; Saint Vitonus, the school and Lawson's Lumber Yard. As I approach the diner, I stop and look in the window. A group of old men sit nursing coffee at their usual table, minus one. Old Bus passed away last month and almost everyone in town turned out to pay their respects, even those who didn't know him personally but knew of him. The faces in the window seem melancholy, and there doesn't appear to be much in the way of conversation.

Walking a few doors further down, I look up at a hanging black sign with gold letters that say "*J. Coyne: Attorney-at-Law.*" Next door is the Sugar Bowl where we seemed to live as kids.

Pushing the door open, I step inside a small room with floor to ceiling bookcases on both sides of an empty receptionist desk. They are overflowing with books, with some stacked on the red carpet in front of them.

Mrs. Cardell walks out of the back hallway and, spying me, says, "Hello, Danny. I'm so sorry for your loss. You can go on back. Mr. Coyne is waiting for you in his office."

"Thank you," is all I can manage as I shuffle by her and down the hall. On both sides, the walls are adorned with pictures from past years of members of the Dutchess County Bar. Reaching his office door, I knock.

Hearing a "Come on in, Danny," I push it open.

Standing behind his desk, Mr. Coyne extends his hand saying, "My heartfelt condolences, again, Danny. Your parents were not only clients of mine, but lifelong friends since high school." Taking his hand,

I give it a firm shake as he says, "Please, Danny, take a seat and be comfortable."

Sitting down, he does likewise. Surveying me for a few seconds, he asks, "How are you feeling these days, Danny? You look good."

"You are a bad liar, I laugh. As you probably know, I have been back in treatment for some time now since my relapse. The last year or two I have felt really well, but since I restarted treatment, not so much."

"What has happened has to have taken a toll. I'm sure with the passage of time, and a little distance from what has transpired, you will be your old self in no time. Speaking of that, do you mind if we get down to business?"

"Certainly."

Opening a folder, he stares intently at it for a few minutes before closing it and saying, "First thing, we have more than a strong case. The driver of the car that hit your parents was legally intoxicated. Furthermore, he was driving without a license and his vehicle was unregistered with no insurance. Luckily, he comes from money so I have filed a civil suit on your behalf. Unfortunately, these things take a long time to resolve, but eventually you will get a nice settlement."

"I appreciate your efforts."

"In the meantime, as you requested, I have arranged for an auction of the contents of your parents' house and then it will be listed for sale. With the way I.B.M. is expanding here and in Ulster County, it is a seller's market. I would expect it to go quickly and, again, you will be receiving a nice sum. Are you still planning on leaving town soon?"

"Yes."

"To where?"

"That is uncertain as of now. Could you do me a small favor? I will leave a few boxes with your name on them on the kitchen table at my parent's house. When I get settled, could you send them to me?"

"Of course. When you have it, call me with your new address and I will send the boxes along with any necessary paperwork. And, of course, the checks. The most immediate one will be for the sale of your father's business and then from the house and its contents. The accident settlement, as I said before, will take more time to reconcile. I think that about covers it for now, unless you have any questions."

"Well, there is one more thing I would like you to do."

"Name it, anything."

"As I understand it, anything I tell you cannot be repeated and is protected?"

"That is correct. It is called attorney-client privilege.

"Excellent. This is what I would like you to do for me, and the sooner the better."

28.

September, 1974

Dutchess County, New York

Looking up as I am walking slowly down James Street, I can see leaves starting to turn. Lush summer greens are teasing hints of red, orange and yellow that will burst in the coming weeks like fireworks. Ahead, Bob the mailman is crossing the street with his leather mailbag overflowing with letters, flyers and magazines, like some mobile library.

Strolling diagonally across the street, I walk up the familiar sidewalk at number nine. Pushing the door open, I enter and move to the receptionist window. The receptionist with the fire engine red hair is on the phone, her hand cupped over the speaker as she is trying to quietly argue with the party on the other end. Spotting me, she says curtly, "I have to go," and bangs the receiver into the cradle with a plastic thud.

Recognizing me from my many previous visits, she says, "Take a seat, Danny. The doctor will be with you soon."

"Thank you," I say as I enter the waiting room. In the corner is a heavy-set woman with badly dyed greasy blond hair, a foundation of brown crawling out her scalp. She is holding a wailing baby like it is an annoyance. Bouncing the child up and down on her knee, she is vainly attempting to quiet him down. Mercifully, the door opens and the nurse says, "Mrs. Kinary, the doctor will see you now."

"About time," she mutters as she pulls the child up with one arm like she is holding onto a melon while grabbing a purse the size of a steamer trunk with the other. The child continues wailing as the door closes, becoming less shrill as they walk down the inside hall and then, finally, silence as they enter an examination room and the door closes.

Reaching for a magazine, I grab the June issue of Sports Illustrated with big George Foreman on the cover. Randomly opening it, I see the article 'History in Making' with a photograph of jockey Ron Turcotte on Secretariat stealing a look behind him as he is on his way to a thirty-one-length win at the 105th Belmont Stakes. Remembering that day, I was home alone watching the race and can still sense the feeling I had that I had just witnessed something truly remarkable, a once in a life-time event, pure perfection. It still gives me goose bumps just thinking about what I witnessed. Just as I am completing the article, the door opens and the woman and child emerge. Sucking contentedly on a lol-lipop, he is no longer crying, the mother looking much less aggravated.

Calling me, a new young nurse I have never seen says, "You can come on in, Danny, second door on the right." She is wearing the same white blouse and skirt, stockings and shoes as all of the other nurses which makes her jet-black hair appear even more stark.

"Thank you," I say, sliding by her and walking down the hall, enter-ing the room. Sitting down, I feel like I know every object, nook and cranny of this room since I have been here so often over the past several years. Looking out the window, I see that the old fence has been taken down and a row of Norway Spruce have been planted. A bulky crow the color of obsidian perches lazily on a top branch, bobbing up and down in the slight breeze.

Hearing the door open, I look up as Dr. Pappo strides in with his stethoscope swinging like a plumb bob, the omnipresent chart tucked under his arm. His bald head has wrinkled over the years, matching his craggy face. Extending his hand as he always does, he asks, "How are you doing, Danny?"

"You tell me, doc," I answer as we both laugh at this standard exchange we share.

Dragging his chair close to me, it makes a scratching sound like the voice of a life-long smoker. Sitting, he opens his folder and reads in silence. Looking up, he says, "Danny, I hate to have to tell you this, but your white cell count has not improved, even with the new treat-ment you have been getting at Sloan. As we have discussed previously, this is affecting the functionality of your red blood cells which is why the fatigue you have talked to me about on several previous visits has slowly resurfaced."

"I assume this means an increase in the number of my visits to Sloan?"

"Well, Danny, that is why I wanted to talk to you today. As you know, your oncologist, Doctor Carter, and I have been monitoring your case together for years. Since his new treatment program has not been effective, it was on his recommendation that I reached out to a colleague of his, Doctor Austin, at the Mayo Clinic. Your case history was sent to him and he agrees that you are a prime candidate for a new treatment they have been using there, getting great results with patients very similar to you. There are, of course, no guarantees but both Doctor Carter and I strongly suggest you go."

Feeling slightly deflated at this news, I say, "Can I sleep on it?"

"Sure, Danny, sure. There is no pressure, but it is something that should be started sooner rather than later. You think on it and give me a call. If you decide to go, I will set everything up for you. If not, then we can talk to Doctor Carter and see what his next recommended treatment would now be."

Standing, I shake his hand saying, "Thank you, Doctor Pappo. I'll be in touch."

29.

September, 1974

Dutchess County, New York

Leaning against my bureau, I stare at the reflection in the mirror dressed in a blue sweat shirt and green sweat pants. After my initial remission, my weight increased, my face filled back out, my color returned as did my hair. Staring at myself now, since I started this new treatment, I once again sport a bald head with red patches, chapped and bleeding lips and all of the other assorted after effects of chemotherapy. An uninvited guest has moved into my house again and is slowly, inexorably pushing me out of the back door. Feeling sorry for myself, I fight back the emotions whirling within me as tears trickle down my cheeks. The worst part of all of this is that I have to go this alone.

Glancing to the upper corner of my mirror, I pull down the photo tucked under a mirror clip. It is one that I took in the summer of nineteen sixty-four, I remember, up at Mirror Lake. In it, Billy, Jo and Tommy are standing on the old canted wooden dock with their arms around each other, wearing the carefree expressions and smiles of youth. Taking a finger, I slowly touch each of them in succession. Sighing, I stick it into a pocket in my sweats while taking a last look around my room. Going to the bed, I pick up the change of clothes I have piled there, stuffing them haphazardly into a brown paper bag.

Glancing at a cardboard box sitting there, I pull open the top and reach inside, removing a stack of letters and postcards bound by a rubber band. Sliding it off, I shuffle through the stack. As she promised, Jo has sent me either a letter or postcard every single week since she left. I feel like I have been with her the whole time as she diligently and lovingly described her travels and experiences in detail.

Where did the time go? I remember the few times she had arranged to come home for a visit. It seemed it was not meant to be. The first time, she took ill and could not come. The next time, her father had a heart attack from which, thankfully, he made a full recovery. Then there was the trimester college and graduate school schedules which left precious little free time for her. It seems almost impossible that I have not seen her for so long. Is the fear I expressed to her so many years ago, that a relationship can't survive distance, coming true? I can't help but wonder if she has changed. Have I?

With a lump in my throat, I pick up the most recent letter, received just yesterday, and rub my fingers lightly over the stamp and postmark and smile. Folding it, I return it to the box and pick it up along with the bag of clothes.

Walking out to the hall, I start down the steps but stop in front of the portrait of The Last Supper. Looking at Jesus in the center, my eyes trace over to the face of Pontius Pilate and I can't but help feel that, in a way, I have met the twentieth century version of him.

Wandering into the kitchen, I look at the old clock on the brick chimney that has stopped at two-fifteen. To the right is my dad's tidal chart, last updated on the day he died, the tides permanently frozen in time like memories. By the gas stovetop is a can of A&P Red Circle coffee.

Putting the box on the table with others I have packed, I take a pen and write in bold black letters "For Mr. Coyne."

Strolling into the living room, I take a final look around as a floodgate of memories opens and comes pouring over the dam; all the birthdays, holidays, the laughs and cries, all of the setbacks and life's milestones that we all shared over the years. Feeling like a vital organ has been removed, I will miss this house, my parents and the memories.

Picking my bag up from the table, I let myself out the front door, locking it behind me. There is nothing left here for me.

Shuffling down the walk lost in my thoughts, I look up to see a state trooper car pull over to the curb. As the window rolls down, I see

Paul Agnos sitting there with his sergeant chevron visible on his sleeve, his bushy eyebrows seemingly advancing ever closer to one another.

"Hey, Danny," he says. "How are you feeling?"

"Hey, Paul. Okay, I guess. Dr. Pappo is recommending some changes in my treatment to see if we can get a better result." Shrugging, I say, "One day at a time."

"I hear you, Danny. I heard you are leaving town, so I wanted to stop by and tell you once more how sorry I am about what happened to your parents. They were both good people. I'll keep a watch on the house for you until it sells."

"I greatly appreciate that, Paul. So, how are things going with you?"

"Busy. The promotion to sergeant was nice, but the work load tripled, the pay grade not so much. I am considering applying for under-cover work in the city for a change."

Suddenly his radio blasts static followed by a dispatcher saying, "10-31 at the Booson Dehli on the block of Mill and South Clinton Streets. All officers respond."

Grabbing his microphone, he pushes in a button and says, "Car twenty-two responding." Pushing the mic back into its clip, he says, "Got to run, Danny. You take care, pal," as he takes off with his deck lights whirling and siren wailing.

Walking to my rental car, I open the door and toss the bag of clothes inside. Turning, I walk to the garage as the siren fades in the distance, open the side door and enter to a musty, mildew smell. Going to Dad's workbench, I pull a pair of bolt cutters off a hook, grab a scratched orange flashlight as well as a half-used book of matches which I stuff into my pocket. Moving to the lawn mower, I stick the flashlight under my arm and bend and pick up a red plastic gas can. By its weight, I can tell it is about three-fourths full, which will be more than enough.

Pausing by the door, I look at a dirty and faded photograph that is hanging there, the bottom and top having curled like ancient dead sea scrolls. The picture is of Dad and me fly fishing in the Esopus Creek at twilight. We both are in the process of releasing our cast as we stand in a rock-strewn rapid, Mount Tremper looming in the background.

Looking closely, I can see the tiny insects of the hatch emerging from the water and bursting free into the air, rising towards the sky. Smiling at the memory, I walk outside closing the door behind me.

Moving to the car, I open the trunk placing the bolt cutters and gas can there, then shut it taking the flashlight with me. Getting behind the wheel, I pull the matches out of my pocket and deposit them in the ash tray. Starting the ignition, I back out of the drive. Turning parallel to the street I give one last glance at what was once my home.

30.

September, 1974

Dutchess County, New York

A meteor streaks across the ebony sky, dissolving into darkness as the ancient lighthouse blinks its warning. It's time. Standing by the river's edge, the delicate breeze teases me with droplets of water thrown like insults at my sunken, defenseless body. The earlier rainstorm that came quick as a thief has fled like a coward, leaving the river calm with only slightly rolling waves. The waxing gibbous moon of several days ago has been replaced by an ascending bloated full moon that brilliantly casts an eerie white light on the surface, sparking in the waves like millions of rough-cut diamonds.

Pulling my wet sweatshirt up and over my head, I toss it on the beach. Bending uneasily, I pull down rain-soaked sweat pants that cling to my skin like a vine to a tree. With great difficulty, I step out and kick them away. Walking slowly into the low tide river until it is up to my shaky knees, I bend and scoop up the chilly water and throw it onto my emaciated face, burning my chapped lips. Creeping forward until I feel the edge of the underwater cliff with my toes, I fall forward as a wave comes in, gliding smoothly underneath me, caressing my body. The cool water shocks me like an electrical charge but it fits like a tailored suit, comfortable as an old friend. Breast stroking out twenty yards or so I stop, treading water. Looking to the west, I see the last sliver of a vermilion sun has disappeared over the horizon leaving a delicate crimson border as fine as fishing line extending north and south.

Gazing north, the moon shines its spotlight on the ravaged lighthouse highlighting the plywood-covered windows, yellow and black "No Trespassing" signs fixed in the middle of each, the caved in roof and shattered lantern glass. The wrought iron fence is rusted, bent and twisted like a Korean donut, the washed-out foundation leaning at such an impossible angle it appears the building could slide off as easily as an egg from a plate, all courtesy of weather, neglect, vandalism and age. It appears to be slowly wasting away, like from a terminal disease, with no hope, no dreams for a future. The automated lantern now seems to be more of a plea for help than for caution.

Hearing a faint rumbling sound, I look to the south and can see the running lights of a huge tanker heading my way. The moon backlights the deck cranes and booms, making them seem like the masts and riggings of an ancient whaling ship, a lone man roams the front deck like Ishmael. Moving swiftly, it angles towards me and the deep channel.

The reverberation gets louder and louder as it approaches, the advancing bow looking as tall as a skyscraper. Suddenly, it is passing by so close that I feel I could reach out and touch the steel skin. Looking up, the water line on the empty tanker is far above me, the cranes seem to be floating in the sky. Massive waves billow out from the bow and travel down the side. Rising high on the first crest, I then drop into a deep trough, then am pulled up to the top of the next crest, then fall into another trough. This is repeated over and over until I rise on a final crest, the stern passing by. The massive propellers roar like a jet engine and agitate the water like a giant blender as I fall to calmer water.

Turning around, I watch the trailing waves crashing onto the shore, moving north in a slow march in a futile attempt to catch up with the tanker. The leading wave reaches the atavistic looking cove and charges in, crest high, followed by another, then another. The water bulldozes into the shale rock on all three sides of the cove, the disturbed water appearing to be at boil, grasping up at the cedar trees with bubbling fingers trying to pull them down. Shortly, the energies cancel each other out, the surge slowly retreating into the river.

Floating onto my back, I gaze up at the millions of stars just appearing above in the ink-colored heavens. At first, I feel alone, abandoned like the injured goose I saw as a teenager on Mirror Lake.

Sometimes you just know.

But then I realize that I am not. Above me etched onto the fabric of the universe are the smiling faces of Billy, Jo and Tommy. They are not the faces of Billy coming home in a flag draped box from Vietnam, or Jo's crying face at the train station or of a damaged Tommy, wherever he is. Rather, they are the faces from my youth, ingrained into my very being, a part of my DNA. Life's winds and tides have pushed and pulled us all in very different directions but I feel that we have never really left each other. My friends are a measure of me, I now realize. And I have been a part of them. This has always been. This always will be. We all truly loved each other; because of this, I never will be alone and neither will they.

It may have taken all of my years to understand, but I now realize that love and trust can be both a finite and an infinite entity. In my experience, more often than not, they are finite with a definitive beginning and end just like each new day. Love and trust are the starting line, lost love and mistrust the finish, the gut punch that leaves you breathless with unseen scars that never completely heal. Yet the unspoken love and trust with my friends appears enduring and will exist, I am now certain, to the end of time itself.

Suddenly, they are all screaming and jumping up and down with joy; we are back at the base of Lenter's Hill swimming in Mirror Lake. With my head face down, my graceful arm effortlessly comes up from my leg, angled at the elbow, reaching over and far out in front making a powerful pull as my body surges forward as if propelled. This is repeated with the other arm and then again by the first, followed by a half head turn, just enough to breathe in air, my face then turning into the water as the whole process repeats. My weakened body suddenly feels resilient. The wilted muscles are no longer raddled but are flexing, adrenaline pumping through my veins. I suddenly am as light as a feather and strong as emotion. I feel as if I am made of steel, indestructible and implacable. I am actually enjoying swimming once again. I can hear the river's song, feel its magic, its life, and I feel wonderful.

What a terrific night to be alive.

"Go Danny! Faster! You can do it! Two minutes and thirty-four seconds!" they all yell in unison from above. "Go Danny, go!"

One, two, three, friends forever, I think. Like a man pardoned from a death sentence, the weight of the world has suddenly been lifted off of me. I am out of body. I can feel the water parting like from the bow of an old naval destroyer. Ahead I see Nag's Boulder looming in the moonlight. On top of it stands Father Donovan blessing me by making the sign of the cross as I pass. At the far end sits Dee Purdy rocking in his chair while whittling. He looks up at me and gives a smile that only a truly content and happy man can give and which, for the first time in years, I can return in kind. I am smiling. I am content. I am happy.

So be it.

Swimming past the boulder, I do not circle around and back towards the shoreline of my life, to the memories of my friends. Instead, I continue onward towards the possibilities of my future, wherever that may be. Cutting through the water like a torpedo, my feet throw a rooster tail spray. As I swim past a faded and tattered orange life preserver, a dragonfly swoops down and parallels my path for a few seconds, then flies away.

Not today.

31.

September 1974

Dutchess County, New York

The sky has cleared and the full moon shines like a brilliant torch on the countryside. I slow my rental car to a stop in front of a rusted sagging chain that lazily blocks the road. The headlights shine on a yellow "No Trespassing" sign that is wired into the chain links like an afterthought. The convent was shuttered in nineteen sixty-five, months after Father Donovan died, when the sisters who resided here consolidated at another facility as a cost saving measure, or so was said. As with many properties owned by the Catholic Church, this one sits in desolate, sluggish decay, mothballed and forgotten. Yet the collection plate continues to be passed. I do not feel the least bit guilty about what I am going to do.

Turning the ignition off, I take the key and walk to the trunk. Inserting it into the lock, I turn it and the lid pops open. Reaching inside, I grab the bolt cutter and walk to the chain. Putting a link into the cutter, I push the handles together and the chain snaps like a leg in a shark's jaw, falling with a dull thud to the gravel road surface.

Walking back to the trunk, I throw the cutter in and push the lid closed. Getting back in, I notice it is exactly three a.m. as I ease the car slowly up the drive. Weeds cover most of the road with only a trace visible here and there of what was once a beautifully manicured bluestone cover. Looking out at what was once a sprawling lawn, on both sides I see that it is overgrown with copses of locust that threaten the towering oaks along its edge. In a few years they will have reclaimed the entire area and the old lawn will be just a rumor.

As the car approaches the tenebrous mansion, I turn the wheel counterclockwise and my headlights traverse across the floor-to-ceiling windows and matching massive white columns that shield the front door. After putting the car in park and turning off the ignition, I grab the flashlight and step out. Shining it on the front door, I see the handles have a chain through them with a heavy-duty padlock securing it. Sticking the light into my back pocket, I walk to the trunk and open it, reach down pulling out the bolt cutter and gas container.

Striding to the door over sullied black and white diamond patterned granite tiles, I set the gas can down and insert a link into the mouth of the cutter. I again push the handles together, which is followed by a snap before the chain sags. Pulling it through the handles, it sounds like the rat-a-tat-tat from a machine gun. Dropping the cutter, I pick up the gas can and place a hand on the door.

Pushing, it moves inward with a protesting squeak. Pulling the flashlight from my pocket while entering, I survey the room. Surprisingly, it looks very much like the last time I was here a lifetime ago. Most of the furniture is the same, though dust-covered, and the huge crystal chandelier still dangles from the towering rotunda ceiling like an abandoned high wire artist.

Turning left, I walk across the dirty granite floor and, upon reaching the pool, I step down. The intense moonlight is cascading through the massive floor-to ceiling windows, dappling the marble floor. Taking a few steps while shining my light down on the floor, I trace a path back and forth until I see the faded maroon colored mark imbedded deep into the grout, a revolting reminder of what we did to poor Father Donovan. Just like the blemish on my memory, this grout stain will never be erased.

Suddenly a splatter appears on the tile, followed by another, then another. The tears run unabashed down my cheeks and off of my chin like water flowing over the collapsed tunnel end in Lenter's Mine. Emotions swirl within my being like a Kansas twister: sorrow, rage, repentance, anger and, strangely enough, relief. The uncontrollable sobs come from deep within my being, flowing freely after being damned up for so many years. Releasing a primal, guttural howl, it echoes throughout the mansion's vacant rooms which scream back at me from the darkness like a mockingbird before slowly fading to silence. Through my sobbing I mutter, "I am so sorry, Father Donovan." Setting the can down, I drop unsteadily to one knee then to another while instinctively blessing myself and saying, "Forgive me Father, for I have sinned..."

Minutes later I stand, grab the can and walk to the edge of the pool shining my light down into it. There is no water and the concrete bottom is weathered with yellow creases and cracks like on an old sailor's face. A dead rat is rotting on its side in the deep end, its teeth fully exposed by receding flesh.

I walk the length of the pool and turn left at the door for the changing room. I see it has come off of the top hinge. Shining the light upwards I can plainly see the door frame is rotted. Stepping back, I take my hand and gently push on the bottom hinge which instantly comes free as the door crashes to the marble floor causing a dust cloud to blow out from each side like a haboob.

Stepping onto it, I walk to the second door. Pushing the handle down, I shove it inwards as a breath of stale air hits me. Turning my head, I take a breath of what fresh air I can find and then step inside.

Turning my light onto the needle shower, it stands in the shadows like some dormant beast waiting to be unleashed. Imagining first the horror, then the pain and shame that Tommy must have felt in this room, I put the gas container down. Pulling the top and spout out, I toss them into the corner. With the container in my hand, I walk into the middle of the shower and turn in a slow circle while sprinkling gas over the horizontal tubes. I splash gas up onto the overhead fixture. Tilting the can, the liquid flows out onto the floor as I work my way backwards towards the door. Stopping by the inner door frame, I douse it and then the door. Continuing backwards, I soak the outer door frame as well as the door lying on the floor. Walking rearward a few more steps, the can empties. Throwing it into the pool, it bounces wildly to the bottom as the sound echoes around the room.

Taking the book of matches from my pocket, I pull free a match and strike it to life. Grasping the book by the edge of the cover, I hold the lit match to it until it ignites. Tossing it onto the floor, I watch as the room comes alive with flames that race down along the floor and up both door jams. The bluish flame trail continues along the floor to the middle of the needle shower where it suddenly rises and then spreads along the horizontal spray bars. It continues to spread upwards until at last it reaches the overhead fixture.

Looking at the flame-ringed doors, I feel like I am looking through the portal of hell at a vision of a flaming beast. The metal pipes appear to be moving, beckoning me inward. They are glowing a mesmerizing bright raspberry and coquelicot when, suddenly, they disappear into a raging inferno as two eyes the size of saucers and a mouth like a bear trap come racing towards me out of the flames. Startled, I step aside as an orange comet trailing black smoke races by me, hissing and chattering like an engine without oil, racing away parallel to the pool. Suddenly it starts galumphing to the left, then corrects to the right and then again back to the left before the front collapses like the damaged landing gear on a jumbo jet. It nosedives to the tile floor and slides forward a few feet before coming to a flaming and smoking rest like a meteorite crashing into a field.

Walking down to it, I look down at the charcoaled and smoldering remains of a rat.

Turning, I walk to the end of the pool and step up into the foyer as spitting fire and crackling wood sounds fill the air. Stopping, I turn around and watch the reflection of orange and candy apple red flames dancing in all of the pool's huge windows which look like dozens of trapped spirits behind a glass curtain.

Reaching the still open front door, I walk towards the car, bend and pick up the bolt cutters, then climb in. Starting the engine, I swing the wheel to the left and then straighten it up as I head back down the drive. Just before driving over the chain, I glance in my rearview mirror and see the entire east wing of the mansion engulfed in flames. Fire pokes up through the roof like hundreds of glowing, accusing fingers and I can see a cherry red furnace glow through the open front door. The roaring sounds of fire and crackling wood sounds like the death roar of ghosts. For me, this place is now a charnel house for the needle shower and the memory of what happened to both Father Donovan and Tommy.

So be it.

Upon reaching the main road, I turn left and head down Fishing Grounds Road as the dazzling moon casts its beam onto the Catskill peaks, turning them silver. Making another left, I head for the thruway as Roberta Flack starts singing 'Killing Me Softly with His Song'. Crossing the high arched bridge over the Hudson, I glance to my left to see that the whole southern sky appears to be on fire.

32.

September, 1974

Clayton County, Georgia

Walking down the jetway, I step into the passenger lounge amongst the hectic sounds of the airport arrival and departure announcements, people talking, babies crying, music, and luggage being dragged across the floor on squeaky wheels. The aroma of various anonymous foods saturates the stuffy air like at a county fair.

Surveying the crowd, my eyes lock onto a man staring at me with a huge grin. He has protruding ears and his right eye looks like a window shade half drawn. Smiling, I walk to him and stop. "Hey, Tommy," I say.

"Hey, Danny," he says while enveloping me in a bear hug, his voice still as high pitched as when he was a kid.

Hugging him back, I say, "Good to see you, old friend," as I pat him firmly on the back.

Stepping away, he says, "Great to see you too, Danny. How are you feeling?"

"You know, day by day," to which he nods.

"You have any baggage?" I ask.

"Plenty, and you?"

"Same as you, pal. Same as you. You have any luggage?"

"No. You?"

"Me neither," I say with a smile. Looking at my watch, I say, "We're running late. Come on."

Walking down the crowded concourse, we make small talk on how our flights were and the weather with cautious familiarity, dodging around what has brought us back together. I can't help but notice the sideways glances from some adults, the stares from children, at my emaciated, withered body and bald head as we walk past them.

Reaching the top of a narrow escalator, I step on followed by Tommy. Descending, I survey the crowd until I spot a familiar face. The rest of the crowd seems to blur until she is the only one. The bandana is missing, the auburn hair now trimmed in a fashionable shoulder-length shag cut. The high cheekbones and strong jaw have become more prominent with age, making her even more beautiful. The livid eyes sparkle with love as she gives a small wave with a huge smile, both of which I return. I feel as if I am about to be overwhelmed by emotion and I do my best to keep under control.

Grinning, she steps out of the crowd and starts walking towards me when I see she has a small girl by her hand. Stepping off the escalator, I move to the side as her hand goes up to her mouth, eyes opening wide, as she recognizes Tommy.

Reaching us, she says in a noticeably excited voice, "Hey, Danny," as she stands on her tip toes giving me a firm, tearful hug and a kiss as I breathe in the familiar perfume. "I can't believe you are finally here. I don't want to ever let go," she whispers into my ear followed by, "I love you so much."

Pulling away, I smile and say, "I love you too," as I choke back long held tears. I feel as if I have just been kicked in the chest, but in a good way.

Turning to Tommy, she says, "Tommy, so good to see you. I've missed you," as she gives him a hug.

Bending down on one knee, I am face to face with the little girl. She has her mother's bone structure and hair color, her penetrating eyes the color of bluestone. Cocking her head, she gives me that quizzical look only small children can give, looking first at one of my eyes, then the other, then back.

"What is your name?" I ask.

Hesitating, she replies, "My name is Ashleigh."

"Well, it is so very nice to meet you Ashleigh. My name is Danny."

Looking at me, as if she is studying, she asks, "Are you my daddy?"

Feeling as if I have been hit by lightning, I glance up at Jo. She and Tommy have their arms around each other, her head resting on his shoulder. She gives me a slight nod as tears stream freely down her cheeks.

My whole body feels constricted, my throat as if it has been glued shut. The room seems to be spinning in slow motion as I put a hand on the floor to steady myself. My face feels flushed. Looking back to Ashleigh, I say softly, "Yes, I am your daddy, sweetheart," as tears wet my cheeks. As I say the words, I get the same inner feeling that I had the first time I took Jo to the waterfalls behind Lenter's Hill. I feel scared and wonderful all at the same time.

Staring at me questioningly for a few more seconds, she takes a tiny step forward and throws her small arms around my neck, pulling herself to my chest so that my chin is resting on her shoulder.

I put my left arm around her holding tightly and glance back up at Jo and Tommy. Tommy has a sheepish grin, Jo a bright smile, as tears gush from both.

Smiling, I extend my right arm out and hold my palm face up.

Looking down, Jo's left hand goes to her mouth, her eyes widening, as she stares at a piece of gold jewelry in the shape of a rock axe.

33.

March, 1975

Dutchess County, New York

We have returned to town for the funeral of Paul Agnos, who was tragically killed in the line of duty. He was a friend, a good man, true to his word. As far as I know, he never discussed with anyone what really happened in Lenter's Mine, leaving what he knew sealed behind a concrete and steel barrier forever. The least we could do was come pay our respects, along with the hundreds of state troopers who came to town from every corner of the state. It was a touching ceremony and we are proud to have known him.

After the cemetery ceremony, Jo and I take Ashleigh to visit my mom and dad's graves. Then we made the short walk to Billy's snow-covered grave. Though Ashleigh is far too young to understand the sacrifice he made, someday she will.

Later on, as Jo and Ashleigh both napped in the motel, I take one last ride around town. Pulling onto Oak Street, I stop in front of Tommy's old house and stare in amazement. The weathered yellow and green paint has been replaced with bright white with black trim, a cheerful blue entrance door shrouded beneath a new front porch supported by circular white columns. The landscaping is meticulous, with dormant shrubs everywhere. On the right side of the house sits a huge glass sunroom addition. Inside, a family is at a brightly lit dinner table, busily passing plates of food while talking and laughing. Smiling, I think *this old lonely house has finally been made into a loving home.* Tommy will like that.

I then drive over to the town war memorial. As I get out of the car, small whirls of powdery snow slap against the tarnished stone. Frozen weeds stand at strict attention around the base. Two small tattered flags sadly bookend the memorial while the old empty schoolhouse looks down from its lofty perch with vacant eyes. Reaching down, I brush away snow and slowly trace my fingers over Billy's name. On each side of his are names of the other six boys from our town who also were swallowed by Vietnam. Closing my eyes, I remember my lasting image from the war being the footage of the chaos, panic and terror at the U.S. Embassy as the last helicopter lifted off, fleeing away like a dog whipped with a stick, abandoning our so-called allies of South Vietnam, leaving them alone to an almost certain fate. In that moment our politicians totally disrespected Billy and all of the fifty-eight thousand plus soldiers who died there. It was the first time I have been embarrassed and ashamed of our government. I have to think Billy would have felt the same way. Just when I thought they couldn't possibly do anything worse, along came the Kent State massacre. No one person ever takes responsibility. Instead, blame dissipates into a black cloud of unaccountability that is Washington and disappears forever. On and on it goes.

My last stop was full circle, back at the cemetery. Sitting in silence in my car for several minutes, I finally muster up my courage and get out. There is so much I need to say, so much to explain. I wonder, *where do I start?* Tentatively, I walk through scattered snow flurries as I head towards Father Donovan's grave and a long overdue visit.

Viewing his headstone, I read his date of birth and date of death, fully realizing that Billy and I etched the last date on that stone for all eternity. As I was during my last visit to the convent, I am overcome by what we did, and finally recognize that forgiveness is not possible. Not from Father Donovan. Not from myself. Not from some spirit in the sky. Certain things in life are just unforgiveable. That is my yoke, my burden to carry to the end of time.

Suddenly, I am a fourteen-year old boy again standing over Father Donovan's body as blood pools under his head, water dripping from my swim trunks pitter-pattering on the crimson floor tiles, horrified that a childish prank could have gone so terribly wrong. Slowly, I drop to my knees, desperately searching for something that no one can give me, something I will never find.

Standing on top of Lenter's Hill, we watch as the blustery March wind blows wisps of snow like smoke over the valley below us. Alabaster puffs of cirrus clouds are scudding across the sky in front of a blinking sun. As has always been the case, the view is stunning. From high up here you can still see Mirror Lake below, with a snowy Nag's Boulder protruding skyward out of frozen ice like a giant tooth. Pine trees decorated with a white lace of ice and snow encircle it like a wreath.

Directly below us to the west is my home town, looking the same as it always has. You can still clearly see snow-covered rooftops of houses that sit close along paved streets, all lined by leafless elm trees sporting shrouds of snow. Several streets south of Market Street, you can spot the war memorial, and beyond it, perched up on a forlorn hill, the old abandoned red brick school house with the field behind. Farley's Stream meanders from the base of Lenter's Hill to the edge of town, then south around the backside of the playing field to eventually disperse into the Hudson. A lazy county road snakes out of town towards us, past Oakley's Farm, the sun blinking off of the greenhouse window panes, twisting and turning around coated drumlins that look like Hostess Sno balls. Looking directly at Saint Vitonus Church, the black steeple still rises majestically above all else in the town, like a giant accusing finger pointing skyward to a vast emptiness above. It is a building where good and evil once lived side by side, praying together, sharing a bed. I'm not so sure anymore that there really is an omniscient, omnipresent essence above, floating somewhere up in the clouds, that people barter with through prayer, asking for this and promising that, not being able to accept the finality of mortality. What I do know and believe is that pure evil is buried in limestone and shale hundreds of feet below where I currently stand, and will remain entombed there for eternity.

Contrary to my strict Catholic upbringing, I now like to think that everything and everyone is the real God. God, I believe, is in the valley below and in the river and mountains beyond. It is in this hill upon which I stand, in Mirror Lake far below. It is in the grass, trees and sky. It is in every living creature, as it is in Jo, Ashleigh and myself. It is in our hearts. This is the religion we are teaching our daughter.

Further out, beyond the town and below the Catskill Mountains, the frozen Hudson River still snakes lazily down through the valley. The mid-afternoon sun busts through the clouds, gently caressing the landscape with cranberry rays, casting the river's ice like a giant colored popsicle.

In the last letter Jo wrote to me, she told me that she was back in the country. She said in it that this was the final letter she would ever write me. That was because she wanted me to come and be with her. Forever.

Jo and I married a few weeks after Tommy and I came to Atlanta. Tommy was, of course, my best man and Ashleigh was the ring bearer. Jo's father gave her away to me, the glowing pride evident in his moist eyes. I will never forget what Mr. Nelson did in helping my dad while I was in my initial treatment. He is an honest, decent man, much like my father, and I am proud to now call him Dad. We were married in a park on an overcast day, not in a church.

We purchased a house outside of Marietta with the proceeds from the sale of my parent's house, my dad's business and the accident settlement. It is a small three-bedroom home on a postage-stamp sized lot, but we love it. Ashleigh has a small back yard and a swing set to outgrow.

Jo still feels guilty that she could not come to my parent's funeral, to be by my side, to comfort and console me. She also is still struggling with her decision, made years ago, to not tell me about being pregnant and the birth of Ashleigh. Through tears on her first night back with me, she laid her heart bare telling me the conflict that she had gone through. From my letters to her, she knew my disease had come back and that I once again was going for a new treatment. She also knew my dad's business was still struggling, the medical bills were piling up and, as sick as I was, that I was working long hours with him in an attempt to save it. At the time, she thought knowing I had a daughter that I could not see since she was in Italy, and could not travel to due to my illness, would only torment me and add to my pain. She promised herself that she would tell me when she thought the time was right, and, true to her word, she did the day Tommy and I arrived in Atlanta.

I have assured her over and over again that she did the correct thing. None of us can change what has happened anyway, so why waste time worrying about it? *So be it.* Besides, how in the world can I be upset? The very first time I saw Ashleigh was the first time I knew I had a daughter. How is that so different from a birth, I had asked her?

Perfection, I believe, is a rarity in this world. Most people never get to experience it and, if they are lucky enough to do so, it is forever imprinted onto every fiber of their being. Reflecting, it seems that I have been lucky enough to have witnessed perfection twice in my life-time. The first time was when Secretariat won the Belmont Stakes. As the lead grew larger and larger to thirty-one lengths, you could feel you were witnessing a once in a lifetime event, something unprecedented, magical, spiritual even. I remember the horse racing commentator Heywood Hale Broun telling the tale of what Jack Nicklaus relayed to him: that he had stood alone in his living room watching the race and cried. Heywood said to Nicklaus "Jack, don't you understand? All your life in your game you have been striving for perfection. At the end of Belmont, you saw it."

The second time was when I first saw my daughter. Again, I felt I was witnessing something magical. Perfection has a way of reaching into your heart and gently tugging at it, leaving you speechless, breath-less and in utter awe. On both of these occasions, I openly wept. That is what witnessing perfection does to you.

Shortly after coming to Atlanta, I took Dr. Pappo's advice and flew to Minnesota to meet with an oncologist at the Mayo Clinic, Doctor Austin, who specializes in my disease. Jo and Ashleigh came with me, staying for nearly five months while I was receiving a new treatment. We were put up in a motel that had an indoor pool, much to Ashleigh's delight. On days when I would come back to the motel feeling nauseous, weak and depressed, I would only have to look at the sunny smile on her face as she splashed about the pool to feel uplifted, thankful to be alive, and think, not for the first time, *not today.*

Some nights, I would sit poolside with her and demonstrate my mother's overhead crawl saying, "One, two, three and breathe; one, two, three and breathe; one, two, three and breathe," over and over again as she tried her best to parrot my movements. Jo would then swim out into the pool and we would both watch as she clumsily tried to mimic the strokes while wearing her oversized, orange lifejacket.

I harbor a secret dream, deep in my heart, that one day when I am old, that I will be able to return to this town and the pebbled beach with Jo and a full-grown Ashleigh, and perhaps her children. That we can walk out at low tide holding hands until our toes feel the edge of the underwater cliff. Together, we would fall forward into the river and swim side-by-side towards the distant lighthouse. Dreams like this were the beacon that got me through my days, what sustained me through those most difficult and trying times.

Last month I was told that my disease is once again in remission. They also informed me that there were no guarantees. I can live with that.

Thanks to the monies I received, these days I am able to spend every waking minute with Ashleigh, watching in amazement as this little person learns and grows. When I was a kid, it seemed like time lasted forever, flowing on seamlessly, endlessly, carrying me in slow motion in its never ending sleepy current. Then time seemed to move on faster and faster, the current quickening to a raging torrent. Now, once again, I look to steal time between the seconds, dodging the grains of sand raining down through the neck of the hourglass the best I can. I finally have a grasp on what is really important in life, and I am holding onto it with everything I have left. It is not how long you live that matters, at least to me, but rather how you live how long you have. Jo once asked me, as we sat by the waterfalls behind Lenter's Hill as kids, if I knew what I wanted to do with my life when I got older. I couldn't possibly have known then, but this is it.

Two nights a week I teach a beginners swimming class at the local YMCA. It may not be my dream of teaching in college, but I couldn't think of a more satisfying age group to teach. I smile just thinking about the kids I am fortunate enough to work with.

Jo completed both her four-year degree and graduate school work abroad and became certified to teach in the state of Georgia upon her return. She is now teaching kids with learning disabilities at our local elementary school. Her eyes light up when she comes home evenings, telling me of what progress she made today, with what kid. She never gets discouraged, never lets the inevitable setbacks get to her. She is living her dream and I couldn't be more thrilled for her. She deserves it.

As for Tommy, he is living with us, for now. I sat down with Jo and Tommy on our second night together and told him exactly what really happened to Father Sipp. With Jo hearing this for the first time, I explained my confession to Paul Agnos and his reasons for not reporting us, and his return of the earring. I also told Tommy that the needle shower was no more. Even though neither of these things can erase his pain, he seemed, to me, to take some solace in what I told him. When I finished, Tommy stood, walked over and embraced me while gently sobbing. He whispered in my ear, "Friends forever."

Tommy shared with me that after his mom died, Father Sipp ceased sending the monthly checks like he had ever since they left town. He paid for her burial and that was the last he heard from him. Since he was doing only menial jobs, he could no longer afford rent and was forced to live in the streets. He soon discovered he could make more money hustling than working, so he ended up spending all of his time there. When foul weather came, he would head to a homeless shelter located not far from where their apartment had been and this is where the private investigator sent by Mr. Coyne, on my behalf, found him.

He said it didn't take long after learning about my illness to accept the plane ticket to Atlanta that he was presented with.

Tommy completed his high school equivalency diploma and got hired by I.B.M., with help from Jo's dad. He is going to college nights to become an engineer. He is on his way and I have a feeling that he is going to be a corporate star someday soon. He also had corrective surgery on his eye and looks more and more like the young kid I remember. We all enjoy having him around, especially Ashleigh who dearly loves her Uncle Tommy.

I have never told him what Billy and I did to Father Donovan, and I never will. He has had enough to deal with in his life, and I would never burden him with any guilt he might feel, rightly or wrongly, over the horrible mistake we made.

As I look out over the town and the surrounding valley, I feel an inner peace. Still, I often am haunted by what Billy and I did to Father Donovan. Regret, remorse, guilt and shame are my nightly bed companions. I must admit that sometimes, late at night, when I am unable to sleep, I find myself succumbing to my Catholic upbringing and silently pray for his soul and mine as tears flow. I guess many of us have dark secrets that we keep hidden, pushed deep down into the darkness of our personal mines like hibernating animals, hoping that a spring thaw never comes and that they never, ever, again see the light of day. Mine is a secret never to be revealed, one that will share my death bed. I have to live with that.

But the thing that bothers me the most, that shakes me awake nights sweating with fear, especially for Ashleigh, is the thought that if evil could penetrate the Catholic Church, is there any place on earth that it can't?

What would you do for love? For me, the answer that was once a blurry, nondescript contemplation crystallized the first time I saw Ashleigh with Jo: anything and everything.

"Come on Daddy!" Ashleigh impatiently shouts. "I want to go!"

Smiling, I look at her tiny face peeking out of a red snow hat that is pulled tightly down around her head. Her cold cheeks glow the color of cherries, her steel blue-gray eyes deep as a sea. Behind her sits Jo, looking as beautiful as ever, with love radiating around her like Saturn's rings. They both are looking at me with smiles that only truly content and happy people can have and which, joyfully, I am able to return today in kind.

Walking to the back of the sled, I gently place my hands onto Jo's back and ask, "Are you ready?"

"Born ready!" they shout in unison.

"Here we go!" I yell.

Racing downhill, I push the sled as fast as I can, the ice-covered snow snapping and cracking under each footstep like popcorn on a stove. Just before I feel as if the snow will reach up and grab ahold of my feet, I jump onto the sled and put my arms around Jo and Ashleigh. The wind whistles in my ears like it is announcing quitting time at a factory as a startled squirrel darts out of our path in a frantic zig-zag through miniature swirling snow twisters. The snowflakes blind me, sticking to my eyes as I wipe a gloved hand across them. Holding on for dear life as the sled increases in speed, the bottom slaps a beat on the rough snow like a jazz drummer keeping time as the hay stalks stroke the sled like drum brushes.

Advancing towards the half way point on the hill, our sled is rapidly approaching the jump. Ashleigh is half-screaming, half-laughing in pure delight as only children can do. Jo is laughing and it is contagious, as I also start.

Reaching the jump, I yell, "Hang on! Hang on!"

Laughter fills the air as the toboggan leaves the ground.

With tears of joy in our eyes, and pure love in our hearts, we are flying.

34.

August, 2001

Dutchess County, New York

Standing in knee-deep water at low tide, my toes hug the edge of the underwater cliff like an Olympic swimmer on a starting block, as a newborn sun peeks over the eastern horizon blanketing the landscape in saffron radiance, warming the early morning air, as stars above say their goodbyes. The Hudson is smooth as a mirror, reflecting bright sunlight with images of puffy cumulus clouds floating above etched onto the surface as if by laser. Looking up and down the river, there is neither a person nor a boat in sight.

Turning to my left, Jo is staring at me with devoted eyes that still make my heart melt, my knees weak, my throat constrict. Age, I think, has been her friend and, if it is at all possible, she has gotten even more beautiful. She smiles, grabs my hand, giving it a slight squeeze.

Looking to my right, Ashleigh is intently staring at the peaceful, tranquil sight before her as a tear skates down her cheek. "Dad, your description did not do this place justice. It is even more beautiful than I could have ever imagined," she says. Smiling, she gently takes my right hand as giggling fills the air.

Bending, I look past Ashleigh at her twin girls, Quinn and Riley, who are hand in hand with Ashleigh holding onto Quinn. They both have on faded and tattered orange life jackets, the water just below their tiny chins, with Riley moving her right hand back in forth in the water like a rudder in an attempt to keep herself upright.

Glancing down the river, I spot an amorphous dot moving towards us. Observing closely, I recognize what it is and say, "Guys! Everyone quiet! Don't move and watch!"

Seconds later, we see the dot transform into a huge bald eagle flying towards us only a few feet above the surface, its reflection a picture-perfect mirror image. Its massive wings move up and down in a slow, fluid, synchronized motion like a ballet. White head, piercing eyes, stun us all with its beauty. It flies by us not twenty feet away, the only sound the air moving under the wings like someone gently blowing in your ear, so close I feel I could reach out and touch it. In a matter of seconds, it is just a speck against the distant northern horizon.

"Wow!" screams Riley.

"That was cool!" shouts Quinn followed by innocent laughter as Jo gives my hand another gentle squeeze.

Smiling to myself, I think, as I do every morning, *not today*. I have been fortunate as well as lucky in my life, and I still savor every second, realizing, better than most I would guess, that the next one is not guaranteed. Like a sapling under the weight of winter ice and snow, I have been bent by illness, heartache and time, but not broken. My future is filled with both promise and uncertainty.

The dream I often had during my stays at the Mayo Clinic, the one that kept me going, that picked me up when I was down, that cast a beacon like a lighthouse, showing me the way, has come true.

Dare to dream, dreams do come true.

"Are you guys ready?" I shout.

A chorus of, "Born ready," bounces across the water surface like a skipping stone, followed by laughter, giggles.

"On the count of three," I say. "One, two, three!"

As one, we step off the cliff falling forward, releasing our hands, as we fully enter the summertime water which tenderly engulfs us like love. Treading water, I watch as the twins attempt the crawl in their buoyant life jackets. Suddenly, I go back in time and visualize Ashleigh, when she was their age, swimming in the motel pool. Then I imagine myself at the same age, arms chaffing on the bulky life jacket sides, breathing hard, mouth full of water, eyes blurry, as I swim towards the awaiting open arms of my mother, and I smile.

As I watch, they all start swimming north, towards the lighthouse, as the sun ignites the building and water on fire with crimson and amber brush strokes, the painted, round topped Catskills loom in the distance like giant scoops of sorbet. A silver scaffolding circles the building, a rusting metal barge with a stooped yellow crane moored off to one side. New windows shine and glitter, a fresh black wrought iron fence stands protectively in front of immaculately painted white siding. A new red mansard roof supports a half-completed catwalk that dangles precariously below a modern glass tower, the automated light flashing a welcome to the rising sun. The structure sits on a brand-new stone foundation, no longer looking lonely, desolate, dying; instead, a bright, promising future looms.

"Come on Grandpa, catch up with us," yells Riley, arms still flailing against her lifejacket, laughing, water splashing around her like a sprinkler head.

"Coming," I reply, smiling.

With my head face down, my graceful arm effortlessly comes up from my leg, angled at the elbow, reaching over and far out in front making a powerful pull as my body surges forward as if propelled. This is repeated with the other arm and then again by the first followed by a half head turn, just enough to breathe in air, my face then turning back into the water as the whole process repeats. One, two, three and breathe. I am the river's song. One, two, three and breathe. I am the river's magic. One, two, three and breathe. I am the river's life. I feel I could swim forever.

I'm home.